THE GLASS CHARACTER

THE GLASS CHARACTER

MARGARET GUNNING

thistledown press

Thistledown Press Ltd.
410 2nd Avenue North
Saskatoon, Saskatchewan, S7K 2C3
www.thistledownpress.com

Library and Archives Canada Cataloguing in Publication

Gunning, Margaret, 1954-, author
The glass character / Margaret Gunning.

Issued in print and electronic formats.
ISBN 978-1-927068-88-5 (pbk.).--ISBN 978-1-77187-000-9 (html).--
ISBN 978-1-77187-001-6 (pdf)

1. Lloyd, Harold, 1893-1971--Fiction. I. Title.

PS8563.U5754G53 2014   C813'.6   C2014-900741-8
C2014-900742-6

Cover photograph, *Harold Lloyd 2014* courtesy Harold Lloyd Entertainment Inc
Cover and book design by Jackie Forrie
Printed and bound in Canada

 Canada Council Conseil des Arts
for the Arts du Canada

 SASKATCHEWAN
ARTS BOARD

Canadian Patrimoine
Heritage canadien

Thistledown Press gratefully acknowledges the financial assistance of the Canada Council for the Arts, the Saskatchewan Arts Board, and the Government of Canada through the Canada Book Fund for its publishing program.

*For Matt Paust, friend and colleague, who never lost
patience with my Harold Lloyd obsession
and offered me more support and encouragement in my work
than anyone I've ever known.*

Glass Pictures

How I hate them, hate them more than life itself! Every few years, one of the studios cranks one of them out, a compilation of the "funniest moments from the silent screen": bleeding chunks torn from movies that were once hilarious and enchanting, now clanging with absurd sound effects, tinny piano music, jerky projection and a booming, insensitive narrator. This sort of manhandling destroys all the charm and superb comic timing that made these films such a pleasure to watch.

And though I hate them and hate myself for giving in, I am dragged to them irresistibly, for they are all I have left of my memories. Yesterday I endured the squirming discomfort of this desecration, with the same old irritating announcer: "*Ye-e-es*, it's Buster Keaton, the Great Stone Face, whose antics rivalled the Little Tramp's in worldwide popularity!"

Then came a few snippets of one of the greatest entertainers of all time, falling down and spinning around on his back and jumping back up, morosely facing the audience while the entire front of a building falls down on him from behind (with a perfectly-placed window saving him from being pounded into the ground), and launching a boat that immediately and gracefully sinks.

We were treated to only about two and a half minutes of Keaton (since Chaplin was considered so much more important), briskly followed by the abominable Keystone Kops, a segment which went on interminably, accompanied by shrieking police-whistles and obnoxious cowbell clangs. The aptly-named Charlie Chase went by in a blur, and the infantile Harry Langdon, surely one of the strangest characters in film history, rated only a few seconds.

I was about to leave the theatre in disgust, when the moment came that I had paid my dollar-fifty for: a desperate figure in a straw boater and a snug three-piece suit hanging off the hands of a huge clock, twenty stories above a street teeming with magnificent Model Ts. While the announcer yammered that "his daredevil skills were a thrill-packed third after comedy's two greatest geniuses", I saw the figure execute twist after twist, hand-hold after hand-hold, his body swivelling perilously through the air, then lurching in terror as the entire face of the clock popped out on a spring.

I had not seen this footage in forty years. To me, it was not a gimmick achieved through "clever trick photography" as the announcer boomed, but the memory of an elaborately-built aerial set creating the illusion of extreme height through perspective.. Clinging to the clock hands was an acrobat so gifted he could vault straight up into the air and gain purchase, even with only one good hand.

For his right hand was so imperfect it could only be used as a sort of claw. Look at the stills of this incredible scene, take a closer look at that hand, and you will see that it looks virtually dead, with a false rubber thumb and an index finger stretched completely flat.

As he flails, swings, whips, turns, grasping hand over hand, every move worked out in advance so he won't fall and kill himself (for the padded platform beneath the clock was perilously close to edge of the precipice, and one bounce, one bad landing could have sent him over), you can see flashes of terror in his eyes.

I know about that terror. It was real. He hated heights, and pushed himself to scale to them again and again because he recognized the nearly-invisible line between laughter and fear.

Even now, when I saw the clip again, my eyes prickling with an almost unbearable nostalgia, I noticed the audience crying in unison: "Oh . . . oh . . . *ohh!*" Then, a great burst of laughter. ("*He made it! Thank God!*"). But it couldn't be real: they wouldn't put him through danger like that, would they?

They would. And they did.

Forty years ago, everyone believed he was twenty floors up, and the truth is (amazing as it seems), he was. The wall and the giant clock were part of a set built on top of a twenty-storey building. Almost no one knew about the hand, or the actual degree of danger. No one had any idea they were looking at a figure who epitomized his era, or what would happen to him at the end of it. Grappling with the clock, hanging off it with his damaged half- hand while the other side of his body swung and flailed to grab a rope, this antic figure, willing to risk his life to make people laugh, was wrestling with the hands of time. The end of the dazzling decade, the decadent Jazz Age, would come in a dramatic and sickening fall, from high times into poverty and ruin.

The country never did fully recover, in spite of all the social and political gyrations that followed, and all the civil upheaval and false Camelot glamour of the here and now. 1962 will never equal 1926, I tell myself, either for unrealistic political idealism or sheer stardust magic.

Oh, I know I can't live in a time that has expired, and I realize there is nothing more pathetic than a woman rotting away in her former glory. But try as I might, I can't blot out those times altogether. For the truth was, they *were* enchanting (I sometimes felt, in direct proportion to the pain): every day that I reported to work, I was sifted with stardust. Do some people carry a spotlight around inside them? How else to explain the extraordinary beauty and luminosity of the only man I ever really loved?

∽∾∽

When young girls heard the word "Hollywood" in the 1920s, their reaction was immediate: an intake of breath, a pang of yearning, an awe that still hasn't lost its power after two generations of disillusionment. The word epitomizes the shimmering grace of those first stars (celestial beings: how aptly-named!) who seemed to live and breathe on the silver screen. In those days the screen really was silver, glinted through with threads that shone like fireflies in the theatre's flickering night.

Back then we called it *Hollywoodland,* and the huge ramshackle sign that decked the Hollywood hills seemed to stretch on forever. Young girls came to this place, girls who had very little experience with living in the real world, tired of being worked to death on the farm and sick of the boredom of the secretarial pool, pretty girls, ambitious girls yearning for excitement and florid romance, and just aching to be noticed.

We knew who we liked, who we wanted to work with. For many of us, Valentino the Sheik was first on the list. We wanted to be thrown over his shoulder and tied up in his tent and decorously ravaged. Graceful and heavy-lidded, his homosexuality veiled by the ignorance and idealism of the times, his premature death from peritonitis prompted fans (both male and female) to line up for twenty blocks to view his embalmed corpse. Legend has it that several fans, unable to carry on without their imaginary beloved, committed suicide.

Then there was John Gilbert, stoked with amphetamines to counteract his chronic drunkenness, and the Great Profile, John Barrymore (though he was a bit too intimidating for romantic fantasies), who had appalling breath and would never look at the camera face-on . These men were actors (or, more accurately, "*ek*-torrs") trying to pantomime Shakespeare, gesturing hugely, their faces more heavily made up than the local hoochy-koochy girl.

But true to the times, most girls equally worshipped actresses, their Sapphic urges sublimated in adoration of women who were almost supernaturally beautiful: Norma Talmadge, Louise Brooks, Gloria Swanson. They yearned for the gowns they wore, the soft drape of cool satin on bare skin, tiaras dripping with artificial gems. The slender stems of their bodies, almost devoid of breasts or hips, made us look at our own dumpy, spindly or spongy frames in despair.

Quite a few of us specialized in the worship of comedians. They were entertaining, they were dear, but under the façade was a ferocious athleticism, ambition, and competitive drive. Being funny is a serious business, and I was to find out that, in spite of the modest stature of its greatest stars, comedy does not attract lightweights.

Some of us (*many* of us! If our husbands and boyfriends only knew) yearned for Chaplin, the legend who was said to be only five foot four and slept with fourteen-year-old girls; some longed for Buster Keaton, though there was something disturbing about his melancholy eyes and body-punishing acrobatics, as if a great void existed at his core.

But my passion was for an actor who so grasped my heart, who so bedazzled me with his sweetness and grace, that I dared not even speak his name.

I was infuriated that the press always called him things like "the third banana," a bronze medal grudgingly bestowed after the Olympian brilliance of Chaplin and Keaton. I had always believed the celebrated Little Tramp was nothing but a pompous ass (or so said my "secret Hollywood connections", questionable sources who helped me get hired for my first job as an extra) with a snooty, irritatingly high-pitched English voice.

And Keaton — why, Keaton was more than once thrown in jail for drunkenness, and sent to sleep it off in a mental hospital.

The man I loved seemed to shine so, to effloresce, not just in the classic white makeup he wore for his character, but in his soul. Like Koko the Clown leaping nimbly out of an inkwell, he was better than human, a pure creation, a character dear and befuddled, good-hearted, sometimes downcast and a little lost, but valiant, and in his own unique way, full of passion.

The man I loved wore a white straw boater hat, saddle shoes and a suit that looked a tiny bit too small for him, so that the cuffs of his jacket crept upwards as if he had not yet stopped growing. He had a boyish things-are-looking-up expression which I now realize epitomized the heady days of the 1920s every bit as much as F. Scott Fitzgerald and bathtub gin. Whether he was in character or not, he was headspinningly beautiful. And below and beneath his sweet and eager expression, there was something else — barely glimpsed, just barely present, but there: *fear*.

This was a man who wouldn't step on a crack, dreaded black cats, backed into his driveway because driving around the fountain in front of his mansion was bad luck, dressed and undressed in exactly the same order, always left buildings by the same door he had entered, and hid money in books and forgot about it, believing that finding it again was a good omen. And what is superstition except disguised fear?

But in spite of this visceral dread, he hurled himself at life, innocent as a puppy, willing to cross any river, climb any peak, walk through fire and do anything (except take his glasses off) for his lady love.

Ah, the glasses! This was the stroke of genius. One day, this young actor, already well-established in movies but still casting around for a persona that would bring his many talents together, found a pair of thick, black, prop glasses, turned them over in his hands, and put them on.

When he looked in the mirror, he jumped.

He looked nothing like himself. The elegant leading-man face (almost a detriment in comedy) had suddenly been transformed.

He was looking at a slightly awkward, somewhat studious, well-intentioned but hapless, eager young man.

He smiled; it was nothing like his own smile.

The smile said, "Here I am!"

The smile said, "Never give up."

The smile said, "Love me."

His director Hal Roach looked at him and said, "Good God, what have you done to yourself?"

"I'm not sure."

"Keep those glasses on. Let's shoot a scene."

They shot a scene. It turned the film completely upside-down.

"Now what do we do?"

"I'm not sure."

"For Christ's sake, Harold! Quit saying that. We have to figure this out."

"Let's change the character."

"Oh, no, we can't! Lonesome Luke is the most popular — "

"Get rid of him. I'm tired of Lonesome Luke. He's boring and he just isn't funny. I think I might have something here."

And so, in the middle of the film, in the middle of the year 1917, Harold Lloyd's alter ego was born. Tellingly, he was not given a consistent name, so closely did he reflect a youthful, hopeful Everyman. In all his early films, he was known in the credits simply as The Boy.

From then on, he would refer to his screen persona as the Glass Character (not a name but a label, and one that was completely unknown to his fans), the wellspring of all the versions of himself he played on film: Harold the department store clerk, Harold the hypochondriac, Harold the country doctor, college freshman, harried husband, millionaire. He liked to refer to these movies as "glass pictures". The singular form was an eccentricity, not to mention ironic, for the frames (not horn-rims, as most people assumed, but made of an early form of plastic called Bakelite) had no glass in them at all.

Harold intuitively realized the significance of the Glass Character's most recognizable feature. "No gags with the glasses," he insisted. "No snatching them off. No turning them upside-down. No breaking them." He believed the glasses were not a prop, but an intimate part of his face, like his eyes, his nose, and that irresistible, razz-ma-tazz smile.

The convergence of the actor and his character, the way they met in the middle, was a rare alchemy, for the Glass Character both was and wasn't Harold. He projected the elements of himself he wished to, held some back, invented more, and thus an Everyman was born.Whatever character he played was fully three-dimensional, whether ranch hand or sailor or social snob, his past implied by the way he inhabited the role. So well did he beguile his fans to follow him that most of them were not even aware they were being seduced.

How on earth did we know so many things about a man who didn't even speak, who didn't in any obvious way convey this information? Subtlety, to be sure, but the rest was sheer genius. There, I've said it: the word that is bandied about so carelessly, often applied to overblown self-promoters, or men who have hardly any talent at all. (And have you noticed that it is almost never applied to women?).

I have come to realize in the many years since my passion for Harold flamed high that he is trapped in a glass bottle, a tiny figure who never ages, who plays out the hilarity and charm of his stories forever, never touched by vagaries like the stock market crash, the Depression or the disaster of sound film. By the time the bottom dropped out, Harold Lloyd was a very wealthy man indeed, and powerful beyond measure.

❧❧❧

I was a teenage girl when everything changed. Propriety seemed to have gone out the window, formal tea dances with all their chaperones and rules knocked flat by wild new steps with arms and legs flying in every direction. Formerly dutiful, obedient young people were now described, often with great disgust, as "flaming youth".

Since it was the only form of entertainment available, people went to the "picture shows" four or five times a week. I knew a lot about movie stars then, even more than I knew about myself. I had been reading about them in the fan magazines for years, and lived for those pictures: good movies and bad, comedies and dramas, movies of such bathos that the negative should have been burned, and others so lovely I could barely force myself to leave and would sit through the second show, hoping the usher wouldn't see me slumped down in my seat.

When I watched dear Harold, whether in one of his whimsical shorts or a two-reeler, I was warmed all over, as if my entire body were smiling. I would pray: oh, let me stay in this spell for as long as I can! When The End appeared in the final frame, my spirit sagged in me, and reality dragged me back. I wanted to laugh that way again, so that I was achy and teary-eyed and had to blow my nose.

I loved Harold's pictures for so many reasons, some that I didn't even know about at the time. He always had some formidable obstacle to overcome, something that seemed so impossible that at a certain point the audience threw in with him and just wanted the little guy to win. He's so hopeful, so heartbreaking, he wants the girl so badly, he needs someone (*anyone!*) to like him, and he just can't make it happen, but . . . give up? How can he let the love of his life (and the purpose of his whole existence) slip through his fingers? This is a man who doesn't know the *meaning* of "give up"!

I was stirred, stimulated in ways that sometimes frightened me. In the gloaming, walking home from the movie, I would silently take his hand and stroll homeward, wondering: will he, won't he kiss me? These were such innocent times; it wasn't a question of "having sex", although at the same time, I somehow suspected that everyone else was having it.

∽∽∽

Though I did not fully realize it at the time, Harold lit a sacred taper in me, a secret flame that melted me from the inside like paraffin wax. I had always been grateful that we were alive at the same time, but now something new had been born in me: I wanted to be in the same world with him.

I ached and yearned, not just in spirit but in body. I spent nights in bed tossing and even weeping with restlessness and discontent, but unlike a lot of girls, I had enough gumption (or so they called it) to do something about it. I had a plan: I would slip out of my bed at night, hoping not to wake my parents, walk the three miles to the bus station carrying only a small wicker suitcase, and head for Hollywoodland.

So that my Ma and Pa would not send the police after me, I left a letter with my cousin Beatrice explaining my need to pursue my dream, assuring everyone that I would be safe. I told them I was staying with an older girl friend (someone I had actually gone to school with, so they never checked the phony address), who had already found me a secure job at a nice restaurant called Frankie's Place on the Sunset Strip.

This letter was one of my early attempts to write fiction. Practically none of it was true, or I would have been dragged home immediately. An acquaintance of mine, not someone I particularly trusted, had told me about Frankie, who supposedly had some contacts in the business, though it was more likely his "restaurant" was the sort where you needed to know the password to get in.

I knew Beatrice would envy me, but also be afraid for me. We all dreamed of going off to Hollywoodland: but to actually *go?* It was as unthinkable as allowing our boy friends to touch us below the waist. Necking, yes; petting, no. And this was more like going all the way.

What I would do when I got there was not entirely clear, though I did have previous work experience at the Rexall Drug Store and Soda Fountain (I was what was ignominiously called a "soda jerk") in the dull desert town of Santa Fe, New Mexico. This was a nothing little place made up of dust, lizards, and pink adobe houses that looked as if they were melting in the sun. Several of my regular customers, men with protruding stares, claimed to know agents and producers in Hollywood, promising dubious information in exchange for even more dubious "dates".

I had $49.98 in my purse (I had been saving for two years, cleaning houses, mending clothing, minding children, even starching and ironing men's shirts), a phenomenal sum for a sixteen-year-old girl. I was a virgin, but somehow suspected I wouldn't stay that way for long: for if I could not keep my hands in the proper place as I lay in bed after a Harold Lloyd movie, what on earth would happen to me if I met him in person?

Anyone with sense would have seen that my venture was a foolish, ill-considered, even harrowing risk. Bea begged me not to go, arguing that I could satisfy my Hollywood yearnings with magazines and picture shows (as if I weren't glutted with them already).

"We can go every night, cuz."

"Bea, I can't. I just can't stay here any more."

"I'll talk to your Ma. Maybe she'll let you work somewhere else. You like to write. Maybe you can go to work for the newspaper."

I stared at her blankly. "Newspaper?"

"Sure. Typing, or typesetting, or whatever they do."

"I have no experience." I knew the words were hollow, given my total lack of experience as an actress.

Bea looked at me, her face full of anxiety. "You're too young,"she said. "Men take advantage. I'm afraid for you."

"I can take care of myself."

I was sure of this, or thought I was. I was pretty. I knew it, but not in a stuck-up way. I wasn't pretty like the fresh, corkscrew-curled Mary Pickford, a star so huge none of us could even approach the possibility of resembling her. But based on what my soda fountain "contacts" had told me, it was important to determine which actress I looked like, because the studios would likely want more of the same. I wasn't dark, thank God, or I'd be relegated to playing some Mexican tart in a Ramon Novarro picture.

I wasn't fair either, or even a dark brunette. I was — well, brown, but had thick lustrous hair with a coppery sheen, a nice nose, friendly blue eyes that danced when I was happy (or so my cousin had told me), and a nicely-shaped mouth. Mouths were very big in those days, with lips described as bow-shaped or bee-stung, though no one notices them at all any more.

My body was unremarkable, slim, not overly developed in the bust or hips. I hoped this would make me adaptable to many roles. I could not imagine myself in Theda Bara's skimpy costumes, so I hoped I would not be pushed into seductive parts (at least not right away) by casting directors.

I had to make a decision which one I resembled. So I picked Mary Miles Minter. Not that I particularly looked like her — in fact, I flattered myself with the comparison — but her name was lovely, sweet and cool, like something newly-minted. I would not have believed back then that years later, she would be caught up in one of those dreadful Hollywood scandals and lose her career altogether.

The bus ride was interminable, the longest I had ever endured. I drew stares, not just from men but women, automatically disapproving of me just because I was a young girl traveling alone. I concocted a story about going to visit an aunt, before realizing that this was what girls said when they were "in trouble" and being sent away.

At times I wondered if I were making a terrible mistake. Failure seemed inevitable, and I knew what happened to girls who failed in Hollywood. Naïve, lonely, scared, but doggedly determined, I rented a bare, distasteful room in an old hotel (and as I looked at the rates, I puzzled over why it was possible to rent "by the hour"). I went downstairs to the rank, cat-smelling lobby and telephoned the first number on my list, the one I had paid for with all those endlessly-postponed "dates".

"*Yel*low," the voice boomed, like a cartoon fist springing out of the receiver. I could hear raucous laughter in the background.

"I'm sorry, I . . . Is this Frank Lancaster?"

"This is Frankie's Place, girl. Haven't heard of it?"

I could practically see the flies buzzing around, and I could definitely smell grease.

"I think I may have the wrong — "

"Guess you haven't been here too long, huh sis? If you wanna job, we're full up."

"No, I'm not a waitress. This is Muriel Ashford. I'm an associate of Johnny Parker."

"Johnny who?" My heart dropped into my shoes. "Not *Jailbait* Johnny."

I had no idea what he meant. Desperate, I began to improvise

"He works for the Rexall pharmaceutical company in Santa Fe."

"Oh, the soda jerk!"

"That's him."

"Well, missy, what can I do for yuz?"

"Johnny told me you might have some connections in the film industry."

"You gotta be kidding. Who did you say you were?"

Desperate, I gave up on my ruse. "Jane. Jane Chorney."

"Oh, *Jane!* Yeah, he said something about you once, told me he couldn't get to first base with you. You wanna be a big star, like all those girls. But Johnny, he don't know from nothin'. Everybody knows he was Harry Langdon's love slave. Only reason he got in as a prop man."

I had no idea what he meant, wondering if it was a nasty joke.

"Excuse me, I don't — "

"Listen, sweetheart, you don't know anything about this business, do you. You don't even know where I'm talking to you from. Ever been to a speakeasy? Do you even know what a speakeasy *is?*"

"Of course I do."

"Listen Jane, or whatever your name is. I'm guessing you're, oh, about sixteen?"

"Eighteen," I lied again.

"Right. Do your parents know you're out here?"

"I haven't got any parents."

"So you ran away. Old man put his hands on you? Touch you the wrong way?"

I stood in shock: bad as it was, living bare to the bone, in constant fear of my father's rages, no one had ever treated me quite as badly as that.

"You're only going to get your heart broke, sister. Better have a backup job just in case."

"Just give me the information. Do you have any connections or not?"

"Sure I do! Charlie Chaplin owes me twenty bucks." His coarse laughter made a mockery of my request.

"So you don't have any connections. Why didn't you just come out and tell me?" I knew my voice was petulant, I could hear the waver in it, but I was tired, and didn't want to call the second name on my list for fear he'd be a gangster outright.

"Oh, listen, girly, I didn't mean nothin'. And yeah, I know where you can go try out for extra work. It's easier to get than you think, 'cause the studios need them all the time. They're kind of like scenery that walks around. Pays a buck a day or something. They're having a big cattle call tomorrow."

"Cattle call?" Oh, how dreadfully ignorant I was!

"Yeah, you know, a . . . well, sis, you're gonna find out." When he read me the address of Rolin Studios, I nearly dropped the receiver.

"That's Hal Roach," I said, my voice shaking.

"Yeah, that guy. Grinds 'em out like hamburger, as far as I'm concerned. He needs females for his next picture. You're in luck. Something about a girl's school."

A girl's school! It would need girls, would it not? Pretty, fresh girls from Santa Fe? Good God, what was I going to wear?

"Ten o'clock, sister. You sound like a nice person. I hope yuz makes it."

"Thank you so much, sir. I will be forever in your debt."

"Lemme give you a little bit of advice. Don't lay it on so thick, huh? This ain't a stage play. Refined manners won't work in this town. Just show up on time."

"Thank you for the information. Goodbye."

The man had spoken like an absolute cartoon, but never mind, he had given me what I needed. Every inch of my body was electric with excitement. I had never seen gooseflesh on my face before, but there it was. I had been jolted with a charge so potent, I knew I would never be able to turn back. I did not sleep, and worried I would be hollow-eyed or too pale the next day, but fortunately youth was on my side. (Ah, the stamina of adolescence, when staying up all night only brings out the bloom!)

In fact, I don't think I had ever looked so fetching. I didn't need to pinch my cheeks to bring out their blush. I put on my one good dress, a faded blue that hugged my contours (modest as they were). I agonized over my one sad pair of brown shoes (Mother said you can always tell a lady by her shoes, prompting Father to say, "Or a chippie"), but buffed them up as well as I could. "Remember," as Beatrice used to say when I needed encouragement, "*act* attractive, and you'll *be* attractive." I prayed it would be true, if I could only muster the confidence.

I reported to the studio at nine o'clock, imagining I would announce myself at the gate with my newly-minted, grand-sounding name, and quickly discovered that I was in the wrong place. Rolin Studios didn't have a gate. It was located in an old house, which threw me off-balance. No one wanted to talk to me. At one point I was ordered to go home. I had heard stories, most of them likely fabricated, of people sneaking or lying their way into movie studios. Harold himself had started that way, disguised in heavy makeup. Then, incredibly, I mentioned the name of the man I had talked to: Frankie Lancaster, that rude, ignorant, horrible man in the speakeasy who seemed to know nothing about the picture business (whom I described as "a close friend of Harry Langdon"), and, stunningly, that invisible gate swung wide.

I had no idea, at the time, that Frankie was a keeper of secrets, one of many I would encounter during my heady days in Babylon. If he ever chose to spill them to the press, any number of careers might totter and fall. This was never more true than in the case of Harry Langdon, a bizarre and baby-faced man who might have been homosexual but was shielded by public innocence and wishful thinking (not to mention a complete lack of evidence). My so-called useless contact was more powerful than I could imagine, and his influence had pried open an impossible door.

This was it, my road to stardom, straight and clear!

The place was a hive, everyone going somewhere purposefully, heads down in a forward charge. I stumbled around for what seemed like hours, ignored and dismissed by everyone I approached. Following everyone else's lead, I decided to name-drop: "I'm looking for Mr. Roach." This seemed to draw a blank face, an incredulous look, or a sneer. Then, my throat closing up with anxiety, I took a brash step: "Have you seen Hal?" Finally a severe-looking woman, some secretary no doubt, looked at me and said, "What audition? What are you talking about? Oh, over there," and pointed me in the right direction. She actually gave me a push.

I opened the door and stepped into the room.

What I saw was a sea of pretty girls.

Pretty young girls, most tricked out to look like Mary Pickford, even with huge bows in their curls to make them look more juvenile.

Some looking like novitiates, others like vagrants.

So where did I fit amongst this motley assortment? And when would I have my screen test?

A harried-looking man strode into the room, his eyes slicing up and down the rows of chairs, dividing us up like sheep and goats. This must be the casting director, I thought, and it looked as if he had about thirty seconds to do the job. So each girl probably had less than an instant to be assessed, accepted or rejected.

Not fair, I thought; didn't most stars take years to develop their careers? Why was I being forced to bloom like a hothouse rose? .

"You." He pointed at a girl, a pretty girl with luminous eyes, who shrieked and jumped up and down.

"I changed my mind. *Not* you." The girl sat back down again, stunned and deflated.

"Okay, you. And no funny business, do you hear me?" This girl, a dead ringer for Pickford, managed to contain herself, though her smile was smug.

I sat trying not to squirm with the intensity of my yearning, wondering if this would be my one and only chance. At least thirty girls were combed over, apparently on their looks alone, picked and dismissed, picked and dismissed.

"Nah . . . " He was looking directly at me. I could not control myself; to my utter humiliation, I felt tears rush into my eyes. Surely this was not what he wanted (for the jumping up and down had been fatal). One giant tear trembled on the very brink of my eyelid, and I dared not look down or close my eyes for fear it would splash down my face.

He had already moved on to the next girl. I sat still as waxworks.

To my astonishment, he glanced back, took my chin in his hand and gently lifted my face.

"Okay, miss, now — smile."

I looked at him, incredulous, praying the tear would somehow stay unshed.

"You heard me! *Smile!*"

I gulped, took a quick catch-breath, and I smiled.

I knew it was the worst, the most false, most unattractive smile I had ever smiled. But the tear stayed in.

"Okay, you're in. Go through that door over there for a fitting."

My legs turned to jelly, but I somehow made it over to the swarming, bustling, yelling mass of bodies, was grabbed by a wardrobe mistress and wrapped around with a tape measure. Someone was putting a sort of corset on me and pulling it in tight, incredible, since my waist was only twenty-two inches (about three inches too large for Hollywood, I was to find out).

I made the mistake of asking her what the film was about. "I stick to my work, little miss," she said grimly, her mouth full of pins, "and you should, too." I hoped she'd sneeze, gasping them all in and choking to death.

I was told to report for work tomorrow at 6:00 AM. The early hour floored me briefly, but then I vowed to buy an alarm clock with my dwindling cash. I wouldn't eat that day, for who needs to eat when one is going to be in a Hal Roach comedy? They seemed to want me slimmer anyway, and since I eventually learned I was supposed to be fourteen, it was no wonder.

∾∾∾

Dear Beatrice:

My sweet cousin, since I saw you last, I have plunged headlong into a land of pure enchantment. To my astonishment, I was hired on my first audition for a comedy directed by Mr. Hal Roach, whom you will remember from some of our favourite comedies. The movie is called Girls Galore!, but so far I don't know any of the details. Never mind, I would walk through fire to appear in this film! Please tell Ma she shouldn't fuss about me, as I'm doing just fine, living in a lovely little apartment, employed, and already making friends.

Dear cuz, you probably know me better than anyone (in fact you are more than a sister to me), so I can't hide the real reason I came out here. Though I don't often speak of it, when we used to go to the movies together and walk home with our arms around each other's waists, I would be particularly quiet or emotional after we saw a film by a certain actor, whom I won't mention by name.

I know you have warned me, Sissy, that my dream of meeting this man is completely unrealistic, and that he may not be the person I see on the screen or in the movie magazines. But I must see him, cuz, because I worship him. I have tried any number of ways to cut it off. I see him on the screen with Bebe Daniels, whom I don't even think is pretty, and I feel as if I could pull her hair out.

Are you shocked by this? They say the two of them are an item, and I can only imagine what they mean by that. I know that they go dancing together, and they always seem to win those contests, you know, where you get the big loving cup. He does make goo-goo eyes at her in some of their films, and she shoots back a worldly look. We all know what "worldly" means, don't we?

Well, Sissy, I need to close now to get my beauty sleep. We begin shooting tomorrow, and I can't imagine what it will be like. I will tell you everything. Wish me luck, my darling.

Muriel Ashford/Jane
(Oh, how I miss you! Oh, how it hurts my heart!)

❧❧❧

People don't mention one thing when they tell their tales of heading to Hollywood. They don't talk about the loneliness. You would think I could have come up to any one of those girls at the cattle call, and talked eagerly and enthusiastically with her about this wonderful experience.

My few attempts were an exercise in stony rejection. Finally I came to realize there was a reason for it. We were rivals, all in line for the same few parts; none of us could afford friendliness. And so I put aside a personal need (and how many of those I would put aside in the years to come!) for the greater good of my career.

For that is how I saw it. Looking back, it was only an incredible stroke of luck (and the ability to radically change my facial expression in a split-second) that got me into a place like the Hal Roach Studio at first attempt. Most girls tried in vain dozens of times, slept with producers, had abortions or nervous breakdowns, and went nowhere, except possibly home.

But Hollywood was a place of wild chances, unlikely successes, precipitous failures, backstabbing, double-dealing, and astonishing, luminous, achingly beautiful illusion. And it was the illusion that I had come here for.

∞∞∞

Girls with tedious lives need excitement, perhaps even more than their male counterparts. There is a kind of seething quality in female adolescents which only goes unmentioned because people are made so uncomfortable by it. Perhaps Chaplin's stable of teenaged maidens could explain it to them.

I was afflicted with movies, I lived in them, I ached to be in them, and most especially I yearned to be near my idols in the flesh. How often had I heard that these legends were even more magnificent in person, a claim that I found hard to believe but which I wanted to witness for myself.

But now that I was supposedly "in", I felt more isolated and set apart than ever. When it became too much to bear, I called someone I had not talked to for what seemed like a very long time. We met in a dingy restaurant on the Strip in which I ordered sulphurous eggs and poisonous coffee.

While he was still "on the bum" in Santa Fe, Tony Firenze had given me the second number on my list, which I prayed I would not need to use: I could only imagine what kind of sordid "connections" he would have. Tony had been out here for nearly a year, and though he said he had worked his way up to assistant director at Monograph Studio (which I had never heard of), he looked more like someone who would assist a butcher. All that was missing was the bloody apron and the cleaver.

"The little guys look better than the big ones," he told me, and I had the feeling I was in for a long and probably boring lecture.

"Why would that be? Tall men are at such an advantage in real life."

"The tall guys get nowhere. They're just too big up there, blown up on the screen. They tower over the women and scare the audience. Only villains are tall. Short guys are almost the same height as the girls, so they can look them right in the eye."

"I never thought of that."

"And you wanna know something? Short guys have big heads. I mean, in relation to the rest of their bodies. Take a look next time you see a real shortie, his head is the same size as a big guy's head."

"Yes, I think you're right."

"So, big-headed people look better on the screen. Nobody wants to see a pinhead. And it reminds them of babies."

"Babies!"

"Yeah. Babies got real big heads, small bodies. You see an actor like that, you think, *awwww*."

"Like you want to baby them."

"Right. Be my *baby*, snookums!"

"How do you know all this?"

"I been around. You notice things. Some actors, they start to look old when they're thirty. Others just keep on looking good until they're forty, even fifty. Wanna know why?"

"Dumb luck?"

"No."

"Clean living?"

"Not even close. Most of them live like tom cats."

"How about . . . an accident of birth?"

"You're almost there. It's bones. Good bones. If you don't have good bones, everything sort of caves in. That and, well, some guys wear all this white makeup. Covers everything up."

I felt my face grow hot, wondering if he knew about my passion.

"So, the ideal actor — "

"Comedian," he corrected me.

"The ideal comedian is five foot four with a big head, good bones, and an inch of greasepaint."

"Now you're talking!"

When I thought about it, which I often did because my life was so hopelessly dull except for movies and magazines, the three greatest comedians in the world were all undersized. Chaplin had a squat, dwarfish quality, Keaton was just a sad-shouldered little shrimp, and Harold . . .

Harold was a couple of inches taller than the other two, but compact and trim. His small shoulders and perfectly-shaped (large!) head with its boyish mop of thick black hair were almost cartoonish, and perfect for the screen.

At moments of extreme danger (and there were plenty of them in Harold's "thrill" pictures), his hair would stand on end like a startled cat's, a charming effect which must have been done with a jolt of electricity. In whiteface and specs, he looked like a doll, a puppet, a clown — but a clown in natty men's clothing. Watchchain, saddle shoes and a white straw boater hat.

When I even thought of Harold's name, it was as if an incandescent light clicked on, as if I heard a note of wild, jazzy music.

Being a rabid fan of the Glass Character since he invented it in 1917, I had seen (and seen and seen) every frame of every picture he had made. More than once I saw Harold vault over a huge obstacle, shoot up effortlessly to grab a bar, or execute a neat perfect flip, all done with such nimble grace that it made us wonder if we had really seen it or not.

Though later critics declared he was more "mechanical" than the other great comics, this was an inaccurate conclusion. He was brilliant at stringing together elaborate chains of gags which would end with a final, delicious payoff. Far from being mechanical, he was more subtle than the others, particularly in his facial expressions. He emoted "below the line", never mugging or pulling faces or crossing his eyes. This gave him a more intimate relationship with his audience, conveying not just emotion but thought.

But Harold lived very much in his body. Though this classic scene did not unfold until the peak of his career, he would forever be associated with the surreal image of the man on the clock in *Safety Last!* His fans didn't know that his maimed right hand had to bear the weight of most of his body while he accomplished all sorts of comic business The strain of holding on with three fingers dislocated his shoulder, forcing him to let go and land on a big mattress two stories below him. (Later he would say in his matter-of-fact way, "Well, you had to land flat, or you went right over.")

I was not present for the accident, the incident that was to change his whole life, and except for bare details it was kept from the public, but it was legend in the inner circles. Harold himself always graced it over, not talking about it for fear of stirring up pity or morbid curiosity from his fans. He carried it lightly, considering that it was a maiming that might have killed him, rendered him bitter, or destroyed a promising career. Harold chose to be grateful, glad that he had been spared, thankful that he had been given another chance and could go on with his work and his life.

∾∾∾

It happened during a routine publicity photo shoot, the sort of thing Harold hated. He was striking all sorts of odd poses, fooling around with what he thought was a large prop bomb (you've seen them: they look like bowling balls and usually have "BOMB" printed on them) with a big fuse that fizzles dramatically, but doesn't blow up. As the flash-powder cameras on the set popped like fireworks, he took the lit bomb, held it up to his face and attempted to light his cigarette with it. It wouldn't light, and there was too much smoke to see it. As the fuse grew ever shorter, he realized there was something wrong with it: it would have to be replaced. He began to lower it away from his face.

But it did not crackle like a cartoon sparkler. Fire ripped through it in less than a second.

And the unthinkable happened.

It exploded with a sickening blast. White smoke was everywhere. The bomb blew a huge hole in the sixteen-foot ceiling of the studio. A cameraman's upper plate cracked apart in his mouth, and the photographer dropped to the floor in a dead faint.

Harold was blown back with tremendous force. At first no one could even see him: Hal Roach usually unflappable and stolid, ran around crying, "Harold, Harold," in a panicky, near-hysterical voice no one had never heard him use before.

As the thick smoke dissipated, someone cried, "Look over there." It was a great dark pool of blood spreading on the floor. The cast and the crew shouted and coughed and prayed. Out of the oblivion of the smoke came a howl like the sound of an injured animal.

"He's alive," Hal cried. Though it seemed impossible, Harold sat up, pale as wax, his eyes staring straight ahead.

"Harold, lie down, for God's sake, you might have a concussion!"

"Hal, I . . . "

"Don't try to talk." Three crew members almost sat on him, but he would not lie back. With awful slowness, he raised his right hand, inches from his face. His left hand was wrapped tightly around his wrist in an instinctive gesture of self-preservation that probably saved his life.

Stunned shock, disbelief and howling hysteria collided as some of the men were overcome by nausea and smoke. This was a scene from wartime, from the trenches of Ypres or Vimy Ridge. For Harold's right hand had been blown to bits. At first it looked as if all that remained were two skeletal fingers. His index finger dangled by a flap of skin, and his thumb was completely gone. A river of blood pulsed as it gushed down his arm.

Harold stared dully, and said in a dragging voice, "Hal, I can't see."

"Harold, it's just the smoke."

"No. It's not the smoke. Christ, I — " Then the pain ripped through him with terrific force, and in a moment of pure horror and mortal agony, he screamed, "dear God, fucking *Jesus!*", like some sort of obscene, horrible prayer.

The set had become a makeshift hospital with a hopelessly inept staff. Someone had the presence of mind to tie off his hand at the wrist with a belt (all they could find) before he bled to death outright. Then it occurred to them all at once: they might be watching their most valuable property expire.

At last the doctor arrived, bearing a proper tourniquet and a towel. When Harold saw the doctor, it was as if his last bulwark against pain collapsed. His face contorted in an expression so full of agony that everyone had to look away, but he clenched his teeth and did not cry out. His eyes reeled, his body tensed and jackknifed, and he fell unconscious.

The crew still milled around in disorientation. Relief that they would not have to hear those awful sounds again vied with stunned shock, and a dread that he would never wake up. The doctor counted his blessings that his patient would not need chloroform, at least not now, and began to pull the rubber tube as tightly as he could. The white towel he used to mop up was instantly sodden with dark blood.

And if his eyes watered a little as he tried to salvage the raw pieces of Harold's maimed hand, watching what might be the final moments of someone who had made him laugh and delighted him for so many years, wasn't it just the smoke? No doctor worth his salt would weep at a few lost fingers, some bad bruises, perhaps a concussion, and a case of hysterical blindness.

But as he walked beside the stretcher bearing Harold Lloyd to the waiting ambulance, his body lifeless and limp as a dummy, he felt a minute crunch under his foot, and looked down. He saw the black Bakelite frames, the persona of the Glass Character in a crush of broken jigsaw-pieces, and it was then that he hoped no one would notice as his face crumpled up in hopeless tears.

Harold hovered between life and death for four days. His eyes would pop open, seeing nothing, then roll back and close again. His temperature shot up. He was wasting before their eyes. The studio held its breath, and kept the news close. A maimed star is not funny, nor is a burn-scarred, blinded one.

Harold never talked about religion, but there were murmurings he had been raised with a simple evangelical faith in which his mother led the way. One did not argue with his mother, so he and his brother Gaylord put up no argument as the waters of baptism closed over their heads.

She believed that even if the ritual baffled and confused them, Jesus would mark them out for salvation no matter what direction their lives took.

For Jesus was a rock in a weary land, a shelter in the time of storm. Years later when recounting his memoirs to a journalist, he felt the experience was important enough to recall in detail, even though at the time it made very little sense. Later his young life was splashed by the influence of his mother's dabblings in Christian Science, a then-popular philosophy which teaches that mind can triumph over matter and the material world is only an illusion.

In any case, this particular philosophy insisted that all is spirit, and the spirit's wholeness can heal even the most grievous bodily wounds. In and out of a foggy coma, Harold saw beautiful things with his beautiful soul, enveloped by an almost unbearably sweet love that saw everything and forgave everything, a love that touched his core and changed him forever.

His right hand, so essential to his work, was horribly damaged, his blind eyes patched, the right side of his face oozing raw, the skin bubbled and seared down the side of his body. It was almost a certainty he would lose his right eye, which was badly burned and appeared to be punctured. His hand had been destroyed, everyone knew that; it would be no use to him ever again. So the stunts were over. The doctors kept scraping away at the infected tissue until he had only half a hand left.

The pain was beyond description. He sweated and clenched his good hand, telling himself it would soon be over, soon be over, soon be . . . then drifted back into coma. The right side of his face was so raw that it looked like the inside of a butcher store. Fear of gangrene forced the doctor to apply harsh antiseptic on burns that had gone through every layer of skin.

Boils and sores and blisters erupted. His swollen lips cracked deeply, causing even more agony when he tried to eat. When Dr. Gleason had to change the dressing, a hellish huge thing that covered his face and side and adhered to him like glue, Harold always refused morphine. Stubborn, sure he could tough it out, he would brace himself, promise himself he would not cry out.

He failed every time. The doctor one day took hold of his shoulder and said, "Mr. Lloyd, I served as a physician in the Great War. With all due respect, this is worse than some of the wounds I saw on on the battlefield. Even the bravest soldiers took morphine for the pain."

So he took just a little, knowing the drug would only dull the agony, holding on to the future, a time when the pain would finally, mercifully remit.

The nurses flitted about, glancing, murmuring to each other. One particularly awestruck young girl named Candy would sneak in and stand by his bed when he was sleeping, and Dr. Gleason had once caught her touching his face. When he dressed her down for it, she blubbered, "But doctor, don't you understand? I love him."

He let it pass.

Treating Harold's wounds was an ordeal all around, and Dr. Gleason was so concerned about him that he sometimes spent the night in a chair beside his bed. This was not just any patient, after all. One night his fever spiked so badly he had to be immersed in a bath of ice water to prevent a seizure. His screams of shock and agony rent the air, a battlefield sound Dr. Gleason had hoped he would never hear again.

The morning after the ice bath, Dr. Gleason nodded awake in his chair as light speared through the windows. He heard a voice, then two. His head jerked up and he looked over at Harold's bed.

He was half sitting up, with Candy perched on the edge of his bed. They were murmuring to each other, and then he laughed with that irritating, high-pitched giggle. Dr. Gleason's jaw dropped when he saw Harold's good hand resting on her knee.

"Mr. Lloyd."

"Oh, hi, doc. Hell of a bad night last night, I had the worst dreams. But I'm getting the best care possible, aren't I, Candy?"

"Nurse, you're dismissed."

"But doctor — "

"Dismissed!"

❧❧❧

Telling his parents about the extent of the injury was difficult. His father, a charming ne'er-do-well nicknamed Foxy, kept shaking his head in disbelief.

His son, his beloved Speedy, burned, maimed, his hand partly blown away: how could this be? Harold had always been a lucky sort. As a young man, a coin-toss had determined his direction, east or west, propelling him to fame as if by an inexorable fate.

His mother, a stalwart sort who could be formidable when challenged, sat staring at the floor. She was braced, knowing there was something more that the doctor was not telling them.

"I'm afraid I have some more bad news about your son."

No more, Foxy thought. I can't bear any more.

"He's blind."

No words, only a gasp.

"Not permanently, surely. Just from the flash?"

"We're not certain. But you shouldn't count on him regaining his sight."

They counted on it. Came every day, even though the two of them were divorced and did not get on very well. Their broken, imperfect love for each other and for their son was stronger than any estrangement.

Healing in itself is remarkable, the unwhole mysteriously made whole, but something about Harold's encounter with grace awoke in him a tremendous power, and his body began to regenerate. The studio's fear that the right side of his face would be horribly disfigured with scar tissue was unfounded. It was covered with new skin, soft and pure as a baby's. Except for a mark on his chin that they hoped would disappear, almost no visible scarring remained, causing Dr. Gleason to shake his head: "Darnedest thing I've ever seen."

Though it took many months, his sight was completely restored. This was a gradual process, one that tested his fragile patience. The first time he could see even a glint of light with his left eye, he was jubilant, but the doctor warned him not to hope too much.

"But I have to hope," he said, his vulnerable blinded face heartbreaking.

"We can't say for sure if you'll see again."

"I'll see again."

Then one morning when the dressing came off, he could see the shadow outline of the doctor's hand. He let out a whoop of joy, so jubilant that the doctor didn't have the heart to try to bring him down to earth.

Then there was the day it happened. "Say, doc. I think I see colour."

"I don't think that's likely, Mr. Lloyd. Your retinas are still very badly damaged."

"But I'm sure of it."

Dr. Gleason whispered to the nurse, "Get something red. Anything."

She stole someone's jacket, asked Harold to shut his eyes, and held it three inches from his face.

"Open your eyes now, Mr. Lloyd."

"It's red, it's red, it's *red*!" They had never seen anyone so deliriously happy.

Slowly, the same process happened with his right eye, the eye that had appeared to be completely destroyed. *This just doesn't happen*, Dr. Gleason thought.

Harold told everyone, "I've never been so glad to see red."

A bizarre publicity photo exists of Foxy aiming a rifle at his son, who sits outside his home on a lawn chair wearing glasses with smoked lenses (more than a prop, for once). Posing in a "hands up" position, he smiles and waves his ravaged hand gaily in the air. It is swathed past the elbow, an enormous white bandage: for show, or for real? And the "nurse", a stout woman in gleaming white who stands by his side, is surely a Hal Roach extra.

But if he was well enough to sit up, wave his maimed hand about, and generally cavort before the cameras, could total recovery be far away?

mmm

The picture I was in was called *Girls Galore!*, and I knew almost nothing about it, except that the part I played in it could have been cast just as well by a large piece of cardboard. I was asked to stand with a group of girls in the back row, and act excited. I was asked to pull back the covers and get into a bed in a dorm room, at the same time as seventeen other girls. At the end of the first day, I began to realize what "extra" really meant.

I knew the Roach studio was still trying to live down a reputation for turning out a dime-a-dozen one-reeler in a week, pictures that were popular but forgotten as quickly as they were made. Though nearly all comedies were made that way at the time, and the quality had soared in recent years, the old perception still lingered. Was that why I no one would tell me anything about it? It made no sense.

My fellow dorm-mates might have had more information, but they would barely speak to me (perhaps because this was my first picture, and most of them were veterans: was I too much of a threat to them?), and no amount of coaxing would open them up. I tried not to allow myself to hope that I would get close to someone famous (or even mildly famous). I had not quite lost hope that I would see the man I dreamed about, but it was pushed down so far in me I could barely feel it. I still could not allow myself even to say his name.

Several hours were taken up with planting and setting off explosions, which gave me a shudder.

Though I had given up on making any friends on the set, I broke down one day during a quiet stretch and spoke to one of the girls. We were all idly lounging around, many of us smoking, and I was making my first brave attempt, attempting to muffle my choking in a hankie.

"How long will this take?"

The girl, nearly as big-eyed and dark as Bebe Daniels, gave me a dirty look at first, then reluctantly said, "As long as he wants it to."

I assumed she meant Hal Roach, trying to curb my eagerness to have my unspoken hope confirmed.

But I didn't dare ask.

"Have you ever worked with, you know — "

"Y'mean Lloyd? Yeah, I know how he operates. Sometimes he shoots a movie and previews it with an audience, then pretty much scraps the whole thing."

"Why?"

"Because they don't laugh." She was obviously an old hand at the smoking, and blew out a long dragon-like plume, shooting me a glance as if daring me to copy her. "If they don't laugh, it ain't funny, and if it ain't funny, it isn't worth putting out. That's his philosophy. So he starts all over again. He works really hard to make it look easy."

"Then the critics don't — "

"The critics don't know spit. He does stuff, stunts I mean, and I don't even know how he does it, take after take. Then he comes back here so hot and bothered, he dumps a bucket of ice water over his head. The whole cast and crew crack up laughing."

"That must be fun."

"Fun! It's the only time he gets to hear other people laugh, except at those previews, and he really sweats them. A few times he's had to get up and go into the men's room."

Aching with anticipation that my suspicions were correct, I asked her, "Listen, have you actually met him? I mean — spoken to him?"

"He looks through me as if I'm just another prop."

"Does he treat all the — "

"Well, you see, that's the thing. No, he doesn't. I don't think he'd go after someone young as you, though I bet you lied about your age."

Caught out, I turned pink with embarrassment.

"All this stuff with Bebe, well, she's moving on now, and everyone says she had a better offer, but the studio is moving her around like a chess piece, and everyone knows why. As if she's the only girl who's ever got herself in trouble around here."

I tried not to gasp.

"So what happened to — "

The girl looked at me, incredulous at my naiveté.

"They took care of it."

"But why didn't — " I had read and heard that they were in love and would marry some day,as soon as their careers allowed it, though I hoped against hope that it wasn't true.

"She's not his type of girl. Not to marry, anyway. He wants someone, you know, *fresh.*" She said the word with withering sarcasm.

This was only the first of innumerable disillusioning jolts I would receive. But at least it relieved the numbing boredom on set. Some days we weren't needed at all, and were sent home.

There was even talk that the whole picture was off.

One morning, I dutifully reported to the set, and noticed several of the crew fiddling with a large wooden contraption.

I had no idea what it was, though it resembled a very large catapult. I assumed a heavy weight would be fired from it, but to my shock it became apparent that it was designed to fire a human being.

Someone was talking to a man on the crew, not just talking but arguing, his voice rising and falling. His voice was almost like a boy's, decidedly juvenile. He had his back to us. He was all in white: white sweater and impeccable white trousers and shoes. It was obvious from his demeanour that he was not just an actor, but a *movie star*.

"Look," said Mabel Bryant, the girl I had spoken with. "Just look over there."

"Where?"

"*There*, stupid."

He turned around, and I gasped.

He was the best-looking man I had ever seen.

Patrician in looks, with a beautifully-shaped head, thick black hair, vibrant blue eyes, a compact acrobat's body, and a casual demeanour that belied his tightly-wound intensity.

If I could catch his eye even for a second, I would gladly die. But I didn't. Female beauty was everywhere, and at the moment, he had no interest in it.

"It can't be — "

"That's what everyone says. They say it's the glasses that make him look different, but I don't think so. He just goes into character, and the real Harold disappears. You'll see."

Even with all the hundreds of fan photos I had seen, it was impossible to match this dashing figure with *my* Harold, the dear boy with whom I had fallen so rapturously in love. I was not disappointed so much as disoriented, even confused.

There was a long and frustrating wait until we shot anything, and then it was just a boring dining-room scene in a communal hall, which we had to keep repeating. I kept wondering what had happened to Bebe. The two had been as joined as Siamese twins, so associated with each other that it was hard to imagine one without the other.

Then we saw a demure-looking woman, very young and fresh-faced, who had the prerequisite Mary Pickford look, but with a slightly madcap quality, almost like a parody of Mary. Her eyes were lash-fringed and lovely. Though she seemed a little old to play someone in a girl's school, the pale makeup on her face erased several years.

Though I had no idea at the time, when I watched the completed picture I saw that she was exquisite, magnified by the camera lens into a peaches-and-cream doll who breathed out adoration of Harold on cue. In other words, she was just what he needed. I learned that the camera enhances some faces and erases others, and it was a quality beyond anyone's control.

I kept hearing loud discussions, sometimes escalating into near-shouting. I heard "all *right!*", and a door slamming. Then someone strode out of the private dressing room, hit his mark, and began.

It wasn't Harold Lloyd. Or, should I say, the beautiful man I had seen an hour ago wasn't Harold Lloyd, making me wonder which one *was* the real Harold. His whole demeanour had changed. The way he walked. His smile. Even his serious face was completely different. He was softer, sweeter, more of a darling boy. And funnier. Everything he did was quirky and amusing.

The scene with the new actress, whom I was to learn was named Mildred Davis, had to be shot over and over again, but Miss Davis (obviously a veteran in the business) did not seem to mind. She was not overawed, yet privileged to stand close to the Legend, to fuss with his tie, to resist his overtures *(resist! Such agony)*.

Then suddenly she was whisked away, and a stunt double wearing a leather flying helmet and a Harold suit came in to ride the catapult over the high (*papier maché?*) wall of Miss Pettigrew's School of Feminine Deportment.

Though I dared not say anything, my face betrayed shock and disappointment that Harold didn't do this himself, but Mabel just rolled her eyes.

"The studio's not risking breaking his neck after they nearly burned him to death. Besides, you'll see what they do. It'll all look like him."

So the double, a not-very-convincing replica (his head was too small!), was propelled into the air as if from a cannon, and barely hit the huge mattress on the other side, sliding off the far edge into the dirt. Though he was well-padded, knew how to fall and was not badly hurt, everything was put on hold while Hal Roach (who seemed to be directing, producing and doing everything but tap-dance) discussed the failure with Harold.

Bits of their conversation floated towards me: " . . . tested the thing beside a lake, you know, so he landed in the water safely. Could we . . . ?"

" . . . trying to do that . . . can't set up a wall beside the water, or it'll . . . "

So this is what it is to be an actress: waiting and waiting, everything shot out of sequence so that no real plot was apparent, having a day's or a week's work scrapped, listening to endless heated discussions, feeling horrible anxiety about Harold's safety, then waiting some more.

The double tried it again, fell short this time. Was this thing too risky to control? Harold begged to try it out himself. I could just barely hear him:

"All right, we've tried potatoes, we've tried flour, we've tried sacks of cement. Even dummies that flopped around like they were dead. And they all more or less hit their mark. But something's wrong with a real human being."

"Would it be better without arms and legs?"

"Cannonball! It might work, let's try it. All right, Vic."

And it did work better. They photographed it from every angle. Then the minute Hal was out of sight, Harold motioned to the prop men.

"Mr. Lloyd, I don't think — "

"Just do what I say. Roll cameras!"

There wasn't any time to lose. He jammed the flying helmet on and leapt into the cockpit of this awful contraption, tucked his arms and legs, then yelled, "GO!"

He shot up into the air and described a magnificent arc, with a great "ride 'em, cowboy" whoop and a huge exhilarated grin on is face.

And fell disastrously short of the mark, nearly landing on his head.

"*Jesus*, Harold!" Hal Roach said. "Do you want to be goddamn killed?"

"Don't worry so much. I'm fine, Hal."

"Well, you won't be tomorrow. No one is going to insure you if you're going to pull shit like this."

"Not in front of the ladies." He shot Hal a look, got up and dusted himself off, wincing a bit. He had lost his helmet and broken his glasses.

"So what do we do?"

Harold stood and thought. He was concentrating so hard, I could sense something like a hum coming from him.

"Lose the catapult."

"*Lose* the catapult? Do you know how much this will cost us in lost time?" Hal dug in his pocket for a handkerchief, couldn't find one, and wiped his glistening forehead with his arm.

"Dead actors aren't funny. Besides, I have another idea. How high do you think a person can pole-vault?"

"Christ in a rowboat! Why doesn't she just *walk* out of this nunnery or whatever the hell it is?"

"No, this will work, I can see it. The wall is what, twelve feet high?"

"It can be any height you want. It can be twelve *inches* as far as I'm concerned."

Then Harold did something that was a treat for all of us. He laughed. When Harold laughed, half-measures did not suffice. He bent over and put his hands on his knees and surrendered to flat-out guffawing hysterics that went on and on. The crew were gradually caught up in it, then the cast, until we were all helpless with it, howling and wiping our eyes, stopping for a bit to pull ourselves together, then bursting out all over again.

Then, without warning, he stopped dead.

Everyone froze, stunned into silence.

"Now *that's* what I want to hear from the audience. *That's* why we're here today, and every day. We're here to make pictures that make people laugh LIKE THAT. Okay, everybody, back to work."

I looked at Mabel, who kind of shrugged with her eyes in a way that said: welcome to the strange and wonderful world of Harold Lloyd.

～～～

Though I seldom saw Harold, the glimpses were heart-thudding. But it was strange, not at all what I had expected or hoped for. His physical presence wasn't quite real to me: I was not accustomed to seeing him as a flesh-and-blood human being. For one thing, transformed into the Glass Character, he looked odd in colour, too much a part of the real world. I was seeing the strings in the puppet show, even while knowing they would never show when the picture hit the screen.

I kept thinking I had Harold all figured out: a martinet, not even allowing us to laugh; a temperamental star, throwing his diminutive weight around. But for the next several weeks, he was an absolute gentleman, and a funny one: laughing it up with the girls, swinging from a set of bars that mysteriously appeared on the set, hanging from one hand (*oh*, the bad hand; he was always testing out the bad hand!) like a chimpanzee. He seemed to be full of unusual energy, except that no amount of energy was unusual for Harold.

It took me a while to find out, but as usual Mabel let me in on the truth: Harold was already falling for his new leading lady, Mildred Davis, the actress he once referred to as "a big French doll". There were practically bets down as to whether or not she was a virgin, but we all knew she wouldn't be for long. She remained professional when the cameras were on her, and so did Harold. But off-camera, he seemed to be full of helium, more hyperactive than usual.

We all watched them carefully while we went through our endless retakes (the hair-braiding scene in which Mildred/ Mollie confesses her forbidden love for Harold Porter to Evelyn/Janice), but could detect no signs of mutual infatuation, not yet anyway. But perhaps he was biding his time. She was an old-fashioned girl, pretty, funny and fresh, and deferred to him as Bebe would not.

This lent a bit of tension and excitement to work which for the most part turned out to be gruelling and tedious. Most of our scenes did not even include Harold, whom we presumed to be off somewhere figuring out how not to kill himself in his stunts. When one of the girls told me it could take several months to shoot a feature, I wondered if I would be able to last it out. I was paid $2.00 a week, a dismal sum, and had to resort to working for Frankie Lancaster at his dismal den of iniquity in the evenings. Now I knew first-hand what a speakeasy was: thick with smoke, running with illicit booze and full of writhing couples executing the latest dance craze, most of which struck me as obscene. Stuffed into my skimpy costume, I tried to play the part of the fetching cocktail waitress, sliding her precious tips under her garter while men hooted with delight.

But was the set much better? Sometimes I saw and heard things I knew I shouldn't, things that turned me crimson, but my curiosity was so excruciating I had to give in to it. One afternoon while loitering around the exterior set, practicing my smoking to avoid embarrassing myself in front of the others, I heard voices approaching.

I knew who they were, but could not make out all they were saying.

"(Something something), Chaplin's a child molester and Keaton's a drunk. And a mental case. So what's your weakness, as if I didn't know?"

"(Something) a paragon. (Something) you always come third, you have to make up for it.

"I think every girl on this lot has your fingerprints on her."

"Oh, no, it's the other way around. That's why (someone) has to polish me up every day."

"Please, do not tell me who that is."

(Laughter) "(Something) why I have to get married."

"*Have* to? What've you been up to, Harold?"

"If you don't get married by age twenty-five, they say you're a pansy."

"Are you?"

"Hardly ever." (Guffaws).

"You know what Mabel Normand calls you?"

"No, I don't know what she calls me. But I wish she *would* call me."

" 'An Adonis in horn-rims'."

"Mabel said that? That's awfully nice of her. I should look her up some time."

"Or — look up her?" (snickers)

They were getting closer now, would soon walk past me, so I tried to busy myself tidying up stacks of props.

"Can't you even go one day without having sex?"

"You know what they say: an apple a day."

"So for you, it's like brushing your teeth or something."

"Yes, except that I don't brush my teeth as often. Only two, three times a day."

"So you mean to tell me you're going to get your itchy fingers on our best actress . . . "

"Oh, she'll be retiring."

"*What!* She's just starting."

"I have a plan."

"God help us if you have a plan. Please, just leave that girl alone!"

"No, Hal, I mean it. I really love her." He sounded so convincing, so innocent, contradicting everything he had just said about sex and apples.

"So you're saving her for marriage, Harold?" His tone was sarcastic.

"If I can stand it."

"Just let us finish the picture?"

And then they were away, and gone.

But that was nothing. One day I walked into a sort of second prop room that hardly anyone ever used, looking for combs for my hair.

They were both still in costume. They stood pressed together. I was shocked to see she had her foot up on a chair. He was rubbing himself against her, catlike. She stood with her head tilted back, letting out a long, shivering sigh. Her silky black hair cascaded down her back in the requisite curls.

Mabel Bryant.

"Harold, you have to stop now, I have a scene."

"Why stop?"

"Someone will see us, that's why."

His left hand swam slowly southward, then rested on its target. He began to massage her, first very gently, then more quickly and firmly.

"Harold . . . *stop!*"

"Harold, don't stop!" he teased her.

"Oh, oh, *oh* — "

Her head jerked back, and cries of hopeless pleasure erupted from her. Harold held his hand over her mouth, and she burst into muffled laughter.

(I was to learn that I had witnessed his famous policy of "ladies first": a specialized sexual technique, much appreciated by his numerous girl friends, in which the goal was to bring his partner to a paroxysm of pleasure before allowing himself to experience his own. He had threatened to use the notorious phrase as a movie title, but so far the studio had vetoed it.)

I was astonished, offended . . . envious. I wanted his lovely red bow-shaped lips on my mouth, his ravaged hand on my breast. But when he reached over and pulled her silky unmentionables down (as if he'd been doing this for years) and began to fumble lefthanded with his trouser buttons, I could stand it no more.

Incredulous that they would actually think of completing the sex act here, I strode away, shaking my head in disgust. I heard Harold say "oops" in a childish voice, followed by a chorus of giggles.

A crew member saw me stalking away and draped his arm around my shoulders. "So, is old Harold at it again?"

I couldn't get out of there fast enough.

❧❧❧

I must confess that that last scene didn't happen. Given Harold's level of professionalism on the set, it was impossible to even imagine, except in my evil mind. Whether I willed it or not, and even in the land where dreams come true, my fantasies were on the rampage. Every day when I wrote in my diary, I indulged in several pages of pure fiction, in which I was the major player.

The page was the only place where I had complete control over Harold and what he did and said and thought. I would tear the stories up, furious with myself, then start all over again. I even thought about writing a novel, cursed myself for such moral turpitude, and swore I would give the whole shameful practice up.

My stories were ridiculous, as crazy as the scenarios with Rudolph Valentino I had written a couple of years ago. Harold would never do anything remotely like that on the set, would he?But in the moral abyss of Hollywood, "would never" was a relative term, sometimes meaning, "I *hope* he would never" (or "maybe he does"). The truth was, I didn't know if he was as promiscuous as he claimed to be, or if it was only idle boasting designed either to impress or to annoy Roach.

Much later, my screenplay based on what I had seen and heard in those early years (which at the time I believed was my finest work) was universally rejected. Did that mean I had somehow scratched the bejewelled surface to bare the sleazy sequins beneath?

And though my Harold scenario was definitely concocted, "ladies first" may have had a basis in fact: the girls kept clucking about him, almost as if they had first-hand experience. Mabel was curiously silent during these discussions. I had a strong feeling they had had a direct encounter of some kind.

It was not enough to crumple up or even tear up my absurd, disrespectful scenario: I burned it in the ash can, watching with relief and dismay as it curled and blackened into ashes, wishing I could incinerate the passion that ruled my days and nights, whether I wanted it to or not.

Dearest Bea,

Hollywood is not at all what I thought. Oh, yes, it's exciting; but it's also such hard work that when I get back to my shabby little room in this awful hotel, I want to cry from fatigue. Just trying to manage meals (on a hot-plate), washing my clothes in the dingy communal bathroom sink, and keeping myself clean and groomed with a lick and a promise, is even more of a struggle than what I had to deal with back home, where we at least had a decent wringer-washer.

And then there is work. So often we just sit and wait for hours on the set, accomplishing nothing, and somehow this is more exhausting than actually working. And I can't help but overhear the gossip.

I have given up on Mabel, and have started to befriend a nicer girl, Alice, who is about my age. Alice is nice, and very pretty, but naive. I worry about her, sometimes. Girls like that can get into trouble, so I have become a sort of unofficial big sister to her (as you have been to me).

And then there is Harold, a much more complicated man than I thought he was. For the most part, he is businesslike, methodically working through the gags until they feel right to him. The temper storms are rare, and he always apologizes after them. It is impossible to stay angry with him.

I will confess I try to overhear what he is saying.

"These girls . . . yes, I know, but each of them . . . next big thing, and really . . . don't know if we want to . . . might lead to problems if she doesn't know how to . . . "

I wonder if he's contemplating using one of us for a scene? Please, God. Oh cuz, I am already too ambitious!

Then there is the never-ending babble from the girls. One of them got onto the subject of Harold's accident, about which there had been much speculation.

"Everybody knows that if he hadn't lowered the bomb when he did, his head would have been blown off."

"But howcome somebody as smart as Harold —— "

"Mr. Lloyd!"

"Oh all right, Mr. Lloyd, His Highness! How come he couldn't tell the prop bomb from a real bomb?"

"Because it wasn't a prop bomb."

"What, you're saying Charlie Chaplin was trying to blow him up?"

"Well, somebody was. He was becoming a serious threat. They say he makes more than those other two guys put together."

"Oh no."

"Oh yes. He makes more pictures, and people come to them. His fans are extremely loyal."

And then the talk would meander around to such sinners as Clara Bow, Pola Negri and Elinor Glyn. Remember, Bea, how we laughed over that silly verse:

Would you like to sin
With Elinor Glyn
On a tiger skin?
Or would you prefer
To err
With her
On some other fur?

Honestly, cuz, this is a den of iniquity rather than a movie set, though idle slander is often the only way to kill the boredom.

Still, we don't know what will happen next. We live for those few minutes a day when we see him, hear him wrangle with his gag men or clash with Hal Roach.

The two butt heads all the time, and it's interesting, because I can see that something better comes of it than either of them could produce alone. They couldn't be more different, Harold slim and elegant, and Hal a stocky, snub-nosed prizefighter. Even with the constant arm-wrestling between them, one detects a mutual respect.

How far would Harold have gone at another studio? Would he have been given years (years!) to develop a character with any real originality? Maybe there's some truth to the criticism that before Harold, Roach was merely turning them out. I think he is beginning to recognize what he has and is bringing him along as carefully as a promising young racehorse.

I see all this every day, and I know that I am in a position most girls would envy. Whether I appear on the screen or not, I am in a Harold Lloyd movie. And that is more than I ever thought possible. Though it's not the way I envisioned it, my dream is nevertheless coming true.

I know Ma is angry with me. I know she wants to come out here and bring me home, but I'm sure Pa is just as glad I'm gone. No, Bea, I mean it. I know you're supposed to respect your parents: "Honour thy mother and thy father." The Bible tells me so, so it must be true .But how can you honour someone you're so afraid of? There were reasons why I had to leave, and they had nothing to do with Hollywood.

So please tell Ma that NO, I am not involved with any dangerous men, and NO, I am not going out to clubs and drinking at night. And I don't need any money. Just keep telling her that I am working steadily, have lots of friends and am having a marvelous time.

And truly, Bea, being here, lonely and hard as it is, is so much better than enduring Papa's drunken rampages and all the terror that goes with them. The truth is, I'm safer here than I am at home. (My goodness, this is a lot of pages — a movie script in itself!)

I send you my heart.

Jane/Muriel

∾∾∾

Gossip was the only thing that made the interminable days bearable.

Most of all, the girls buzzed about Harold.

One could hardly blame them. He was heaven incarnate. I loved the sweetness of his character, the cartoonish walk, the adorable facial expressions.

Off-camera, he was all business, walking around looking like Harold's distant cousin and scanning the scene as if he were hunting partridge.

I loved it when he was out of breath and sweating like a racehorse, and Hal Roach called out, "Harold, stop, stop, *stop!*" This was an athleticism that seemed effortless, but it was not.

But I was as frustrated as ever, knowing I would probably never even speak to him directly. Shouldn't I be happy just to stand in his mighty shadow? I should thank my lucky stars I wasn't trapped in some wretched Slim Summerville movie.

Meanwhile, *Girls Galore!* seemed to be going nowhere. If it ended with a chase scene, which I hoped it would, I would never get to see it. The girls were nothing but part of the set, just props that were worse than props because they needed to be clothed and fed. So there was a certain unspoken resentment towards us as we were ordered around, or abandoned to sit and wait.

Harold would watch what he had shot, shake his head, slash this and scrap that. He would preview it before audiences, and if they didn't laugh in certain places, those scenes would be ruthlessly cut and destroyed.

This was why Harold Lloyd was so funny. He could not afford *not* to be funny, with two comic legends constantly on his tail. Sometimes he seemed more workmanlike than inspired, and I began to understand what his critics were referring to. Was he too mechanical, or just getting by on that darling boy charm?

But as the experience wore on, I gathered a strange impression of him, one that seemed most unlikely. He was more like a minister than an actor. The work was his calling, his devotion, and he pledged himself to it. At the end of the day, sweaty and out of sorts, he would go home, then appear the next morning once more ready to give himself to the work.

I was to learn that every one of the extras on the set was in love with him, and longed for special favours. Though he seemed to glance at Mabel more than the others, I had no evidence they were actually involved. Would that flickering eye some day light on me?

Meanwhile, I noticed strange things happening around Harold. He was standing near the edge of a very high building when someone dropped a large heavy hammer from the roof. It was going to hit him on the head full-force, maybe knock him out (as he had been knocked out so many times before).

In less than a split-second, he stepped back, his left hand shot out and he caught it. My scalp prickled: what he had done wasn't possible. He hadn't even seen it. It was as if he had slowed down time, or sped himself up to some higher frequency.

It wasn't the first or last time I had seen this. Other comic actors relied heavily on camera effects; Harold used them sparingly, trusting his lightning reflexes. To see the darling boy land a punch was very funny, because the punch was a hard, straight-from-the-shoulder *whomp* that seemed to knock his nemesis flying. But at the same time, it didn't connect at all; that was all part of the illusion.

Such flashes of violence were unexpected, because the Glass Character wasn't conventionally masculine. I knew that even then. His skin was smooth, his movements graceful. Audiences didn't yet know about his juvenile, gee-whiz voice, still stamped all over with small-town Nebraska and not deep or resonant enough to overcome the shallow, tin-plated sound of early microphones. But they didn't know about Chaplin's abominable nasal dithering or Keaton's ugly whiskey baritone, either, so, for the moment, Harold was safe.

∾∾∾

Harold's movies often had elements of fairy tales: the poor, oppressed boy, the unrecognized prince in exile from his rightful title. Regaining himself, proving his virtue and worth by being true to his own principles restored him from Harold the Boy to Harold the Man.

The fact that this pattern repeated itself over and over in his pictures may have said something about Harold, revealing a certain need that was somehow never fulfilled. Some film historians would later make unkind remarks about his emotional immaturity, as if oblivious to the fact that creativity is the province of childhood: not many mature men know how to play on a level that entertains the world.

To be cut down just as his star was ascending was monstrously cruel. The accident was a huge blow, not only to his body but to his sensitive soul. Resilent as he was, he often felt he would never fully recover, though he hid his anxiety from everyone. The boy prince was truly oppressed, faced with a dragon he might not be able to slay.

After three weeks in agony in the hospital, Dr. Gleason guessed he would do better at home with a private nurse. He was flooded with so many visitors (twenty-eight on one afternoon) that his no-nonsense mother stepped in to impose some order.

People were required to call in advance to reserve fifteen minutes with him, after which he would have fifteen minutes of rest. This was precisely observed. Hal came a couple of times, but was uncomfortable, not knowing what to say.

Dr. Gleason saw him one day, noticed his discomfort and took him aside.

"Tell me, what were you filming when the accident happened?"

"Two-reeler about a haunted house."

"So what happened to it?"

He gave the doctor a "what do you think?" look. "We had to scrap it."

"Oh, no. You will not scrap that picture. Shoot around him, then put it on hold until he comes back."

"What?" *Comes back?* A one-handed comedian, facially scarred and almost emaciated, with only partial sight in one eye?

"You heard me. Harold is in a bad way, no matter how he acts on the outside. He needs a goal. Needs to feel needed. If this young man sinks into depression, we'll lose him, body or mind or both."

Hal cast around wildly in his mind. It would never work. It would cost them an arm and a leg. The scenes wouldn't match. He had no hand!

Then he closed his eyes, rolled the dice, and said,

"All right, we'll do it."

The gamble was on Harold's will to get better. When he could see well enough to look at his right hand out of the bandages (his right eye gradually regenerating from a seemingly hopeless condition), he shuddered. He was missing not just the thumb and forefinger, but nearly half the palm of his right hand. The remaining fingers were so stiff and immobile that he could barely move them, and only with excruciating pain.

No one knew what to do.

Hal had told him about the plan to finish *Haunted Spooks,*, and he looked at him like he was crazy.

"I'll never be able to do it."

"You'll do it."

"How do you know?"

"Because you're a tough-minded little cuss who never gives up, that's why."

"No, you're thinking of my character."

"Listen to me, Harold. You didn't see that accident. You were so close, one more inch would have blown your head off. The doctor told me that at one point your fever was 104 and he couldn't find a heartbeat. All these things you're facing now, they're just . . . " He waved his hand. "They're nothing. Just challenges."

Startled, he asked, "How do you know all this?"

"Because you're goddamn *Harold Lloyd.* Look, I hate being mushy, and sometimes I think you're plain crazy. But the truth is, you're not like those other comics. Your character is completely original, and you're just starting to hit your stride. I see it every day I work with you. All your best work is still ahead of you."

"With this bollixed-up hand?"

"*Yes,* with a goddamn bollixed-up hand! Haven't you figured out how to use the other one yet?"

Catching the crude double meaning, they both guffawed. The doctor heard Harold laughing, sighed. Maybe they were making progress, after all.

∽∽∽

After a few weeks earning a pitiful salary on the set, I began to almost appreciate my distasteful job at Frankie's, if only as a strategy for survival. In a few hours I could make more than Roach paid me in a week. My life as a "hostess" mostly involved slapping men's hands away and learning to balance huge trays of elaborate cocktails. We all lived in constant fear of a raid.

It wasn't until much later that I found out I had been working in speakeasy heaven. In spite of the smoke and grabby men, Frankie's was considered high class. It was a literal underground of pleasure, a smoky wolf den below-stairs, with young girls performing bizarre Maypole rites and dancing on the stage in costumes that left nothing to the imagination.

Unlike most of the less-than-law-abiding joints of the day, Frankie's had an orchestra and a dance floor, not much of one, but enough for the flailing arms and legs of the patrons as they threw themselves into the Shimmy or the Baltimore. Tender young men sang in swooping high tenor, and the beat was full of primitive joy. As the evening wore on, dance steps were disposed of, to be replaced by a lot of uninhibited grinding.

Frankie thought of himself as a brotherly figure, when the truth was I really didn't like him. He had never tried anything, unlike Tony the butcher boy who once put his arm around me as we sat at the Bluebird Soda Fountain enjoying a cold Coke. But since I was desperate for companionship and needed protection, I allowed Tony to stand in as my beau.

"Y'know, Janie, sometimes I think you must be seeing somebody."

I knew I looked flustered. "Oh, no, I'm — well, it's no one serious."

"Because, you know, a lot of little girls like you end up with, well, some of the big stars. But it's not what you think."

"I know that," I said in irritation.

"They're just out to use you."

"It won't happen to me."

"It could. I know what's going on."

"What?" I was horrified. How could Tony know anything?

"Mabel. She talks to me sometimes."

"Mabel *Bryant?*" Wasn't this the nasty little pot calling the kettle black?

"She said you have a big crush on, you know, Mr. Glasses."

"Well, she's wrong. It's all business. Mabel is the one who's acting like a tart."

"She saw you staring at him once."

"So what? All the girls stare at him. He's a movie star."

"Through a hole in his dressing-room wall?"

"That's a lie!" I had patched it up weeks ago.

"Even if he does like you, Janie, he's only going to use you. They all want the same thing."

"You have no right to say that about Harold."

"You know how he got where he is? He was willing to do anything, I mean *anything* to get there. All these famous guys are the same way. He *has* to get what he wants. He's dangerous, sis. You just don't see it."

Accusations of danger did nothing to dull my curiosity. Sexual antics on-set were discussed, but usually unseen, if not invented outright. Alice came up to me shyly one morning and said, "Muriel, why did that girl over there call me a name?"

It was as if we were trying to settle a dispute on the playground. "Well, Alice, she's probably not a very nice girl, so maybe you should stay away from her."

"But none of them are nice. Except you." She smiled, teary-eyed, reminding me of my ridiculous audition.

"What else have they been saying?" I could only imagine Mabel's influence.

"They talk about boys all the time."

"Alice, don't listen to them. You're only fourteen."

"What does 'cherry' mean?"

I blanched. To be honest, I wasn't sure.

"It's what they put on top of a sundae," I said.

"Oh. That's what I thought." She planted a little kiss on my cheek, sweet as a five-year-old. Sometimes I wondered if this was a case of the blind leading the blind.

Then the waitresses at Frankie's began to buzz and giggle. Something big was in the works: a bacchanale of sorts planned for April 1. All of Hollywood would be there, Frankie insisted, and I'd get the best tips of my life. And I'd have a chance to see all the big stars of Hollywood, drunk and falling down! This didn't sound appealing, but I did hope they would tip me before passing out.

The air was swampy with smoke, making it almost impossible to breathe. I wielded my trays as best I could and mercifully didn't spill my load of cocktails in Chester Conklin's lap. My scanty dress — if you could call it that — did very little to protect me from grabs and slaps. And in spite of what Frankie had promised me, I didn't see any big stars, drunk or sober.

I had ducked into the kitchen for a desperate attempt at tidying myself up, the swinging doors blew open, and my stomach turned over.

This was a star, all right, but one I loathed: Roscoe Arbuckle, known by the unappealing nickname of Fatty. At nearly three hundred pounds, he deserved the name. I had heard stories about him, and none of them were good.

I instinctively backed off, but he kept on coming. I wondered where everyone else had gone. Dear God, had Arbuckle arranged it that way? "Hey doll face, come on out and dance with me."

"I'm sorry, Mr. Arbuckle, I'm working right now and I don't want to lose my job."

"Your job. Doesn't that cockroach pay you enough?"

How did he know about all this? Did Frankie tell him?

"Please don't insult Mr. Roach that way."

"Why not? He grinds out garbage and calls it 'art'. A two-reeler a week starring that pansy with the glasses."

I felt sick with shock and disgust, but could do nothing.

"The guy isn't funny. Everyone in Hollywood knows it. Even *Roach* knows it. Only keeps him on because he's cheaper than the other guys, the real stars, and he knows how to work to formula." He seemed to be slowly getting larger, as if he were inflating himself.

"Then why does everyone go to his pictures?"

"Because they're sick of all those other no-talents. All they have is gimmicks. Turpin, Conklin, Chase. Sure, crossing your eyes makes you funny!" He threw his cigarette butt on the floor, making me wonder if it would start a grease fire.

Even for Arbuckle, this was extreme, and I cold only conclude he was so drunk he didn't know what he was saying. What was it Harold had said about him? "Oh, he has talent, big talent, one of the best, but he'll trip himself up if he doesn't watch out." He meant booze, the dangerous pleasure that had destroyed so many,and would undo Arbuckle in the worst way possible.

He fished around in his pocket and pulled out a $100 bill, tucking it into the front of my uniform. "This ought to keep you going for a while."

"Mr. Arbuckle, with all due respect — "

He yanked me by the arm. It was clear that we would be dancing right here, not on the dance floor. Where was everyone? *Where?* Why had the entire staff disappeared?

Mr. Arbuckle's idea of dancing was mostly horizontal. I hated his filthy fat hands on me and wished I could smack him across his bloated face. He jammed his fingers into my crotch, and though I squirmed with loathing and disgust, I was horrified when a jolt of electric pleasure shot through me.

Then the doors blew open and Frankie strode in. "Okay, mister, that's enough Your time's up." Relief at being rescued overcame my shock at what he was saying. His time was up?

Arbuckle was at that tipping point between extremely drunk and unconscious, so was unable to resist when Frankie rolled him out of the kitchen like a piece of scenery. I slumped against the counter, my heart thudding hard. Had I been rescued, or set up, or both? It was something I was never able to figure out.

ↄↄↄ

Having thrown away the catapult (which likely would have broken his back anyway), Harold, who had never pole-vaulted in his life, began to experiment. He reacted to the series of falls in various ways: sometimes with laughter, sometimes bitten-off curses (for he generally didn't swear in front of women), sometimes with winces and limps that he tried to hide.

Hal took him aside more than once to ask him, then ask him please, then beg him to let his double do the stunt (which wasn't likely to work anyway, as the wall was just too high). Harold had that furrowed brow, that I'm-thinking-about-this-and-I-don't-like-it look.

"How am I going to get inside?"

"Why doesn't someone just let you in?"

"Could work, but we'd have to set it up."

"Why don't you use your head as a battering ram, and Miss Pettigrew opens the door — "

"That's the oldest gag on record. Why don't I just blow the place up?"

"We don't have enough explosives. Place is built like a fortress. Plus it'd kill everybody and we'd have no story." As was common then, our exterior set had been used over and over again, as a jail on the frontier, an army barracks, a hospital, and any number of other institutions.

"Throw up a grappling hook and climb the wall? A thief in the night."

"With a black mask on."

"No black mask, it'll make me look like a cat burglar or — worse."

(Titters from the girls.)

Harold spent the rest of the day climbing up. Though the wall looked fragile, it somehow held. I should not have been surprised that he was able to do it, as he seemed to be able to master physical challenges almost effortlessly.

But it just wasn't working. He didn't even need to see the rushes to know it. It didn't feel right, and it wasn't going to be funny.

"Why? Looks okay to me."

"It just doesn't have the right energy to it."

Yet another day went by when we all sat around doing our nails, brushing and braiding each other's hair. Roach liked the look of it, so it became part of the movie. It was as if we really were in the same dormitory, virginal schoolgirls instead of glorified waitresses and runaways.

As far as Alice was concerned, sometimes I thought I was nursing her like a puppy. When I found out she was only thirteen, I was horrified and tempted to turn her in, but she begged me not to, telling me her father liked to drink and once knocked her across the room. My stomach turned over in empathy and shock: were we a kind of sorority, then, all the girls who had fled to Hollywood to escape violence and pain?

I shuddered for Alice's safety. She was so naive about men and sex that she did not even seem to understand basic reproduction.

"We used to say that a girl could get . . . you know . . . "

"In trouble?"

"In trouble," she blushed, "from kissing. You know, that special kind of . . . "

"French."

"Yes, French kissing."

"Alice, has a boy ever kissed you?"

"On the cheek. Well, he was my cousin."

"Alice, you're going to have to be very careful. Men can take advantage of a girl like you." As I said them, I heard the irony in those words.

"Oh, no, I'm sure Mr. Lloyd would never do anything like that! He's so sweet and gentle, like a boy. I love him so much!"

The glow in her eyes no doubt reflected mine. I felt ashamed of myself, and knew the next words I said were more for me than for her:

"Alice, be very, very careful around Mr. Lloyd. He is not who he seems. He is a grown man who chases after women until he catches them, and he sometimes takes advantage of them."

"I don't understand."

"Alice . . . " How could I spell this out when she seemed so completely ignorant?

"Alice, he is the sort of man who doesn't wait until he gets married. Do you know what happens between a man and his wife?"

She looked confused. "They kiss, and . . . "

"They do more than kiss. And you can end up . . . expecting, whether you're married or not. (She looked incredulous, as if such a thing were not possible.) Be very, very careful, Alice, and don't ever be alone with a man. *Any* man. And especially not with Mr. Lloyd."

She looked grateful, but also hurt and confused.

◦◦◦◦

Miss Pettigrew's girls sat and fidgeted and waited. We could hear talking, arguing, male voices rising and falling. This was the usual battle over the next move (for none of Harold's movies were scripted, just worked out gag by gag, the plot inventing itself).

A winner emerged.

"I don't think it will fly."

"I know it will work, Hal, I know it will be funnier than going over. Just trust me."

We looked at each other. Was he contemplating — going *under?*

"I don't see how we're going to get that cross-section where the audience can see you in the tunnel. And what happens to the dirt? This is all wrong, Harold."

"But that's just the point, the dirt is piling up behind him so there's no escape. And he digs and digs, and suddenly his head hits this solid wood — "

"And he suffocates."

Harold just gave him a look, and he subsided.

"So you think, that's it, he's done for! He's hitting this wood which turns out to be the floor of the place, and just when he's about to give up — "

"The trap door in the floor opens, and — "

"His head pops up, and here come the girls!"

It did seem like a weak idea, one that even a Harold Lloyd would have trouble executing. A whole day was taken up with digging holes. How to dig a hole and make it funny? Then came the logistics of the side view, in which he turned himself around like a mole in a burrow: this was shot away from us, so there was more sitting around.

Voices drifted around me.

"Have y'ever, you know . . . "

"Not with him."

"I think he's doing it with Mabel."

"*Everybody's* doing it with Mabel."

"I hear he's . . . " My dorm-mate whispered something in her ear, then pretended to fan herself.

"Well, yeah, he's pretty cute."

"His character is pretty cute. *Harold* is completely gorgeous. What about that smile? It's a dazzler. And he knows what he's doing, you know what I mean?"

"He seduces everybody. Everything in sight."

"Who told you that? It's a lie. He's, well, he's particular."

"Is it your turn this week?"

"*Bitch*!" The two of them looked daggers at each other. I wondered if hair-pulling could be far away.

As if a whistle had been blown, we were all martialled to our places in the dorm room. Once again we were instructed to look demure, in partial undress (though nothing to offend the code of decency). Just having your hair loose down your back was considered risqué back then..

Then Mildred Davis walked in, her smile enchanting. The girls breathed excitement and awe: we would be *this* close to someone who was *that* close to Harold! Miss Davis sat in the middle of the group reading a letter, the significance of which we did not know (though it would show up later in the titles). Instead of talking, she moved her lips. (Harold always talked out loud, thinking it would look more natural.) Then she exited.

I was thinking that it would be very helpful if we knew what was going on. Then, in the middle of the confusion, the trap door in the floor flipped open, and Harold's head popped up like a prairie dog's, his face a study in confusion.

There came a chorus of giggles from the girls, but the cameras were rolling, so Harold held his expression. He could screen out dynamite if he wanted to, with that concentration of his. He seemed to shoot straight up from the hole (how did he achieve these things?), and climbed out, with six feelings on his face, *confusiondismayjoydisappointmentcuriosityfear.*

The next direction was, "Girls, come forward now, and make a fuss."

We looked at each other.

"Make a fuss over Harold. You know, you haven't seen a man in how long — "

This wasn't a women's prison or a convent, so the direction seemed silly, and none of us knew how to proceed. We were timid, unsure, needing individual direction.

Hal started moving girls around like chess pawns. "You, yes, you, come over here, you just stand there with your hands clasped and sort of sigh over him. You, come on over, kneel down and look up at him. You . . . "

Though it seemed ridiculous, the tableau shaped up and worked better than I thought it would, especially with Harold's mercurial facial expressions and eloquent body. The man could act with his back, I thought.

"Wait," Hal said. "Where's the little girl who smiled while she was crying?"

Dear God.

Harold gave a comic shrug, still in character. He had no idea who Hal meant.

I wanted to scream: *me, me,* look over here!, but I had been trained too well to efface myself, to bite the inside of my lip and keep quiet. Then I thought of Gloria Swanson, and wondered if she would keep her mouth shut in the same situation.

But I wasn't Gloria Swanson.

My one, my only shot at fame was dying in front of my eyes. Hal scanned and scanned, sweeping back and forth. "What was her name, Marabelle, Millicent, Melinda — "

His eyes stopped.

And then he said the most wonderful word an extra could hear.

"*You.*"

"Yes, sir?" (I really did sound like someone in a girls' school.)

"Come on over here." Heart thudding in my chest, I came over.

"Stand close." I thought I *was* standing close.

"Closer."

Dear God . . . such sweetness; such helplessness! Tumbling headlong down a long flight of stairs. Falling into the well . . .

"Now I want you to muss his hair."

It was like being close to an exquisite wild creature, a deer or an exotic butterfly. I could not believe his beauty: I could see his skin through the pale makeup, his eyes so full of eager intelligence behind the boyish black-rimmed glasses, his thick head of shining dark hair. I was so close I could breathe him in, and he smelled *so* good.

I reached out, but I was trembling. I cursed myself; it would show in the take and ruin it. I had to be casual, to run girlishly up to this stranger and fuss over him while he dithered in confusion.

He looked at me, not through me, smiled just a little, and said in a low voice that no one else could hear, "Nervous? You don't have to be."

I nodded.

"Remember, you're the character, not you."

While he had spoken those few words to me, he looked completely different, that combination businessman/pastor who came in to plan the stunts every day.

Then, instantly, he snapped back to the other Harold.

His creation was a sculpture made of translucent ivory, wrought with his hands, his feelings, his mind. His creation was not a real person, never born, just made. Only God makes people, so he would be punished for it, I was sure.

But such beauty! Such invented beauty, refined out of the raw ore of his nature. And I stood in awe, so close to him I could feel a radiant nimbus of heat all around him.

So I did what Hal told me: I mussed his hair. I tried to make it convincing. With all the other girls swarming around him, the comic effect was quite good. He was in heaven, but also awkward and embarrassed. Though touching his hair had been heart-lurching, there was another girl holding on to his leg.

We did seven more takes. A lot of hair-mussing. When I was alone, I could not stop smelling my right hand, with its faint tinge of orange-blossom pomade overlaying the warm scent of his hair.

"And — cut!" Hal seemed happy with the effect.

Harold stood there looking down, with his brow in a knot.

Oh-oh. We all knew that look.

"I don't think this is working," he said.

It was likely that all our hard work would end up on the cutting-room floor, while Harold came up with yet another variation on a theme.

But I had touched him. And he had spoken to me. I had stood so close to both of them, the two Harolds. It was more than I could have asked for in my wildest dreams.

Harold could not stop looking at the remnants of his right hand. His career was over unless they found a solution. The most they could hope for was a dead hand, something that would look grotesque and show up in every scene, making his audience feel sorry for him.

But his mother, a strong woman who believed that everything was possible with faith, prayed for an answer as she stood by his bed at night, her hand resting on his dark hair.

The boys tossed around ideas, all bad.

"Okay then. He won't have much mobility. But can we at least make it look realistic?"

"I don't see how. Makeup people do faces, maybe noses. Not thumbs and fingers."

There was a long, awkward silence.

"Jesus," Hal said. "I just thought of something."

"What?"

"Samuel Goldwyn."

Now they knew he was crazy.

"What did Sam Goldwyn do when he first came to this country?"

Silence.

"His name wasn't Goldwyn then. You couldn't even pronounce it, so when he got to Ellis Island they changed it to Goldfish."

"He sold fish?"

"Can the wisecracks. You know what he did? He swept the floor in a glove factory in the garment district. Worked his way up to being a cutter. Ended up as their top salesman before going into the picture business."

"Get to the point."

"Sam Goldwyn knows gloves."

Another silence.

"Not any little two-bit gloves, either. The finest kid gloves, custom-made to fit. You know how you can never get gloves to fit?"

A light was dawning.

Sam Goldwyn paid a visit to Harold Lloyd. It was 1919, so neither had crested in their fame, but both were ascending fast.

Harold offered his left hand to shake.

"Mr. Goldwyn."

"Mr. Lloyd. What can I be doing for you?"

Harold awkwardly unbandaged his right hand, still pink and tender and not completely healed.

Sam Goldwyn gently turned the hand this way and that. Measured it. Got a feel for the shape of it. Looked carefully at the other hand, did the same things to it.

"We need a match," he said. "See, we make cast of this hand here. The good hand, we call him Lefty, say? We reverse him. Then we make the glove from it."

"It'll never stay on."

"Stay on, I have to show you how that works. I think this all out before I come! You fasten way up here (he touched the crook of his arm), up here, see? It's going to be tight, but you'll get used to it. It will fit like — what? Fit like a glove! The leather will be thin and tight as we can make it. And we'll make new of these." He tapped his index finger and thumb together so enthusiastically, his hand looked almost like a puppet.

"I don't understand."

"The first finger (he grabbed Harold's left index finger, to his alarm) will be sewed right on to your middle finger, so — (grabbing his middle finger and pinching them together so hard it smarted). Now move them together."

"Say, what's this all about?"

"Move fingers, now. They're stuck together."

Mystified, Harold did what he was told. A light was dawning.

"Now, let me understand this. You're telling me you'll make a glove with a false thumb and first finger, and the first finger will be attached to — "

"Yes, yes, yougaddit! Attached to next finger. Wave the fingers now, that's right, up and down. Just like you're saying toodle-oo! Or Judy making the punch in the puppet show."

Harold wondered what he was talking about. "But I still don't see how it'll work. How can I make it look natural?'

"You a betting man, Harold?"

"I don't go to the racetrack."

"What I'm betting on, you're shuffling cards by the end of the year, once you figure it out."

"It will show on screen."

"Not unless they're looking for it. Don't hide it, they won't see it. Magic trick, it's like. Hide in full sight, son, they can't help but miss it!"

In spite of his labyrinthine quirks of speech, Sam did exactly what he said he would do. It took several tries, but he designed an elegant glove impossible to spot at a glance.

Harold, being a talented magician well versed in sleight-of-hand, learned to do almost everything left-handed, and hardly anyone noticed. There were a few ragged edges: sometimes the right hand hurt like hell when he used it too hard, which was most of the time. While playing a particularly ferocious game of handball, he broke his right arm. And his left-handed writing was so crabbed and ugly, he forced himself to switch, spending hours practicing script like a schoolboy.

But on camera, his new hand passed. Look at photos of it now, all these decades later, and you will spot it so plainly it's a shock. The skin is wrinkled, and the thumb looks peculiarly inert. But back then, we didn't see it because he didn't want us to see it. It's the oldest magician's trick in the world. The hand is quicker than the eye.

By all accounts, Harold returned to work in only eight months, filled with gratitude for his survival and bubbling over with the sheer joy of living, eager to return to his beloved pictures. Just full of ideas, all the ideas he had been hoarding during his relatively-short recovery period.

He overworked himself, of course, and did stunts that he wasn't ready for, because that was Harold, more driven and insecure than anyone knew. And in more pain. He had pills for it, even shots, but they dulled his reflexes, so for the most part he didn't use them.

After a particularly gruelling shoot, when the right side of his body felt like it was on fire and his vision was terrifyingly blurred, he was wiping the pale makeup off, splashing cold water, drying his face with a towel, when something happened which shocked him to the spine.

All at once he broke into loud sobbing, powerless to make it stop.

Panicked, he tried to hold his breath (no use), stuff the towel in his mouth (futile). He could not even keep it quiet. The crew outside his dressing room looked at each other. What on earth were they to do? Cause him even more embarrassment and pain?

They ran to get Bebe Daniels, his leading lady.

"Bebe. You've got to see Harold."

"See Harold? What's the matter with him?"

"It's . . ."

"He's not hurt?" Her voice was full of genuine alarm.

"Not exactly, but — "

"Oh, just tell me what the problem is."

"He's . . . well, he's crying."

"*What?*"

Happy Harold, crying? Never-say-die Harold, who always got back on the horse? Bite-the-bullet Harold, who silently endured pain after stunts went wrong? Sunny-side-up Harold, the Harold who would not even allow long faces in the cast and crew?

By the time she got to his dressing room, she could still hear the harrowing, difficult sound of his sobbing. He jumped when he saw her, then quickly turned his face away.

"Oh, Harold," she said softly, drawing his head down on her shoulder.

Her tenderness released whatever self-control he had left.

"My baby, my baby." She knew she should not be saying it. Those feelings were long over, weren't they?

His whole body heaved. She wondered if this was the expression of all the pain and fear he had bitten down on for months.

"I can't stop it, Beebs."

"Don't try. You've had such a shock. You nearly died, and it wasn't that long ago."

"I feel like such a fraud."

"You're the bravest man I ever knew. *Too* brave. In fact, you're a complete idiot for coming back to work so soon."

"The boredom was killing me. I didn't want to start drinking, like everybody else around here."

"You won't. You're not the type." She caressed his back, and he sighed, shuddering a little. Like a small child who has been howling, little involuntary sobs rose in his throat.

"I miss you, Beebs."

"We've been over that."

"I don't know why the studio has to run our personal lives." He was regaining himself, standing a little taller. The shoulder of Bebe's dress was soaking wet.

Bebe looked at him, knowing there was more to it than that.

When Harold first came to Hollywood, he was eager and full of ideas, but very naive. He fell hard for Bebe and was astonished by what she knew, particularly about sex. She was shockingly young, but no younger than Chaplin's innocent maidens.

Some people saw her as "fast". Later in her career she would be known as the "Good Little Bad Girl". Harold wasn't exactly a virgin, but he soon found out how ignorant he was. Things happened with Bebe in the backs of taxis, things he had never even heard of, madly pleasurable but somehow suspect.

Ingrained with the notion that sex meant marriage, and ignorant of what a lifetime of commitment meant, he impulsively proposed, then quickly realized it would never work. Though he was almost ten years older, his maturity lagged far behind hers. When a good offer came from another studio, she took it, not realizing her career would never be the same without him.

He leaned in to her, his face still tear-streaked like a little boy's, cupped her face and gave her one of his voluptuous, soul-sucking kisses. And another.

"Harold, don't."

And another.

❧❧❧

The tears still broke through at odd, unexpected times. Mortified and confused, Harold went to his doctor to find out why he could not stop crying.

"Shell shock," he said.

"*What?*"

"If you were a soldier in action and got blown up by a shell, burned over half your body, had most of your hand blasted off and gone blind, wouldn't you expect to have some sort of reaction?"

"Reaction?"

"Yes, reaction!" For such an intelligent man, Harold could be remarkably obtuse.

"Such as: 'ouch'?" Harold was playing with him.

"No, that is not what I mean. I mean getting the shakes and crying uncontrollably. I've seen it in the toughest men you can imagine. Your body and your mind are gradually releasing the trauma and shock, which means you are recovering psychologically as well as physically. It's actually a good sign, Harold, a sign of health returning, so don't be alarmed. Just bend over and take deep breaths."

"Oh." The idea of being a war hero appealed to him, but blubbering still didn't seem like a fitting response. "How long will it go on?"

"Until you don't need to do it any more."

This made sense to him. On some level he was still reverberating from the wrecking-ball impact of the accident, which he had endured with his natural resilience but which had left fine cracks of damage in his sensitive soul.

He wondered what a wounded spirit looked like, felt like. He looked in the mirror while in character, didn't see a difference. Still the same old Glass Character, eager and smiling. Took the glasses off, and jumped. He had always looked eerily, radically different from his creation, not even as close as a brother, but this time the contrast was startling. There was something in his eyes, eyes that had been blinded, then restored to sight. It was something he could not put into words.

Putting the glasses back on, he went back to work, taking solace in the adrenaline rush and hard physical punishment of the stunts.

Dr. Gleason spoke to Hal Roach. "Watch him carefully, Mr. Roach. His body is back to normal, but he could be on the verge of a complete mental breakdown."

"Jesus. Harold? I can't believe it. Shouldn't he stop working?"

"It would kill him for sure. Just watch him."

When the feeling came on, Harold treated it like any other insult of his work: stopped what he was doing, bent over with his hands on his knees, and took huge shuddering breaths. The cast was a bit confused, but no more confused than usual, for Harold was full of eccentricities. They wondered if he had asthma or bronchitis.

After a while, he didn't need to do it any more.

On a particularly vile day when we were supposed to be doing outside shots, I got caught in a downpour such as I had never seen before: a California monsoon of sorts. As everyone ran blindly for some kind of cover, I heard an unmistakeable voice under the rolling thunder:

"For God's sake, miss, get in here."

"Mr. Lloyd — "

"Forget that nonsense, call me by my name."

He held out his hand and pulled me in next to him, in a tiny dry patch under a roof. "You're the girl who mussed my hair," he said, beaming at me. "Muriel, isn't it?" I thrilled at the sound of my name in his mouth.

This was a small space, very small indeed, and I was somewhat alarmed. I had never been really intimate with a man, so had no knowledge of being this close to a man's body, clothed or not. It was not just his heat, but the incredible racehorse energy in him which startled me: held back in the starting gate, he was restless and aching to go. I felt dizzy, swoony almost, with a sweet heaviness gathering in me as I felt him tensely breathe.

At one point he turned and smiled at me, and my heart sank, for this was the antic impersonal smile of the Glass Character, jaunty in the face of any pickle. I remembered being allowed to touch his hair, to tousle it like a little boy's. I ached to have him touch me, to *want* to touch me.

I felt ashamed of what was happening in my body, but at the same time I felt a sort of awe at the natural force, the power that seemed to be lifting me up off my feet. Our bodies were literally pressed together, and when I tried to edge out of the tiny dry strip into the hammering downpour, his hand came out, gently but firmly grasped my shoulder, and pulled me back.

"Now Muriel, there's no need to get soaked. Let's wait it out." He talked as if he had all day. He was using a different sort of voice now, the kind you'd use at Frankie's to get in. He did not look directly at me; that would have killed me. I was close enough that I could not ignore the smell of his dampened, stunt-dusty clothing, the white greasepaint that transformed his face, the hot scent of his sweat.

I wasn't aware of the large drop of rain hanging off the end of my nose, but he saw it and smiled — a real smile this time, with marvelous relaxed eyes — reached out with a forefinger and flicked it off. My face was awash with a rising warmth, the blossomy scent of my hair released by the freshness of the rain.

And I would have died right then and there, his unnervingly lovely gaze sustaining me for the rest of my life, when I noticed something about him, something (even in my naiveté) I could not quite believe.

Virgin though I was, I had kissed and petted with boys before, and knew what happened to their bodies as a result. Without having to look, I realized with shock (and elation, and shame, and despair) that I was not alone in the feelings I had been struggling with. Whether he willed it or not, he was responding to me as a man responds. What sort of unknown power did I have to stir him that way?

Then, incredibly, instead of dissipating, the downpour increased in force, gushing down with tremendous intensity. There was a hissing, searing flash of light followed by a terrific, bone-shaking crack of thunder.

Harold let out a mad whoop of laughter, then jumped out into the deluge, throwing his head back, opening his mouth, stretching out his arms like some demented forest creature driven mad by the moon.

"Come on out, Muriel, it's marvelous!" He spun around and around in mad circles, stirring up a tremendous muck under his feet. I would not have been surprised if he had got down and rolled.

"Muriel, Muriel, come on out!" The man was an absolute infant, a case of arrested development, an embarrassment to the acting profession. And — I did what he said. I came out into the rain, a steamy, mucky, uncomfortable mess, my hair sodden and my skirt weighed down.

Harold's clothes were glued to him, not just caked but clumped with mud. He was jumping up and down with a wild smile on his face, and after a while, reluctantly, I joined him. He grabbed my hands and swung me around and around. I prayed that everyone else had run for cover and would not see us cavorting like naughty babies.

"Muriel, Muriel — " And he did the thing I had dreaded and prayed for, grabbed my shoulders and pulled me almost violently close. I knew he was in a state of arousal, any fool could see that, but what worried me was my own arousal, the part of me that wanted to toss caution to the wind.

"Let me kiss you," he said breathlessly.

"Harold, you can't."

"Only once, I promise."

"Harold, no."

"Muriel, *mmmmmmmmmm*." He grazed my mouth with his lips. For a long time he just stood there, barely making contact.

Then I remembered what the girls had said. *Ladies first.* The way he carefully prepared his . . . victims.

I knew I should have pulled away, and I didn't because I was crazy in the head for him. I understood at last what being drunk must be like. We swayed slightly, almost as if we were dancing. His mouth pressed gently on mine, then just the tip of his tongue parted my lips.

This is what it should be like. Not having some stupid boy stick his tongue down your throat, with beery breath and fumbling, clumsy fingers. Harold lightly caressed my face while he kissed me, soft as roses. *The man is an absolute master,* I thought.

By the time he grew a little more bold, I was in such a state that I wondered if I could even remain upright. The rain had just about stopped. The ferocious black sky was breaking up, the clouds dissipating.

We were two mud statues embracing, our tongues entwining as everything dripped all around us. The heady freshness in the air mixed with the smell of sex, a smell that was beginning to be familiar to me. And below and beneath that, the rude smell of mud.

Then, oh horrors, the worst thing possible: "Harold! *Jesus!*"

What happened next was a scene straight out of one of his movies: he jerked back from me, looked at me in shock, turned around and looked at Hal, then back at me, as if he had no idea who I was.

"Harold, if I've told you once, I've told you a thousand times. Don't screw around with the extras!"

"I'm *not!* We were just having a little . . . talk."

"Christ, right out in the open. Haven't I warned you about that?"

"It was raining out. Everybody went inside, nobody could see us. I promise."

"You're an idiot."

"Yes, I guess I am."

"No more 'little talks'. He talks with his hands, miss. And other parts." Hal stalked past us, and shocked me by reaching out and slapping the back of Harold's head, hard.

Harold ducked, winced, looked truly contrite. His little innocent dalliance had turned out badly, and he knew he had embarrassed me.

"I'm sorry," he said, with his sad little-boy face, his eyes.

I didn't know what to say. To cry would be disaster. It was plain he'd kiss anything with a pulse. It occurred to me that I would be within my rights to slap his face.

Just as I had the thought, as if he'd heard it, he said, "I deserve to be slapped, Muriel."

"Oh, Harold, don't be ridiculous."

"No, I mean it. I broke the code of honour. Slap me."

"Harold!"

"*Slap* me." He grabbed my wrist and wrestled with me. I was dealing with a crazy person. I wrenched away from him.

"You deserve to be slapped, you self-important, ignorant little hick! Don't you think people see through you?" I was appalled at myself even as the words came out: I knew that nothing could hurt him more. "But I won't, because you'd probably enjoy it. That's how hopelessly immature you are."

All the air seemed to go out of him. He did not look like a movie star, ankle-deep in mud, his rain-streaked makeup ashy and unnatural. He looked awkward, defeated, a small-town boy out of his depth.

"I don't know what to say. I really am sorry." He was back to Harold the human being again, shocked at his own outrageous behaviour.

"Stay away from me from now on."

"Muriel, I really do like you. I mean it."

"You like a lot of girls, Harold. I see it going on right under my nose."

"But wouldn't it be nice if we could be — "

"*No*, Harold."

"Muriel, you don't know how lonely . . . I mean, I just don't have time for friends. I think you're special."

Even though my body screamed *forgive him*, even though another part of me told me to slap him hard, to give him what he (and I) wanted, I had to walk away from him with my head held high, and not look back.

❧❧❧

After screaming abuse at him, let alone being caught kissing him out in the open, I was sure I would be immediately dismissed. But I was in for yet another surprise. The next morning the wardrobe mistress, the same one with the pins in her mouth, handed me a small folded-up note.

Dear Muriel, I hope you can find it in your heart to forgive me for the way I acted last night becaus I know I insulted your dignity and your womanhod and I would not be surprised if you didn't want to speak to me. ever again, But I hope you will stay with us, we think you have talent and even the chance for a career someday if you keep out of the way the likes of me, I am most awfuly sorry and I hope we can still be friends, Id like that very much.

In my deepest apology,
Harold

It was as if a small boy were apologizing for stealing an apple. It did not help that his handwriting looked almost like grade school printing, that his writing style was awkward and unsophisticated (the remnants of going to a dozen different schools). I wanted to tear it up, throw it out, burn it, but I folded it in half and secreted it in my diary, along with a photo of Bea, a copy of the Twenty-third Psalm, and a lock of my mother's hair.

❧❧❧

Dearest Bea,

I know this is going to sound like some sort of mad dream, but something happened with Harold (I don't call him Mr. Lloyd any more, by his request) that I must share with you before I go completely mad.

I have no idea if he really likes me or not, or is just trifling with me. From everything I've heard, the latter is probably true. But oh cus, he kissed me. I'm not sure why he did it. We were out in the rain and we were alone and I lost my head and he looked so beautiful, and . . .

This is no fantasy, though I am sure it must appear that way to you. He did sincerely apologize, though in my heart I wish he hadn't. I know I should leave this place right now, and think of this picture solely as an experience to put on my resumé.

I want to finish up this shoot, try my luck at Mack Sennett or one of the other studios if Mr. Roach will put in a word for me, or even try to get an agent. Though it seems far-fetched, all the talk among the girls has made me realize that's it's possible. Connections lead to connections. Even Frankie (to hear him say it) knows people. In fact, he claims he knows everyone in show business, all up and down the moral scale.

Oh, I know you think I'm being foolish and exposing myself to danger. But Sissie, if I hadn't run away from Pa, I don't know what would have happened. He can't help it, he's a prisoner of the drink, but it makes him so violent, and then the next day he is so contrite before doing it all over again. Am I in any more danger out here?

Meanwhile, Tony Firenze has gone from friend to good friend to boy friend, and it seems we are actually dating. He's an unlikely choice, I know, but there is real kindness in him, and he wants to protect me. And he keeps the worst of the loneliness away.

I sit and talk to the extras (some of whom have now been promoted to bit players, due to the fact that the shoot drags on and on), trying to avoid anything slanderous or critical of Harold, and Alice fastens herself on to me like a barnacle. But in the midst of all this, in the midst of my wildest dreams coming true, I feel more alone than I ever have in my life.

So you are more precious to me than ever, Bea. Send me more photos of the children, tell me all about them, all their little stories. And say a prayer for your Hollywood-struck little cousin.

All my love,
Muriel/Jane

Jazz-ma-tazz

I EVENTUALLY REALIZED I DIDN'T FULLY appreciate Tony and his steadfastness. Though I was not madly in love with him, I was beginning to genuinely like him, his down-to-earth quality in particular, and I felt secure in having someone for companionship. I even let him kiss me sometimes, though it was clumsy, just like all the other kisses I had experienced. It was nothing like the memory of that impossible moment in the rainstorm, stardust on butterfly wings..

But had Harold really kissed me, or was it the other Harold, the Glass Character? Where did you draw the line? Was one the product of the other? I watched his facial expressions and saw the brilliant smile, the sad little boy eyes, the determination. But he still looked nothing like his alter ego. The two Harolds were distinct.

Tony took me to the movies one night, and wouldn't tell me what we were seeing, even covered my eyes so I wouldn't see the marquee. I wondered what was going on. Then the lights went down, the great Wurlitzer began to play (this was one of the more elegant picture palaces on the Strip), and the title flashed on the screen: *A Sailor-Made Man*. I caught my breath: this was Harold's first feature-length film, so I would have a whole hour with him in the intimate darkness.

It was a funny film, but different ("It's too hot to play croquet. Let's get married.") The pacing wasn't nearly as frenetic as the one- and two-reelers he was known for. A more complex story unfolded. Once again, Harold had to prove his manhood by joining the navy, with all sorts of crazy consequences.

Oh, how adorable he looked in his sailor suit, a nimble little man-doll fearlessly leaping over every obstacle! I wanted to pick up this doll, hold it, toy with it, make it my own.

By the last madcap scene in which he proposed to his girl with semaphore flags, I was as captivated as everyone else in the theatre. And as always, I didn't want it ever to end.

"Well, what did you think?" I asked Tony. I knew he wasn't going to give it a rave.

"It was okay. Didn't like the men dancing with each other, though."

"Yes, that was a little strange."

"A little! Isn't your friend kind of . . . "

"Kind of what?"

"Oh I don't know, a little bit — " He did a sort of curtsy.

"He is *not* a homosexual."

"Hey, I never said he was! But he kind of, you know — "

"What?"

"Skips around."

"What are you saying?"

"He smiles like — " He crooked his fingers into glasses, and parodied a simpleton grin.

"It's *comedy*. People don't go around with poker faces. And if you want an outright pansy, just look at Harry Langdon."

"Okay! Okay, Sissy, calm down. Let's go for a soda."

"Why did you take me to this, if you were only going to make fun of it?"

"Don't be sore, Janie. I thought you'd like it, that's why. Listen, I know you . . . admire him and all."

"I did like it." In fact I had loved it, spending a whole hour in the dark with the man of my dreams.

Then it occurred to me that Tony really was trying to please me. He didn't like Harold Lloyd very much, for reasons of his own, so taking me to one of his films was a real gesture of — what, of friendship, or something beyond? And was I ready for it?

When we came to my door, he stood in a certain posture of hope, but I gently told him, without words, that he could not come up with me. He probably liked me better for this, though I sometimes hated that twisted standard: women had to spend hours making themselves look attractive, even sexy, then rebuff all sexual overtures until they were married, after which they were consigned to decades of boredom and frustration.

When he bent to kiss me in the usual way, I said, "Wait."

I put my lips near his. Very close. I didn't kiss him. I could tell he was puzzled.

I grazed his lips with mine.

I just touched them with the tip of my tongue.

"Oh, Janie."

"Shhhh. Go slow, go slow."

"Oh baby, I can't go slow any more. Don't tease me like this."

"It isn't a tease."

"Where did you learn this? Oh, God."

"Just kiss me, like . . . *this*."

I never thought I could feel any sort of desire for the longshoreman type, and the thrill was nothing like the swept-up feeling I'd had in Harold's arms. But it was nice, pleasant. And I did wonder what effect it was having on my beau.

"Janie, we'd better stop."

"Why stop?"

"I mean, I can't . . . look, I can't stop myself when I get past a certain point."

"Why is that so bad?"

I immediately regretted saying it.

His voice was quiet, serious. "It's not bad. It's just not what we should be doing."

I had come right up against it, that iron rule: there were good girls and bad girls. You could not be both.

"Janey, how far have you gone with this guy?"

"How far? What do you mean?"

"Look, I just want you to be all right." His protectiveness touched me. "These big Hollywood guys, they have all sorts of power and they think they can do anything they want. Most of them have no morals at all."

"I'm not a child."

"Oh baby, you're sixteen. That's a child."

"I'm not Lita Grey, you know." Chaplin's latest teenaged wife was still a scandal.

"I know you're not. But you can still get out of your depth."

"Harold has a girlfriend already." I wasn't sure about this, but it was a pretty safe bet that he had at least one.

"That doesn't mean very much."

"I'm just one more cast member, an extra. I don't mean anything special to him."

"Even if you don't, he could still do a lot of damage."

I heard him looking out for me. Strangely, it was just what I needed.

I said goodnight to him, gave him a quick kiss and ran up the stairs, before I had time to make any more foolish mistakes.

❧❧❧

Though the title of the movie had changed several times (and was now called, inexplicably, *A Miss and a Match)*, certain details were still miring it down. Once Harold had sprung Mildred Davis from Miss Pettigrew's School of Feminine

Deportment (returning to the original method of scaling the wall, this time in a bizarre Alpine get-up), they celebrated by going dancing at a jazz club.

Harold presented the situation to his gag men.

"You mean a speakeasy."

"Can't have a speak, Johnny, or at least not an obvious one. This is a family picture."

Somebody suggested a supper club. "A dry one."

"With convent virgins in it?"

"It isn't a convent. But we might get away with a night club."

"Called the — "

"Called the — come on, Howard — "

"I'm dry."

"Hey, Lex. Come on over here. Name of a classy dance joint, right now. Don't think. Spit it out."

"Moonlight Dance Club?"

"Too sentimental. We need something with a little more punch. And funny."

"The Elinor Glyn Pleasure Palace." Everyone burst out laughing.

"That's going a little too far." But then, Harold's lucid eyes lit on me in their oddly penetrating way.

"Muriel, I can see you're thinking of something."

I wasn't even supposed to be there. I was eavesdropping, pretending to fuss with props. Up to now I had been so insignificant as to be completely invisible.

"Oh, no, I — "

"Muriel, come on, if you have an idea, please tell us."

"I don't think — "

"Tell us." The deliberate tone, the imperative, hinted at the beginnings of irritation, and I knew what would happen then.

I swallowed, though there was nothing to swallow. Then the name leaped into my head.

"Jazz-ma-tazz."

Hal and Harold looked at each other for a second, then at me.

Hal nodded ever so slightly.

"It's good, Muriel, we'll use it. Thank you."

My heart spun in circles on ice as slick as glass. This couldn't be happening. Even a leading lady wasn't expected to contribute to the gags. It just wasn't done. But along with having my picture on the cover of Photoplay, or at least finding steady work as an extra, I had always dreamed of writing the titles (those smart, funny signposts of dialogue and plot), or even creating the stories themselves.

My name in the credits. It didn't bear thinking about.

This gave me one more thing to brood and daydream about during the ordeal of the shoot. It was like a war: hours and hours of numbing boredom, followed by ten minutes of exhausting focus . . . then back to boredom again.

During another dull day of standing around not being used (for, incredibly, we still had not been dismissed from the picture), Hal came up to me, looking a little uncomfortable.

"Say, Muriel."

"Yes, Mr. Roach." I noticed he didn't correct me.

"Harold wants a favour of you." Then why doesn't he ask me himself, I thought. Is he still too embarrassed after his little transgression?

"We need a new title."

From *Girls Galore!* to *Fancy Free* to *A Miss and a Match* to *Hit or Miss*, we'd gone through any number of bad titles during this shoot.

"What sort of title?"

"A, well, a Harold Lloyd title. You know what I mean." Harold's titles were smart (*Why Worry?*), sometimes sweet (*Girl Shy*), and at times even inexplicable (*Never Weaken*). But usually they were simple summaries, the essence of the picture in a few words.

My head whirled for a few seconds.

"*Mind your Manners*," I said.

It hit Mr. Roach between the eyes. Why hadn't they thought of it before? It was so obvious. Miss Pettigrew's was a finishing school, a school of manners. Harold has to impress Mildred's upper-class father with his polished manners, when he's really just a hayseed. So Mildred has to coach him, and . . . yes, this one could work!

"I don't like it," Harold said.

"What don't you like? It's the best one yet, and it even fixes that whole dull part in the middle."

"Muriel isn't a professional."

That was it. He had come up against the Victorian in Harold's heart. Women didn't write titles, create stories. Women could be sweet and winsome like Mildred, but they were to be cherished and kept apart. Girls like Bebe were in a separate category, great to have fun with, but not the right sort to marry.

But smart girls? He had never really heard of them, except perhaps for his mother.

"At least consider the title change, then. It's simple and good. Probably the best we'll get."

"I hate this picture."

"Don't say hate."

"Then I double-dog dislike it." He thrust his hands in his pockets and stalked away.

I was to find out that Harold would try practically anything for the good of the picture, even if it meant putting his own feelings aside.

The title change, tacitly accepted, made for some small but crucial changes in the plot, and rocked the movie out of the mud rut it had been stuck in.

Everyone grew excited

Harold burst out of his dressing room. I had been frankly loitering outside, hoping to catch a glimpse of him half-dressed. He beamed as only Harold could beam, then seized my shoulders and shook them.

"Muriel, you're a genius. All it took was one change in the title. Now we're moving forward again. You should write a novel. You're marvelous." He leaned forward to kiss my cheek.

Then I horrified myself by doing something I absolutely should not have done.

I kissed him: but on the mouth.

I simply couldn't help it. He was in character, and I could see his wonderful sensitive eyes so plainly through their glassless frames. This close, his white-painted face seemed unreal, with a delicate, childlike rouged mouth. His three-piece suit fit snugly on his compact, springy body.

He stared at me, incredulous. Perhaps he was unaware of the fact that he was reacting in character, his feelings playing across his face like weather patterns.

"No," he said in a warning voice, putting me away from him.

"I'm sorry — "

"We can't do this."

"I know. I should leave."

"Wait." For a moment he looked almost distraught, then composed himself. "I really think you're swell, Muriel. You're smart and going places. But my life is pretty complicated right now, and — well, I've been warned." The thought that he might be getting interested in me was a heart-wrenching joy.

"I need to tell you something, and this is meant to help you, Muriel, not hurt you. You don't know who I am, and sometimes I think you've made me into something I'm not. This character I play — sometimes I think he was almost an accident, or maybe just a stroke of luck. It's hard to know exactly where he came from, but I know he isn't real. I think you've fallen for him, Muriel. You wouldn't be the first."

"But he couldn't exist without you, Harold. Surely you use parts of yourself in creating him."

I saw him thinking, trying to come up with an explanation that would help me understand.

"When I was a boy, all I wanted was to be an actor. Got beat up for it a lot, so I had to learn to defend myself in the ring. And we were so poor I had to hold down a half-dozen jobs. I used to tell myself that if I ever made it, I would take a long, hot bath all by myself every night. None of this Saturday night business, with everyone using the same dirty water."

I wondered why he was telling me all this. And how much of it was true.

"My Daddy dragged us from one small town to another, trying to make a go of one enterprise after another, with no success. Never mind, he was restless and couldn't help it. Somehow or other my mother got me into the theatre, and I was beginning to do well. Hooked up with John Lane Connor, maybe you've heard of him, he was my idol and gave me a break. But when I first came out here to make my fortune, I was starting at the bottom again.

"Some days I had nothing to eat but sugar doughnuts. I did manual labour, which was not my idea of success. My hands were callused. Look at this, they still are, from the stunts. And it took me years to put together a character with any real originality. I plugged away for two years without any inspiration at all, and I did it for the money. If it hadn't been for Hal . . . " He shrugged.

"But your character couldn't have come out of thin air. Don't you feel close to him?"

"I guess I'm too busy making him go. He's mine, maybe, but — he's not *me*."

I saw at once that he was right. But I still could not stop myself.

"I'm so sorry, Harold — "

"Muriel, don't ever be sorry. Just try to do better next time." He was withdrawing from me, and it was torture, but I knew he had to do it, for my sake as well as his.

His sudden personal revelations puzzled me, and in spite of his intentions they did nothing to reduce my irrational love for him. I don't think anything would have disillusioned me at that point. I didn't know then about the darker side of his boyhood that he never wanted to admit, the shame of a father who was a failure and parents whose marriage fractured under the strain. Far below the surface of his professional self, the part of him that was under constant scrutiny, there was invisible damage that ached in him all his life, crowding his spirit with crippling superstitions.

I had never known anyone as complicated as he was, yet he seemed simple, probably thought of himself as simple. The charm would stay with him always, but there was a ghost Harold, a trailing shadow, a cold gust of doubt that whistled through him in the night. He could never forget that he was not quite whole. How could I explain to him that I loved that Harold most of all?

So I obeyed his orders, I stayed away. Incredibly, perhaps due to the successful title change, I was given a small role, a scene in which I helped smuggle Mildred Davis out of Miss Pettigrew's school to run away with Harold.

It probably lasted seven seconds and had the unmistakeable quality of celluloid hitting the floor, but I was incredibly honoured. Miss Davis was so lovely and big-eyed, almost unreal in her radiance and beauty. Harold was saving her like a treasure, trying to keep his restless racehorse feelings under control.

Was he being true? Not according to the girls, who confirmed my suspicions about Mabel: she had been his mistress for months now, and had been whisked away by the studio when it became too obvious. Whether she was pregnant or not was up for conjecture.

Were there others? Should I torture myself by thinking about it? I was taken over by irrational jealousy and a despair that caused an actual, physical ache in my chest, an agonizing yearning that would never really go away.

∼∽∼∽

In those high and dizzy times bridging the teens and the twenties, before his peak as a daredevil climber with only one complete hand, Harold kept a team of men around him, steady gag writers, the same crew, even recurring cast members like the bizarre and ubiquitous Snub Pollard. No one was quite sure where Pollard had come from, how Harold had become so attached to him, and why he was there in nearly all his early one-reelers. His role was always the same: he played Snub Pollard, his bizarre artificial moustache taking up half his face. Audiences liked this consistency, a kind of repertory of players shuffled and reshuffled into different roles, novelty mixed with familiarity.

Then there was his brother Gaylord, looking like sunny Harold's shadow side. Gaylord wasn't nearly as good-looking as his brother (in fact, if you averaged the two you'd have an ordinarily handsome man, devoid of Harold's matinee-idol gleam). Audiences didn't realize this, but his voice was as deep and resonant as Harold's was colorless and thin. Gaylord was plugged in wherever there was a hole, and he looked so unlike his brother that no one really noticed him.

Harold kept his entire family on the payroll, even his father Foxy, a charming confidence man who had at one time or another been fired by everyone in Nebraska. (Strangely,

Harold looked more like his stout, charity-working mother, her face sombre except for her unexpected, chramingly toothy smile.) The shiftless Foxy would go on to become Vice President of the Harold Lloyd Corporation, his sole duty signing fan photos in his florid nineteenth-century hand.

Harold adored Foxy, and who could help it? He had inherited all his twinkle and gloss from his shiftless father, along with a strange kind of catch-me-if-you-can quality. Foxy had rechristened his son Speedy at an early age, and it was a name that kept popping up in his pictures. But it was a lad's nickname, a sign of perpetual youth, a quality most evidenced in his classic performance as a college boy at the age of thirty-two.

But his closest practical partner was Hal, the man responsible for bringing Harold into the movies in the mid-teens. They were both scuffling around, taking on odd jobs, squeezing their way in as extras back when movies were still called the "flickers", when Roach came into a fortune — something like $3000 — and started his own studio.

In those days Harold played thin copies of Chaplin, with most of the action consisting of prolonged fights. Audiences loved these "knockabout" comedies, and it was better than living off sugar doughnuts, but Harold grew increasingly restless and dissatisfied with the dull unchanging formula and utter lack of originality. Then came the Glass Character, mysteriously transforming his face and everything else about him. Like Superman in reverse, it was a metamorphosis which was a little hard to understand or even believe.

But all this is the stuff of legend, facts invented, story intertwined.

For all his inspiration and quirky genius, there were days when Harold put his head down and worked like a mule. He would perform chains of gags, methodically working from one link to the next, and I was a little disappointed to realize that some of them weren't very funny. I was beginning to wonder about the truth of Hal Roach's famous and puzzling statement, "Harold Lloyd doesn't have a funny bone in his body." I came to realize there were aspects of this process of dream-spinning that I would never understand.

But there were subtle perks. Because of my modest contributions, I was given certain small but envy-inducing privileges. This meant I was sometimes allowed to stay after the day's shoot to see the rushes. They were rough and mostly out of sequence, and Hal and Harold stood with their arms folded saying,

"Oh, no — "

"Yes, keep that one."

"No, it's a stinker. Get rid of it."

"Do you think we could, you know — "

"Re-shoot it? Let's get Roy in there, he's a lot taller."

But something was happening to me and the gag men and the crew members and the more favored cast members who were allowed to watch.

We smiled, then giggled, then laughed, then began to howl. Harold was the only one who just stood there with his hands on his hips while the rest of us giggled and even guffawed. It was then that I realized the key to his great gift.

Harold didn't do funny things. He did things funny, and the most minute changes in his facial expression telegraphed the pain and fear and humiliation that is the real basis for comedy. In some way no one could quite analyze, he brought the audience over to his side, asking them, "Has this ever happened to you?"

His subtlety in a realm of exaggerated mugging was remarkable. In his stunts, he leaped as gracefully as a stag, ducked like lightning, threw a punch like a prizefighter.

We laughed until we were teary-eyed, until I began to think that exhaustion had made us all a bit hysterical. Watching us watch him, Harold's face was a study in anxiety and hope. But he wanted to know *why* we were laughing, why eating a mothball instead of a chocolate or going to the dictionary to correct a spelling error in a suicide note (*suicide note!)* was so funny.

Some of the gags lasted mere seconds, though the two-reelers approached half an hour. That meant a lot of gags, almost end-to-end, and they had to flow. At the end of the day he must have been battered, exhausted — but no, he leaped to his feet and went out dancing. What was chasing him, I wondered — the fear that if he ever stopped running, everything he had worked for would slip through his fingers and disappear?

∾∾∾

Ambition wasn't a desirable trait for a woman (or a girl) in those times, unless she was brash, mannish, or a com eccentric. When I first ventured into this dangerous world, all I really wanted was to be close to Harold. The tiny bits of screen exposure I'd been given (if they hadn't already been scissored out) had lit a fuse in me, and it fizzled along to who-knows-what kind of explosion.

I wondered if I had any actual talent, if Harold had been right. Looks mattered the most, everybody knew that, and my "look" wasn't special enough to please the pitiless eye of the camera. I practically had "bit player" written on my forehead. That wasn't necessarily a bad thing, if I could manage to live on the pittance I was paid. But I was unlikely to be in a Roach film ever again. Harold would see to that. And would I be able to stand the boredom and frustration of being a living piece of scenery?

I had had a plan for some time now, but I dared not carry it out. I had seen every Lloyd picture, including the early Lonesome Luke films, most of which were completely forgettable. I even endured an atrocious character named Willie Work, to whom Harold later referred with disdain: "Now that one was a real clinker."

Without even realizing it, I had been studying the gags and the titles and the plot structures. Observing the moment-by-moment evolutionary process of filming had been an education. But even the funniest picture needed a framework for the gags (which, for Harold, were more important than anything). It needed a *story*.

After much inquiry, I found out that Hal Roach, along with everything else he did, often collaborated with Sam Taylor to construct the stories. Since it's impossible to tell a very complex story in two reels, they were for the most part fairly simple. Harold's best work was yet to come: the feature films that allowed him to develop nuance and depth in a character that had started off as a charming but violent cartoon.

I had an idea. It was burning away in me, and I agonized over what I was going to do with it. I couldn't exactly come up to Mr. Taylor and say, "Excuse me, sir, I want your job." God knows, I couldn't go near Harold, who was so distant with me I may as well not have been there at all.

I worked on it and worked on it. I could see it in my head. But a sixteen-year-old female extra does not write stories for Harold Lloyd films, or for any films.

What about a man? A man of twenty-four, who is (supposedly) established in the business already? Never mind if his job is mostly lugging around equipment and fetching coffee.

A Tony Firenze?

So how was I going to convince him to stand in for me? With his protective nature, he'd probably try to talk me out of it. This was just another way to get myself hurt.

But how could I *not* do it? I was convinced my idea was unique, brilliant, wonderful. Did I *have* to tell Tony I was using his name and address?

I discovered a ramshackle typewriter under a jumble of props (wondering if it could be the same one that Harold threw on the floor in *Bumping Into Broadway*), and spent a whole afternoon trying to get it exactly right. Oh, this had to work! I envisioned doors flying open for me. If I didn't make it as a screenwriter, then (perhaps) could I set my sights on being a journalist. A magazine writer? But not for the sleazy rags that lay dog-eared around the set, like the *Hollywood Tattler*, in which Mabel Bryant (whose name turned out to be Gertrude Blonsky) would give a "tell-all" interview about the secret life of Harold Lloyd. For what price, no one knew.

My masterpiece lay gleaming before my eyes.

DOUBLE VISION

Story by Tony Firenze and Muriel Ashford

The main character is Harold Hornbill, a poor boy who stands to inherit a fortune from his rich but cranky great-uncle.

This character, Uncle Hepplewhite Hornbill, is very old and a bit dotty, and wanders the countryside studying rare birds.

Thinking Harold is a ne'er-do-well, Uncle Hepplewhite threatens to cut him out of the will unless he "makes good", which means marrying a rich girl.

Harold falls madly in love with Madge Sweet and asks her to marry him. Unbeknownst to him, her family has pushed her into the engagement because of Harold's inheritance. Everyone believes Madge's family is in high society, so Harold thinks he has "killed two birds with one stone", but in reality the Sweet family has lost everything and is only keeping up appearances. Madge feels it is her duty to marry Harold to rescue the family, even though she doesn't love him.

Harold makes Uncle Hepplewhite angry by accidentally stepping on a nest of cuckoos, and thus puts his inheritance in jeopardy. He tries any number of ways to make it up to him (insert gags here), but always falls short. Fearful that he will never inherit the money, Harold begins to feel unworthy of Madge.

Meanwhile she sees him trying hard to please her, and begins to warm up to him. Just as things are beginning to look better for Harold, Madge catches him kissing another girl, becomes jealous and wants out of the engagement.

Madge does not realize that the girl Harold kissed was his cousin Bertha and that the kiss was completely innocent. (Madge saw her from behind so does not see that she has buck teeth and a moustache.)

Trying desperately to get out of the engagement, Madge trades places with her identical twin sister Millicent, a gold-digger who is strictly interested in Harold's inheritance money.

Uncle Hepplewhite sees Harold and the impostor Millicent together, then spies a heart-shaped birth mark on the back of her neck, alerting him to the deception. He despises Millicent for being a mercenary and changes his will, cutting Harold out completely and leaving all his money to the Society for the Preservation of the Red-Crested Burrowing Cockatoo.

Harold is puzzled by the fact that his fiancée (who still thinks Harold will soon be rich) has changed and now seems like a completely different person, vain and shallow and only interested in money. He becomes disillusioned and falls out of love with her, but stays in the engagement due to a sense of honour.

On the morning of their wedding day, Millicent secretly meets with Herbert Strong, her boy friend. He tells her Harold has been cut out of the will and is no longer of any use to her. He also tells her he has just "made a killing" with investments (on Hepplewhite Hornbill's advice) and is now immensely wealthy (specifically, by investing in a rare Rhodesian leghorn which can lay a dozen eggs in a single day).

The ceremony begins, with Millicent shooting longing glances at Herbert. Her twin sister Madge sits at the back of the church wearing a veil and weeping, realizing now how much she truly loves Harold and not caring if he has money or not.

When the vows come to "if any man should object", Herbert Strong stands up and claims the marriage is based on false pretenses and that Millicent was forced into it to help her impoverished family, while all the time Harold Hornbill knew he would not inherit a cent. He proclaims that HE is the man Millicent loves, and she runs to him and jumps up into his arms.

Harold is left alone, jilted at the altar, and looks devastated.

Uncle Hepplewhite suddenly stands up and shouts, "Hold on a minute! This woman is an impostor! I saw the birth mark on the back of her neck." (Everyone reacts with consternation.) "This is Millicent Sweet, the gold-digger. The real bride is Madge Sweet, the sweetest girl in the county!" Madge jumps up and starts to run down the aisle, then makes herself stop and slowly does a bridal two-step towards Harold. He lifts her veil and gives her a Harold Lloyd kiss. Slow dissolve.

I took my name off the manuscript. I put it back on again. I took it off. I put it on (I can only lose!), before finally, painfully extracting it like an infected tooth.

But what if they just discarded it, and I never found out what they had thought of it?

I had to compose a covering letter.

Dear Mr. Roach,
I am a great fan of Harold Lloyd's movies (scratch that out).
　　For the past few years I've been writing (No, no, no!).

Please find attached a sample

All of them seemed wrong. Finally, I scribbled at the top of the manuscript, "Dear Mr. Roach, would you please take a look at this and tell me what you think? Sincerely, Tony Firenze."

I put my own address on it, wondering if I'd ever get a reply.

I folded it up, put a stamp on it, and stood by the mail box with my heart pounding. Then ripped it out of my own fingers and let it go.

What had I done? Even with a fake name on it, this could go disastrously wrong. They might hate it, scoff at it, or — worst of all — completely ignore it. The story was convoluted and needed lots of "business" to illustrate its twists and turns. Harold's gag men were a tightly-sealed brotherhood who had been working together for years. They knew each other's loves and hates, strengths and weaknesses, and worked in graceful, synchronized harmony. How would they feel about a story coming from a complete unknown?

But I also knew they could stumble, or miss something that was right in front of their eyes. There was a weak spot, a gap in their seeming invincibility; I had seen it. More than that — I had even filled it. I told myself I still had some kind of a chance.

❧❧❧

Dear Janie,

Dearest cousin, though I've kept my opinions to myself up to now, I can't hold my tongue after reading your last letter. When you first decided to try your fortunes in Hollywood, I thought you had a sensible plan: to spend one year scouting for extra work in pictures, while at the same time holding down a more practical job in the nicest restaurant you could find. If after one year you could not make a go of it, then you would come home.

You were indeed lucky to land steady work right away, and with a well-known studio. And I thought you had the level head and sensibility to handle the temptations that might come with it.

I was truly alarmed to hear about the kind of girls you work with, their loose morals, meanness and vicious tongues. Though I know you will not allow yourself to sink to such a depth, I pray your innocence will not be stained by such moral turpitude.

I would have let this pass, however, trusting that your religious training would keep you pure in this environment of wanton immorality. But now you tell me that you have allowed someone to kiss you. Sis, you should never let a man kiss you whom you do not know! Even a beau of many months must be handled with extreme care. And if I am to believe your incredible story, you allowed yourself to be kissed by a movie star!

I realize you think this man (no doubt at least ten years your senior) is some sort of a hero or a shining figure. Oh Janey, how you have deluded yourself! When will you learn that all men want the same thing, and that movie stars feel especially entitled. Try to think of the possible consequences of such an act, and of how the studio would treat you. You would be very quickly hustled out of sight to avoid casting a bad reflection on the man who is responsible.

Though this is difficult for me to say to someone I love so much, I cannot stand for any more of this dangerous behaviour. If you experience one more episode of such flagrant loss of control, I shall have to send your mother to fetch you. The only reason she hasn't come to get you up to now is that I keep telling her how happy you are *(and why don't you ever send her a letter, cousin? She feels terribly cut out), and that she's afraid of what your Pa will do to her.*

I realize he has been cruel in the past, that he has called you unfair names and accused you of things you never did. But can't you give him one more chance? Don't prove him right, my darling sissy. We both know you aren't really a harlot, so why not show him? Oh I love you so, and this letter is sheer torture to write. But please listen to me! Mr. Lloyd is dangerous and cannot be allowed to touch you ever again!

Please try to see this advice as protective of your purity. Once lost, it can never be restored. And believe me when I say that these movie stars, no matter how glamourous, don't care about your honour at all. They think their fame places them above the moral standard and that their wealth will buy them salvation, when the truth is they will face their day of judgement just like all the rest of us.

I implore you to listen, and ponder these things in your heart. If need be, you could live with us, though the six of us in two rooms is already pretty tight. We will find a way to make it work, because we are a family. Please, please, listen to your cuz and stay safe!

With all my love,
Bea

❧❧❧

The line between my daydreams, my made-up Harold in his exotic world versus my own grinding reality, was becoming blurred. I was beginning to write down our imagined conversations, which were much more scintillating than our real ones. ("Oh, hello, Muriel. Beautiful day, isn't it?" "Hello, Harold. Yes, it is.") The fact that I was allowed to address him by his first name gave me a certain status among the girls, but that was all.

After Bea's horrified letter, I was beginning to wish this interminable shoot would end. I was always seeing things I shouldn't, annoying things, and this time it was Harold and Mildred necking behind a wobbly flat. His hand was on her breast, but she didn't seem to mind. The wall was crumbling. No ring on her finger yet, so he would likely stop short.

Our brief sexual spark seemed to have fizzled. Just as well, for my cousin was right on all counts: I should never have let him touch me. Then during yet another back-aching, dreary, smoke-choked night serving illicit drinks at Frankie's (password: *chinchilla),* my heart dropped into my shoes.

There he was in the doorway in that spotlight stars seem to carry around inside them, elegantly dressed in a gleaming, expensive suit.

Panic-stricken, I ducked into the kitchen.

"Muriel," Susan whispered in my ear, her eyes huge with excitement.

"Yes, I know."

"He is an absolute *doll!* Even cuter than in his pictures. Who's that he's with?"

I wasn't sure: a petite brunette who somewhat resembled Clara Bow, with bobbed hair, a silvery dress fringed all over, and long strands of artificial pearls. A real flapper. We all knew about the reputation of flappers, which ensured that Harold would have a good old time tonight.

I prayed he wouldn't notice me in my skimpy uniform, but my shift didn't end until midnight, so I had to go on working. Though it was humiliating, I was learning the best strategy for earning the tips I needed to pay the rent. This required a lot of smiling and leaning over.

I tried to avoid his table, turning my face the other way, but it was awkward. Then he and his girl got up to dance.

The crowd reacted with a mixture of pleasure and dismay: Frankie's held dance competitions every Tuesday night, and when Harold and Bebe showed up the result was a foregone conclusion. By now, I thought, they must have rows of those loving-cups crowded together on the mantelpiece.

They walked smoothly together to the dance floor, the piano playing a few chords of fanfare, then stood and waited for the orchestra.to begin. I had never seen this particular step before, but it was complex and lively, and the music was simply wild. Some years later I saw a dancer named Kelly, and Harold had that same effortless, athletic grace. At one point he threw his girl up in the air and caught her, airplaning her around as the audience gasped and the glitter-ball cast firefly rainbows all over the room. The other dancers slowly moved back to watch.

They finished with their version of the infamous tango from Valentino's *Four Horsemen*: both tribute and parody, sexy and funny at the same time. Their great comic gifts were evident, as was their physical oneness. The applause went on and on, and Harold casually reached up and caught the cup as it flew through the air.

Then I knew. It was Bebe Daniels. Officially they had broken it off, and she had moved on. Apparently they still had feelings for each other, for I was to learn that she'd had the diamonds from their engagement ring set into cufflinks which he constantly wore.

So they were still friends, or at least dance partners. Since this place wasn't supposed to exist, they would be relatively anonymous here. I studied her: she was dark, sleepy-eyed, and looked a little dangerous. Not really pretty. I never could get a fix on Harold's type.

Having effortlessly blown the audience down, they walked back to their table. Harold wasn't even breathing hard. Then

Bebe trotted across the room, waving gaily at a group of elegant-looking people.

Harold's gaze swept the room.

His eyes lit.

If only he hadn't smiled, *ignited* that way. I saw him mouth my name. I waved him off, he insisted, then I reluctantly came over to his table.

"Muriel! You look swell."

"This awful thing? It's full of smoke. And too short."

He flicked his eyes up and down.

"Dance with me, Muriel," he said in that wheedling, little-boy tone he had used with me in the rainstorm.

"I can't. I'm on shift."

"When do you get off?"

"At midnight." I never should have said it. It sounded like a ludicrous fairy tale. "Anyway, I can't dance like this. I look like a barmaid. And what about — " I couldn't say her name.

"Oh, don't worry about that. Beebs has friends to talk to. We come to the clubs sometimes, just to dance. We're not dating any more."

"You're awfully good. Where did you learn?"

"Didn't, actually. Just sort of — "

"I couldn't keep up with you anyway."

"I could teach you." He could be so earnest, so Midwestern. Like he was teaching me the box step at a tea dance.

"C'mon, Muriel." I thought: a gleaming movie star, one of the most famous people in Hollywood, is just at the tips of my fingers. Here I am, entering the mouth of the wolf again.

"Susan always brings her club clothes for when she's off shift. Maybe I can change with her."

"Good! Good!" Harold looked intoxicated with excitement, though I knew he was a good boy and didn't smoke or drink or dabble in the white powder.

And at the stroke of twelve, I was led to the slaughter. Susan screamed with excitement and insisted she dress me. First I had to put on a strange undergarment that bound my breasts (not that I had much to bind). The dress was made of a heavy, shiny deep-blue material covered with hand-sewn glass beads, so I glittered when I walked. The neckline was shockingly low, the waistline dropped almost to my hips. The black patent-leather shoes had straps around the ankles, and higher heels than I had ever worn before. This wasn't an outfit, but a costume.

Susan rouged my mouth, pinched my cheeks, and pulled a few strands of my hair out of the old-fashioned combs I still wore, making soft little tendrils.

I caught a glimpse of myself in the mirror, and my pupils dilated. I looked nothing like myself. I could have been anyone. An actress. A flapper. A vamp. I'd have Harold in the palm of my hand.

I turned on my high heel, switched on my brightest smile, and flounced over to greet my swain.

He did a very admiring "whew!', which was pleasantly enthusiastic without implying I looked a mess the rest of the time. Then snaked his arm around my waist.

"Don't be afraid, it's only the fox trot."

"This fox doesn't know how to trot."

"Oh Muriel, you're so funny!" He suddenly dipped me, in fact almost dropped me, then caught me at the last second while my head reeled. *Yes*, I realized, *I am dancing with a comedian.*

"Push against my hand a little. That's it. There needs to be a bit of tension between us. Then with my arm, I'll . . . "

My awkwardness lessened as he steered me around. The music was lavish: mellow saxophones, high keening clarinets, and a single violin soaring above it all in a melody so tender, it made my eyes sting. And my skin prickled with dizzy joy that I was in the arms of the most beautiful man in the world.

He was very gradually easing me closer so that our bodies were almost touching, but I knew it was only another tease, proof of his power over me. This close, I could not help but feel his heat. I wondered if Bebe could see us, if it would even matter.

The fox trot escalated into the "toddle", a sort of hop-step that was much harder to execute. The music grew wild, with razzing trumpets and primitive, thudding percussion. Harold had an almost shocking instinct for the music's hot, sexy rhythms, and was practically lifting me off the floor so I could keep up.

Then came an announcement that made everybody cheer: "*The Black Bottom!*" Panicked, I shook my head vigorously: I knew I wasn't up to this one. Maybe Harold and I could go sit down and talk. But to my shock, he grabbed another girl's hand, a girl he didn't even know, and set to, leaping around like an adorable little puppet. He radiated joy and exuberance like no one I had ever seen before. But he was dancing with someone else, as if women to him were practically interchangeable.

I left the dance floor, devastated, collected my things, changed back into my drab street clothes and headed for the door.

"Muriel . . . " I felt like I was being dragged back.

"I have to go," I said, trying very hard to keep the tremble out of my voice.

"Oh Muriel, I didn't mean to abandon you. How about one more dance?"

"Harold, *no!* Why do you think you can yank me around like this? Go away, come back! Dance with me, but don't touch me!"

"I thought we were having fun."

"You know how I feel. And you told me not to. 'We can't do this, Muriel.' Does that mean I can just turn my feelings off?"

"Be quiet, Muriel, you're making a scene." It occurred to me that a spat in a speakeasy wouldn't be good for his career.

"Go have fun, then." I turned on my heel again, the dramatic effect ruined by a stumble because I was still wearing Susan's ridiculous tottering shoes.

"It's not fun." He said it very quietly.

I had to turn back.

"It's not fun to live like this. I feel like I'm not really close to anyone."

"But what does it matter, so long as there's a different girl for every night of the week."

For an unguarded instant, he looked devastated.

"Oh, Harold, I shouldn't have said that."

"But you did."

"Why can't you just tell me if you like me or not?"

"It's not a question of liking. You're so very young, Muriel, not even out of your teens. Sometimes I wonder if you really know what goes on between men and women in this town."

"You don't have to protect me. I can take care of myself."

"I don't think so, Muriel. You don't know how pretty you are, and in five years you'll be a full-blown beauty with real character, which means your looks will last. And you have talent, I've seen it. If you really want to be an actress, you can be. But you've got to be very careful."

He seemed to be offering me stardom on a platter. I knew enough to suspect it. Still, I watched his face for the most minute chance that he would break his own rule and touch me.

"I might be able to help you," he said.

"So what would I have to do, Harold?"

"What does that mean?"

"I've heard the stories. Don't you like them young?" My tone was provocative, acid, awful.

"That's not fair."

"What about Bebe? Wasn't she just a little underage?"

His face darkened so quickly I had to catch my breath.

"Leave Bebe out of this. You don't know what you're saying."

"I know what other people are saying."

"Why do you pay attention to such trash?"

"Oh, there's more. Like the story of how you got your start."

"Stop it right now. Don't say another word."

"Oh, it's just hearsay, but . . . who was that man who got you into the theatre? Connor, was it? Maybe it's just a rumour, but I heard he was a bit of a nancy-boy."

"What are you implying?"

"Can't you guess?"

The anger escalated into fury. "I don't strike women," he said in a frighteningly low voice.

"That's too bad, Harold, because then I could strike you."

The air in the room was crackling and ready to explode. And he didn't move. Stood vibrating with a fury that would soon turn to rage.

"I've given you every advantage. I only want the best for you."

"You know what you want."

"Show me a man who doesn't." The gloves were off, and I saw the hard, calculating man who had come from nothing and was tough enough to survive in a pitiless world.

I realized with a shock that I had no idea how to deal with him. He seemed to be getting bigger as I gradually diminished. I slowly backed up, and he advanced.

I ducked inside the unlit storage room. I grabbed his hand, and he followed. With Susan's ridiculous wobbly shoe, I kicked the door shut.

❦❦❦

Fairy-tale evenings can have nasty endings, and there is always the shabbiness of reality to face the next day. By the time I took an overly-expensive cab home, I felt dishevelled and even dirty. I knew I would have to face him on set the next day. An awful mixture of unresolved passion and regret surged inside me. I could finally understand why girls were so sternly warned against sex.

It was a mess of confusion, of raging appetites and desperate repression. We had kissed and kissed, and he drew the combs out of my hair so that it all tumbled down in a shining mass that he buried his fingers in. Then he roughly pulled my head back and kissed me so hard I could feel his teeth in me. There was no tenderness this time, no teasing, no subtlety at all.

It was true: I *didn't* know what happened between men and women, in this town or any other town. It could not have been more different from the fond looks and decorous kisses I had dreamed of. The skin on my throat was on fire, and I realized with a shock that I could not stop my body from responding. I wanted him so badly I was willing to expose myself to any kind of danger.

Then I realized with a jolt that he was right: aside from his extraordinary talent, he wasn't magical at all, just a randy young man with too many opportunities and too much worldly power. He had warned me over and over again, and I had ignored him. Now I was in his hands, trembling, exhilarated, ashamed, poised on some sort of brink.

He squeezed me in his arms, almost hurting me, crushed himself against me, groaned, then said, "It's no good, we have to stop." He pushed the door open, began to readjust himself, button up. I scraped myself back together as well as I could.

"Sorry, Muriel. This was a mistake," he said, not looking at me, distracted and a little wild.

"Harold — "

"Here, take a cab." He pressed a bill into my hand, then turned and walked out. I watched him switch on his smile and cross the room, waving with all the elegance and self-possession of a Douglas Fairbanks.

It suddenly occurred to me with a pang that he really didn't have any choice.

❧❧❧

There followed a period of such wretchedness that I wondered if I would ever emerge from it. Everything I had done since coming to this place of dreams had turned bad. I'd held a golden chance in my hands, one that any girl my age would envy: I trembled on the edge of opportunity, of being acknowledged, either as an actress or a writer or both. Something had ripped it away from me, my own ignorance, an unlucky turn of fate, or (most likely) my illicit passion for a man I knew I could never have.

If only I had been content to be friends with Harold, as he kept asking me to (making me wonder how he truly felt. As it said in one of his titles, "Could you like me just a little?"). I had shattered the fragile miracle of our connection by grabbing for more. His fundamental decency had stopped him from taking me as a mistress, or even exploiting me as a casual fling.

The first thing I did was submit my resignation to Hal Roach. We were so close to wrapping on this interminable film that it made very little difference, so he didn't require notice. He was uncharacteristically gentle with me on the phone, asking me if I was all right, if I had found another job, and I lied that I had. He told me that everyone in the cast missed me, that I should call him if I ever needed anything, and wished me well. Though I knew it was probably a lie, it was a kind one, and I thanked him.

But I mourned the loss of this agonizingly beautiful experience, not just in my heart and mind but in the core of me, in my body. I ached all over as if I were ill, grew thinner because I found I was unable to eat. I sat up nights and tried to read sensational novels (movie magazines were out of the question), wrote stories and tore them up.

I didn't leave the shabby, stifling cube of my room unless I had to. I refused to talk to Tony or my so-called friends from Frankie's Place, dumping my disgusting uniform in the trash and telling myself the whole embarrassing episode meant nothing. The telephone in the downstairs hall rang often, but I told myself the calls were for someone else.

But soon there arose a small problem: unless I found a source of income very quickly, I would be existing on nothing. I hated to approach Bea, who had little enough as it was, and would no doubt take an I-told-you-so attitude that I completely deserved. Hal had said "if you ever need anything", but my pride would not allow me to go begging.

Crazily, I even thought of Harold, who was rapidly becoming a very wealthy man from his loyal and growing audience. He could afford it. And he might even do it. But it would draw us back together again into that insane and hopeless dance, powerful magnetic attraction followed by violent blowing apart. I knew that one more of those would kill me.

My landlady, an unlikely source of help, mentioned that she knew people who needed clothing repairs. So for a few weeks I was able to scrape together the rent by taking in mending (and thank God I knew how to do it from my barren days in Santa Fe). At the same time, I began to trek around town trying to find a decent job.

I wondered how to approach this task. Lying seemed necessary. I had already learned that, bizarrely, Frankie's name held more power than I thought possible because of his capacity to keep potentially catastrophic secrets. Could I use his name as a reference? No, that was insane. Officially,

Frankie's Place didn't even exist. I would have to invent something, a nice restaurant or at least a drug store with a soda fountain (oh, what a terrible demotion!).

Could I use my movie experience, or would that work against me? It was unlikely a prospective employer would believe everything that had happened to me in only a few months. But everyone was a star around here, or just about to become one. It seemed ironic that I had to hide my finest accomplishments to find employment, but I found myself making up stories about restaurant work, listing Tony and Susan from Frankie's as references and carefully coaching them in what they should say.

No one pays attention to references anyway, so I landed a fairly good job within a week. "I like the look of you," the proprietor said. "You look like somebody, with that long hair. Can't decide. Maybe Mary Miles Minter?"

Even with my natural reserve, I liked her right away. Shirley Tate had been a businesswoman in Hollywood for a decade, opening first one restaurant, then three or four, then eight (which she claimed to be her lucky number). Her energy was enormous, her manner brusque but essentially kind.

Her popular chain was called Chez Louise (its motto: "How sweet to eat with the elite!", later parodied by Wallace Beery as, "How swell to dwell in film star hell!"), after Shirley's resemblance to Louise Brooks.

The resemblance was mostly imaginary, for Shirley was at least forty, and wore exotic and unusual things like an aquamarine turban, a white fox stole with the head still on, and a sapphire brooch that looked like a reptile. (Though these styles looked a little strange, ten years later they would become almost *de rigeur.*) This glittering gecko, whom Shirley had christened Carlos, was her lucky piece, and one day when it fell into a huge pot of soup she went into brief but intense hysterics.

Shirley didn't pry, but she seemed to know things without being told. It was some time after I started that I slowly began to share my experiences at the Hal Roach Studio, and I knew she believed me.

"Geez kid, you were doing so swell. Why did you stop?"

"Well, the picture wrapped, and I wasn't sure what to . . . "

"Hal Roach. Yeah, I know the man, great guy, comes in here sometimes. He directs the one with the glasses, you know . . . " I knew she was feigning ignorance.

"Harold Lloyd." The name was honey in my mouth.

"Listen, I don't know what happened there, Muriel, but I have to tell you, that man has broken a lot of hearts."

"I felt like such a fool."

"Never apologize for learning something. And you learned something, right? These big stars feel they're entitled to pretty much anything. They've been told they're marvelous too many times. Most of them aren't — they're prima donnas, or they get that way after they've been here a while."

"Harold isn't like that."

"You don't know that for sure."

I even told her about sending in my story idea, but she seemed to disapprove of this far more than my glorified crush.

"This is no business for young girls, no matter how clever they are. That kind of thing could backfire on you. Show business people aren't known for their honesty."

"But I wrote it under someone else's name." Then I blushed, suddenly, embarrassed by my own dishonesty.

"All the same." She sucked on her cigarette so hard it looked painful. "If you try to do a man's job, it comes to no good." This attitude seemed to fly in the face of her unusual accomplishments as an entrepreneur. But perhaps she had learned the hard way, enduring criticisms and poisonous rumours she had done nothing to deserve.

∽∾∽∾

Working at Chez Louise was a dream compared to Frankie's. I could keep regular hours. The tips were more modest, as were the uniforms, but my salary at least approached a living wage. And against all hope, I began to make friends with the other waitresses, most of whom were several years older than me. They made me feel safer, and a little less lonely.

But I could not forget about Alice, naïve to the point of shocking ignorance, who had been in the same sort of little-sister position I was in now. I realized I had done a terible job of protecting her. In fact, I had pretty much abandoned her, assuming (or at least hoping) she had taken my pleading advice to go home to her parents.

Though the wretchedness of those awful post-Harold weeks had subsided, there were still more blows to come: another letter from Bea in the same vein as the last one, practically ordering me home. This time I was honestly able to tell her I had a decent job and some stability, and had left the wicked Babylon of moviemaking for good.

Then came the polite, terse rejection of my story. I was humiliated to see it was scrawled in ink right across the text on my typewritten copy: "Thanks Tony, this has promise but is a little too confusing and hard to follow. Keep at it and don't hesitate to try us again. Yours, Hal Roach."

Confusing. Yes, I guessed it was, with all those ins and outs about inheritances. But wasn't the basic idea sound? Didn't it have comic possibilities? Good sister, bad sister. All right, it was a bit hackneyed, but some of Harold's stories were pretty unoriginal, freshened only by the clever and beautifully-executed gags.

There was one compensation, and a very large one: I received a cheque for $50 in the mail, presumably as a kind of severance pay. This was astronomical for a bit-player, and almost seemed to be a kind of acknowledgement of my other contributions. I prudently deposited the windfall into my savings account, my nest-egg (or hush-money), well-earned with heartbreak and toil.

There followed a dull but stable period in which I worked hard as a waitress, was promoted to a junior supervisor, turned seventeen (or nineteen, depending on which reality you believed in), and waited on Blanche Sweet, Bessie Love, Reginald Denny and a few other minor celebrities. I was to learn they didn't tip any better than anyone else (and the buzz about Harold was even worse: apparently he was a skinflint, leaving miserable tips or no tips at all).

Ah yes, Harold. Just as I was about to put him to rest, the inevitable happened, and *Mind Your Manners* was released to great fanfare. By this time, his loyal fans were excited to see a new two-reeler. His days as a primitive "knockabout" comic were long over. I bought up all the fan magazines I could find, tortured myself with the magnificent photos (I had never seen a really bad picture of Harold), and revelled in the virtually-fabricated interviews, which I knew were a wholesale distortion of the truth.

So there it was: a delicious picture of my former idol in *Photoplay,* along with an interview in which he talked about how magnificent his new leading lady Mildred Davis was, how charming the story, how outrageously funny the gags.

"And yes, we even had a little helper. It seldom happens that a cast member contributes ideas, but in this case we had a couple of useful suggestions from an extra that we ended up using. Most unusual for a young actress."

And that was it. *Say my name!* my mind screamed as I read through the skimpy paragraph. I heard myself, and sighed. I had become as rapacious as everyone else, wanting desperately to be noticed. But I kept the interview, knowing no one would believe that the "little helper" was me.

⤳⤳⤳

In Hollywood during the sizzling era of Prohibition, violent twists and turns were part of the daily routine. Several months after I started at the restaurant, a little-known actor named Hugh Hennessey was arrested for gross indecency (likely with a minor, the disease that seemed to flourish everywhere). The fact that the bust took place at Chez Louise was the only variation on the usual theme.

The press could taste blood in the water miles away, so cameras were flashing, and Shirley was calmly calculating how she could turn this sordid event to her advantage. Because Hugh Hennessey knew the right people, he got off without penalty, his name was completely cleared, and he never worked in Hollywood again. Two years later, he committed suicide.

I tried to ignore the misery of an environment that seemed to wrench people out of shape (or were they already twisted to begin with?). One night I got a call, and was surprised when my heart leaped:

"So how's my girl?"

"Your girl. Do you really mean it?"

"Sure. And I can bet which movie you want to go to."

"Oh Tony. I don't know if I can stand it."

"You can stand it. And if you don't go, it'll drive you crazy."

"Oh well, I suppose you're right. I don't imagine my part survived the shears anyway."

"Don't be too sure. Muriel Ashford's going to be a household name before you know it."

His statement gave me pause.

"You know, Tony, I'm not even sure I want that any more. But I don't want to be a waitress forever."

"You won't. You're smart enough to find a place for yourself. Actresses are dumb bunnies anyway."

"I beg your pardon!"

"Oh, sorry, Miss Ashford, I meant every other actress except you."

We didn't go to the premiere (which Harold would likely attend, wearing a tux and his prop glasses so people would know who he was), but waited a couple of nights for the crowd to die down. But it was still a full theatre, with a good organist who could improvise to the action with great skill and charm.

The credits listed only three names, as usual ("The Girl", "The Boy", and "The Headmistress"), and it took forever to get to the part where Mildred's parents sent her to Miss Pettigrew's school to get her away from Harold the bumpkin. I eagerly watched the first scenes, and caught a slight glimpse of my hair being braided from the back (causing Tony to annoy our fellow patrons by crying out, "Look, there you are!"). I sighed, wondering which one of the half-dozen or so gags they had used to get Harold over the wall.

To my astonishment, it was the digging scene, which I never thought they would pull off. I felt sick with anticipation. But it worked: he popped up like a prairie dog, getting a huge laugh from the audience. Then the girls ran over to him (title: *It's been a long time since they saw a boy of the opposite sex!*), and began to fuss.

I looked for myself. Dear God, I wasn't there. My heart was sinking. And then –

Not just a long-shot, but a closeup of the hair-mussing! The only problem was, the camera was on Harold as he went through his usual mercurial array of facial expressions.

"Well, we know that's my hand anyway," I said. Then for a second, the camera pulled back.

I was astonished, and mortified. I could see myself, and I was looking at Harold with naked adoration, as if I wanted to fall on my knees in front of him. Perhaps it made for good cinema, but the intensity and stark visibility of my emotions scared me.

My later scene with Mildred had been cut to the bone, but I was still there.

"Oh baby, you look so great. You look gorgeous."

Secretly, I was pleased, as I seemed to be more photogenic than I thought. Meanwhile, audience members started to realize from Tony's loud promptings that I was actually in the film, and far from finding it irritating, they seemed to think it was pretty exciting.

Every time they saw a tiny glimpse of me after that, there were whispers of *"There she is!"* Though it was completely ridiculous, I couldn't help laughing and blushing. As The End flashed on the screen, the whole audience burst into applause. It wasn't unusual for audiences to applaud movies back then (though I could never understand exactly why they did it, when the actors weren't even there). But this time they turned around and looked at me.

It was a sweet moment, and I tried to hold on to it, but as with everything else in that illusory realm it dissolved like so much candy floss. Soon I was back to the safe, mundane world of Chez Louise.

But I had underestimated the unexpected kindness that could pop up out of nowhere. No, not out of nowhere: Shirley had been at work here, orchestrating a surprise. When I walked into the kitchen in my uniform the next day, all the girls were standing around in a semicircle. One by one they began to applaud, until the accolades escalated into cheers, and Harriet Golden (Ruthie Brown) handed me a lovely bouquet of daisies dotted with tiny yellow roses.

This time there was no brimming, no tremulous smile. The tears gushed down my face, ruining my makeup and making my nose run in a river (and of course I had no handkerchief). I was overwhelmed by their kindness, their acknowledgement of a major accomplishment (accompanied by a pain and remorse they knew nothing about).

Shirley gave me a brief hug, then whispered in my ear, not unkindly, "Go splash some water on your face, sweetheart, it's time to get back to work." Sentiment had never been her forte.

I was learning a lot from Shirley: don't take things personally (one of the hardest things to practice). Don't trust anyone until you are sure they are trustworthy. And *don't* give your heart away until you are fully aware of the risk of being hurt.

She wasn't saying I shouldn't risk, but that my risks should be considered. Tony seemed beyond risk, but that wasn't strictly true. I often felt sorry for him, in an endless waiting game for something that would likely never happen.

We weren't engaged, and weren't likely to be. I was fond of him, and was gradually becoming more fond, but it wasn't likely I would ever love him. But I knew he loved me and courted me ever so gently, with respect. Stopping at a few kisses was becoming painful for him, and once again I wondered why girls had to pretend they felt no desire, why they were considered morally tainted if they let their boyfriends "go all the way" (for in spite of the so-called liberated atmosphere of the "jazz age", that repressive belief was still very much in evidence). The implication was that girls were responsible for keeping sex under control, and if either of them lost control, the blame lay squarely on their shoulders.

It was a raw deal, but I had to accept it. I was grateful to be seventeen, too young to marry, for I knew that if we stayed together Tony would eventually ask me. He had no other girl, didn't even want another girl, so it was likely he would wait for me. I respected him and was grateful for his protection, but I knew I could never give him what he needed. I was beginning to believe he was entirely too good for me.

∽∾∽∾∽

It was in the middle of a long and very tiring shift that the phone rang again. I did not have a particularly friendly relationship with the telephone. It seldom brought good news. Bea couldn't afford a phone (and our letters had come to a sort of uneasy truce), but I still feared her judgemental voice on the line.

It was ten o'clock, not a civilized time for anyone to be calling. My idiot brain piped up, "Maybe it's Harold. Maybe he's changed his mind about me." But it was someone I'd never heard of, claiming to be a casting director for the Hal Roach Studio.

"Mr. Roach was impressed with your performance in *Mind your Manners*. There's a part in his next picture he'd like you to audition for."

My caution light, the one Shirley had installed in me, was blinking fast.

"May I speak to Mr. Roach about it?"

"Of course. I'll have him call you." He sounded offended, but was trying to cover it up.

"What is the picture about?"

"Ah, it's about a man who's coming into an inheritance from his great-uncle, but he has to get married first. To a rich girl, I mean. And there's this set of twins . . . one of them is nice, and one of them is nasty. Mildred Davis will play both of them. They switch places, and Harold doesn't know the difference."

Harold. Hal. The people I had trusted. Fury sent a hot blush surging upward from my chest to my scalp.

"Your part is — "

"Let me guess. The cousin who kisses Harold."

"How did you — "

"I need to speak to Mr. Roach about this."

"I'll ask him to call you."

"Thank you." I hung up.

Fury vied with a completely irrational excitement — for after all, the cousin's part might be padded into a fairly substantial one. And here it was, another gleaming opportunity to have Harold run over my heart.

I needed a strong dose of reality, so I thought of Shirley immediately. I had come to rely on her horse sense and wry wisdom in tight places, which this one definitely was. We sat over our Cinderellas (fruity pink non-alcoholic cocktails, Prohibition specials which supposedly tasted like the real thing) after the restaurant had closed.

"Okay, sweetie pie. They just asked you to audition. That means they want you."

"Yes, but — "

"Just listen to me for a minute. They *want* you. That means you're desirable. So you have hand."

"Hand?"

"Leverage. Influence. You know."

"Oh, *hand*."

"And that means you don't have to take the first offer that comes along. Or the second, or the third."

"But that means — "

"Play hard to get until you've figured out a plan. Ask Mr. Roach exactly when he needs an answer from you, and make sure it's an actual date."

The clouds were beginning to clear.

"Now, about your story. It was sent in under false pretenses, so if they lifted it — "

"I'm in no better position than they are."

"You can still make this work for you. Keep on pretending to be Tony for a while. That's crucial. If they've stolen it from you, you can get him to go undercover, so to speak. Tony worships the ground you walk on, so I don't think he'd mind co-operating."

I was taking it all in with fascination. I wondered where Shirley had learned all this strategy.

"Send the story back to Hal Roach — the copy with the writing all over it. They might need to compare handwriting for evidence. Attach a note to Mr. Roach — do it on a typewriter, girl's handwriting looks different — saying you've found out from an inside source that the person who scribbled all over your copy stole this story from you. Dollars to doughnuts, Roach didn't do this. It'll be one of his gag men.

"You can't really go legal on them, not yet anyway. But if they won't own up, or won't compensate you for your pains, mention — pay attention now — *Mr. Don Bishop*, Editor-in-Chief of the *Hollywood Tattler*.

"You know, say something vague like, 'I recently sought counsel with Mr. Don Bishop about the plagiarism laws in this country, and . . . ' I hate to brag, but I've got Bishop in my back pocket. He's dying to take Roach down, some stupid old grudge from ten years ago. Stealing stories, eh? Theft of creative properties is a serious matter. And it means they must be desperate for fresh ideas. *Unlike* Chaplin and Keaton. Whom you've also written for."

"But that's an outright lie!"

"Do you know what the meaning of fiction is? Something that didn't happen. And you're a fiction writer, aren't you? You just wait. They'll either drop that story like a stone, or pay you — I mean Tony — very handsomely for it. They were already going to use it, weren't they? Kid, you're on Easy Street!"

"Shirley, you're a genius."

"We'll see, we'll see. I'd suggest you split the proceeds with Tony, for using his name and all. And this way, if you can forgive the bastards for what they've done to you, you'll still have a job."

I put off the audition for as long as I could. I sent the story back to Hal Roach, and I waited. I turned the name of Don Bishop over in my hands, but didn't need to draw that particular card. Two weeks later I received a letter from Hal Roach Studios.

"Dear Mr. Firenze,
We were shocked to be informed that one of our gag men plagiarized your story idea, Double Vision. He sent his rejection note to you before I had a chance to read it.

This fellow is new, and it was the first time he came up with a decent idea, so we should have been suspicious. He was fired immediately, but the fate of the story is in your hands.

We would like to compensate you for any distress we have caused you. Enclosed is a cheque for $100. However, since we like your story so well, we would like to offer you another $100 to develop it into a picture.

If you're interested in this offer, please come to the studio to discuss this matter and collect your fee.
Yours very truly,
Hal Roach."

I didn't know whether to laugh or cry. Tony was becoming a famous writer! And he didn't even have to pick up a pen. I would have to coach him carefully before he went in to collect, for he was far too sincere and honest to make a go of it in Hollywood.

Revealing my deception might be the first serious test of our relationship. In any case, I had a lot of explaining to do.

❧❧❧

We had our celebratory feast at Chez Louise.

"Oh, Tony, you were wonderful."

"Wonderful! I was shivering in my shoes."

"But you got the money. And they're using 'our' story!"

" 'Our', nothing. It's yours, sweetheart. You earned it. All I did was was act for ten minutes, and I'll tell you, you people deserve to be paid like kings and queens."

Tricking Tony out as a studious writer type was hilarious. We found a too-large, motheaten suitcoat in the Goodwill, saddle shoes, a battered felt hat, and a pair of spectacles that were almost identical to Harold's (except they had glass in them).

"Isn't it funny, though — "

"What?"

"The story's all about a switch in identity."

"Which is exactly what we had to do to pull this off."

"Had to? No. You did this for me, sweetheart." I was shocked to hear the word leave my lips. And Tony looked heartbreakingly hopeful.

"Put the money in the bank, Jane," he said quietly.

"Take half. It's $100, Tony. You know you could use it. And I — well, I used you. I feel bad about that."

"I don't. It means you trust me. But maybe you should've told me about it."

"I was a coward."

"But would they have taken the story from a girl?"

I already knew the answer to that one.

Though the public was mostly unaware of it, Hollywood could be a bottomless swamp that sucked people under. Though almost everyone thought he was innocent, Roscoe Arbuckle sank without a trace. The beloved Little Tramp survived, but eventually fled the country, branded a Communist and a sexual predator, unwanted and unloved. Though I was completely unprepared for it, the swampy ground would soon give way under my feet and nearly claim me.

Feverish weeks went by while I waited to hear from the studio. The date for my audition came and went, and all my calls were vaguely brushed off. This wasn't like Hal Roach. Usually he was all business, and honoured his commitments. I tried to let the opportunity go, for after all, Tony and I had already made a bundle. But still I hoped for a call from Hal.

Then it came, but not the one I expected. It was the kind of call that changes everything.

"Listen, Muriel, we have a bit of a situation here that's holding things up."

I prayed they hadn't somehow seen through my crooked tactics with the story.

There was such a long pause that felt forced to ask, "What is it?"

"Do you remember that little girl, that Alice?"

Alice. I had kissed her goodbye, and she had cried on my neck and promised to write to me every week. But I had heard nothing, and I hadn't even inquired.

I felt my face darken with consternation and shame. If she thought of me as a big sister, I had let her down terribly, inexcusably.

"Well, she's — gone missing. No one knows where she is. Her parents are furious with the studio and are threatening to break it wide open."

Meaning, I supposed, to alert the press.

"They want . . . well, what people usually want, and we're talking to our lawyers. But the truth is, though we feel as badly about it as everyone else, we're not legally responsible for her disappearance. But if this gets out, it could . . . "

It could seriously damage their reputation. And Harold's.

"So the *Double Vision* picture is on hold for now. Harold's distraught. I've never seen him like this. The police questioned him for hours, and he came out looking pretty shook up."

Had they thought he had somehow ruined her? Suspicion always hung around actors, whether they were guilty or not.

"I just thought I'd let you know, Muriel. We've had to give the police everyone's phone number. The whole cast will be questioned. But I think I'd better tell you something."

I caught my breath.

"You were in a position of trust with her. You knew her better than anyone else, and she looked up to you. Everyone could see that. It came out that she was only thirteen, and that you knew about it. You had a responsibility to turn her in."

"I didn't know what would happen to her."

"Could it have been any worse than this?"

"I'm so sorry."

"Listen Muriel, I'm just trying to help you here. I think you'd better prepare yourself carefully before you go in. Get your facts straight. I'm not asking you to lie, but be very careful how much you reveal."

I suddenly felt as if I were being thrown to the wolves.

"I didn't do this to her! I hardly knew anything about her."

"Yes, we know that." How I hated the "we", playing the card of studio power against my solitary vulnerability.

"I didn't want her to lose her job. She had nothing else to live on."

"She had no business being in the picture in the first place. She was just a little girl."

I dreaded the "was", prayed it was a mistake, wondered what else he knew and was holding back (or had been advised to hold back). An air of malevolence was seeping in like a gas.

I put in my shifts mechanically, dreading the call from the police. I didn't tell Shirley, but with that spooky sixth sense of hers, she knew something was up. But she didn't pry. My friends tiptoed around me, whispered. What did they know? And who had asked them? I was distant with Tony, and he looked sad. Maybe I was back with that Harold guy again, seeing him on the sly?

Then, bizarrely, a call from Harold himself. This was the last thing I expected, and my heart responded in the usual hopeless way.

"Muriel, listen, we have a situation here."

"Hal already told me."

"No, you don't understand. There's been a — development. I'm just letting you know that you're going to be questioned."

"I'm sure I will be. I've been waiting for it."

"No, Muriel, listen. All the other girls saw you two together, thick as thieves. There are all kinds of witnesses."

"What are you talking about?"

"Well, for one thing, you knew about her age."

"Is that a crime?"

"Muriel, she — "

"Just tell me."

"We think someone white-slaved her."

"Oh, Harold, that's completely ridiculous! She knew nothing about sex. She thought you could get pregnant by kissing."

"They found her."

Nothing was making sense. My head reeled. I could hear Harold choking up.

"They found her in the woods, all banged up. Beaten up, I mean."

"God, no."

"It's worse than that. She'd been garrotted."

I had no idea what he meant.

"What?"

"Strangled with a wire."

I was unable to speak.

"That isn't everything, Muriel. She'd been . . . tampered with."

He was telling lies! No one would violate a child like this. It was past even thinking about.

"It looked as if . . . oh, Muriel, this is too horrible to tell a sweet girl like you, but I think you need to know the facts."

"So I can deny everything?"

"As a matter of fact, yes. You must. You cannot get yourself mixed up in any of this. You came out here all alone, and that just doesn't look good. You were in a picture, and some people think that's improper for a young girl who isn't chaperoned. And you were working in a speakeasy. I don't need to tell you they're illegal."

I felt a flash of hopeless, powerless anger. Was I suddenly being accused of blatant immorality, just for surviving?

"Don't lots of girls work in them?"

"Yes, but you can't let yourself get caught. And there's something else."

How *could* there be something else?

"Somebody saw something. At Frankie's, I mean. I feel just as sick about it as you do."

"What do you mean?"

"That night we danced. My God, how I wish I'd never gone there. Someone saw the two of us — "

"*Who?*

"The police have been questioning the staff."

So much for my friends at Frankie's.

"Fine, so we were dancing together. Is that such a hateful crime?"

"Someone saw us. I mean, when we went into that room."

God, *no.*

"They must have assumed the worst."

"Harold, no, they *can't* say that, we never — "

"Listen to me, Muriel, I will stick up for you in every possible way. I will swear on a stack of Bibles we didn't do anything more than kiss."

"But just suspecting I *might* have done it — does that make me a whore?"

"It darkens the picture with Alice. Just by association. If they think you're . . . intimate . . . with movie stars, it paints a picture of a promiscuous older girl having a bad influence on a minor, no matter how innocent both of you are. People's imaginations run wild in this town, and they love a scandal. I've tried to warn you. There's a whole side of it that's about as far from glamorous as you can imagine."

"You can't tell me a movie star strangled Alice with a piece of wire."

"We don't know. Probably not. But she'd been assaulted, horribly. A little girl. It makes me sick to think about it."

And I could have saved her. Could have put her on a train home, or if home was too terrible to contemplate, could have at least let her stay with me until she found a roommate, and a safe job in a factory or a store.

I could not let my imagination approach what Alice had lived through. It was too frightening to contemplate. I tried to push it out of my mind.

"Harold, I need to see you."

"We can't. There's nowhere that's safe. Don't try to contact me. And please, *please* do not admit to anything beyond a completely professional relationship between us. We could still pull out of this if we keep our stories straight."

Stories!

"So we'll go to any length to protect our own reputations, at the cost of that girl's life?"

"That's unfair, Muriel. We would never resort to those tactics. What happened to Alice was nothing short of a tragedy. But her parents are threatening a lawsuit that could wipe us out. I mean completely. They're claiming the studio knew she was underage. And in a way, they're right: someone in the studio *did* know."

It was a stinging slap, but one I thought I deserved. And yet . . . how many of the girls at Miss Pettigrew's school were underage? More to the point: did anyone care?

"I thought you said you were going to protect me."

"There's only so much I can do. You *knew*, Muriel, and you did nothing. Do you know how her family is going to react when they find out about that?"

"Are there spies around every corner?"

"Yes, there are, when there's trouble like this." He said it wearily. Not yet out of his twenties, he had already seen his youthful illusions fall to pieces.

"You have to help me, Harold. I don't know what to do." I could hear the desperate note in my voice, though I tried to control it.

"It's what you *don't* do that's important. Don't admit to anything except the bare facts. Remember, you had nothing at all to do with the murder. Don't look too upset, or they'll get suspicious. But look concerned."

He was like a director setting up a scene. But I knew we had no choice.

"I don't want you to lie, Muriel. I know it's hard for you."

"It's also perjury. It could send me to prison."

"You won't go to prison. But you might not find work again, or at least not the kind you want."

"Except — *that* kind of work?"

"For heaven's sake, Muriel, that's not what I meant at all."

"Isn't it? I'm already coming across as some sort of scarlet woman, when the truth is, I'm one of the few virgins left in this place."

"We're going to get through this if we just have a little faith."

"'*We*'. Do you really think something like this could damage your reputation as much as it would mine?"

"Yes. Believe me, it could. It's happened to people before, and for reasons far less serious."

"I feel completely alone here. Everyone is about to run for cover. Even you."

"You won't be alone. Just hang on."

The call left me utterly flat with exhaustion, and I called in sick the next day and lay in bed as if paralyzed. I wondered if the police had already questioned the other waitresses, the girls I had come to think of as my friends. Or, worse, Shirley, whom I hoped did not know about this (while suspecting that with her elaborate web of connections, she probably did).

Desperate, not wanting him to know but unable to go on in this state of abject loneliness, I called the one completely unshakeable friend I had, the only one I knew I could trust with my life.

He came over right away.

I huddled in his arms for hours that night, trembling and babbling through uncontrollable tears. "I'm going to go to jail for the rest of my life. I'll take the fall for everyone involved in this. I knew she was young and innocent and a little bit slow. She knew nothing about men, nothing about life at all. And I did nothing to protect her."

"Oh Janey, listen, you're having a hard time even protecting yourself. How can you expect one little girl to look out for another? And that Harold guy, he took hold of you — "

"Leave Harold out of this!" I shocked myself at the tone I was using. Tony looked weary and miserable.

"It's no contest, Janie. The guy is big, he's rich and powerful, and he likes women. He isn't even married, so he can play the field with anyone he wants. And from what you've told me, he's been trying to warn you. But you don't listen! You just keep hoping. Hoping — for *what?* Sure, he likes you, and I think he admires your talent. But that's *it*. He's not going to marry you. And he can't even be seen with you in public, especially now. It's not going to happen. He has to have some snooty actress or a rich, glamorous socialite on his arm."

There was so much truth in what Tony was saying that it made me gasp. I should have hated him for it, but I didn't. It was just the jolt I needed to clear my head.

Still, I had the awful sinking feeling of a prisoner about to be executed. Even Tony didn't really know how I felt. Inevitably, I was called in to be questioned by the police. I sat in the middle of a dark room on a straight-backed metal chair with a big light above me. I couldn't believe it: I was trapped in a bad detective novel, every ridiculous cliché coming true before my eyes.

But the dreadful ordeal was something of a surprise. I wasn't grilled or shouted at. It was a policewoman who questioned me (I didn't know they existed), and she was gentler than I expected.

But her gentleness opened up a place in me that tough questioning never could.

"Muriel, we know you and Alice had a special kind of relationship. Would you say you were like a sister to her?"

"I've never had a sister, so I'm not sure."

"Did you try to give Alice counsel on private matters?"

"I'm not sure what you mean."

"Did she ever ask you any personal questions?"

"Sometimes. But I tried to tell her things a good friend might say. I told her she had to be very careful."

"Did you see any evidence that she went out with men?"

My eyes flew open. "Of course not!"

"Do you think she tried to emulate you?" I was mortified that I wasn't sure what the word meant. But I took a guess.

"She might have looked up to me sometimes. There was nobody else — nobody in her family, I mean. "

"Muriel, what is your relationship with Harold Lloyd?"

My ears began to sing, and I felt weak. This was the crucial question, the one that everything else revolved around.

"I was an extra in one of his movies."

"And isn't it true you went out dancing with him?"

"Not exactly. He was with Bebe Daniels. He asked me for one dance after I got off shift."

"At a speakeasy."

"I think you've heard of them." I immediately regretted my words, but to my amazement, the lady cop only smiled a little.

"Yes, I believe I have. And we know movie stars frequent them. What we want to know is whether you have a special relationship with Mr. Lloyd."

"No. It's not special." The words were heavy as lead, but true.

"Someone at Frankie's Place claims they saw you and Mr. Lloyd in a compromising position."

How was I going to get out of that one?

"Mr. Lloyd warned me about that. He said that certain people are in the business of ruining actors' careers by spreading malicious lies. They do it for money."

"It's called extortion."

"Yes." I thanked God she knew the word for it.

Harold *had* told me about threats made by so-called fans. So far, I had told the truth, more or less.

"Do you still work for Frank Lancaster?"

"No. I resigned months ago. I work for Shirley Tate at Chez Louise."

I swear, the colour of her face changed. This was a whole different story.

"Do you think she would be willing to come in to talk to us?"

"I'm sure she would." I was hoping against hope.

It was my first indication of the potent under-the-table power Shirley wielded. There were layers to the truth, as there were layers in lies, and they were not always as distinct as they seemed.

"Muriel, I have to tell you that I believe your story, and I believe your influence on Alice was mostly positive. In fact, you were probably the only good influence she had. But there is still an element who will choose not to believe you. In a case such as this, it's convenient to have someone to blame. I can't guarantee that my opinion will carry much weight. I'm just a lady cop, and most of the time they don't listen to me. They use me just to keep little girls from getting hysterical."

"So what will happen now?"

"Muriel, you knew Alice was only thirteen. That's the thing that won't go away. You knew, and you did nothing." Suddenly I could not hold back any more — I flew into the kind of humiliating hysterics she had just talked about.

"I was afraid she'd go home, and — "

"Muriel — "

"And her Pa would beat her up, and — call her a whore, and — a slut, and — "

"Muriel, no."

"*Yes!* You don't know what it's like. You can't *do* anything! You're afraid all the time. All the time! And your Ma just sits there and doesn't move, and says you should mind your Pa, and — "

I tried very hard to stop sobbing. I knew now that it was all over, that I would never be free.

"And if I had to send Alice back to all that — "

"Did she tell you about her Pa?"

"No. But I saw it." One day when our costumes left our arms and backs partially bare, I had seen the kind of scars that were all too sickeningly familiar: the belt marks, the cigarette burns, the marks of casual torture.

"So in a way, you were trying to protect her."

"I would never do anything to hurt Alice. I was so afraid for her, but there didn't seem to be anything I could do."

Then she said three words that would sustain me during the sick anxiety of the weeks to come.

"I believe you."

❦❦❦

Then came weeks of silent tension, when I heard nothing. I came to work when I was able, and looked a wreck. Shirley didn't talk to me about it, but I felt a kind of protective field around me which was the only thing holding me together.

I had not written to Bea in a very long time, and now I dreaded she would see something in the paper that would drag my name into the horror of Alice's murder. If it happened, it would be all over for me, and (at best) I would be back flipping pancakes in Santa Fe for the rest of my life. I tried not to think of the worst.

One by one, all the extras were questioned, along with the waitresses at Frankie's. I had only one contact, Susan, one of the girls I hoped was still my friend. But I wondered what she had told them. I remembered the way the girls on the *Mind your Manners* set had played at malice as if it were a sport. I did not think I would survive.

I touched bottom when I got an anonymous call from a woman telling me she was going to bring me down, then slamming down the receiver. I had no idea who she was. I was convinced I had no friends or support in the industry anywhere. I was bitter, depressed, hopeless. Tony advised me to wait it out, then leave the whole situation and move away, get a normal job, and work on my writing on the side.

Then came the most bizarre experience of my life.

I was leafing through the *Los Angeles Examiner*, and found a story that sounded almost like Alice's murder, except that most of the details were different.

"Look at this, Tony," I said.

He read it. "Quite a story, sis," he said. "Especially since it's about you."

I reread it: an innocent sixteen-year-old girl (name withheld) with a strong resemblance to Mary Pickford was living with her nineteen-year-old sister and just breaking into the glamourous world of pictures, when suddenly . . .

She was found in the woods, raped and strangled with a wire, brought down by a complete stranger, a sex fiend fuelled by cocaine. The article included statements from everyone who knew the girl, none of which had anything to do with the truth.

"We all looked out for little Polly."

"We knew she was special. She had so much talent."

"I don't know how this ever could have happened."

Her parents, too distraught to be interviewed, told the press through a third party that no one could have stopped this heartless fiend, that it was plainly a random case of innocence sacrificed.

The policewoman who had questioned me (using my real name!) cited me for protecting the young girl and providing a sterling example of maturity and morality in a dangerous environment.

But there was more. Hal Roach was quoted as saying, "That little girl Muriel was one of the best bit players we ever had. Worked her way up from an extra in a couple of months. I saw the two of them together, they were like sisters. All this stuff about Harold, why, that's nothing but slander, everyone knows Harold Lloyd is a model of deportment, I can trust him in any situation."

My eyes were wide and my mouth open, but there was more: Shirley Tate (a.k.a. Louise of Chez Louise) claimed to be my guardian by proxy, citing my excellent work record and denying I ever worked for a speakeasy: "This girl has too much class for that."

I was astonished. "Tony, what does this mean?"

"Means you're off the hook, Janie. In fact, it looks like you're a paragon of virtue and a minor celebrity."

"What should I do now?"

"Nothing. Wait it out. It'll all settle down soon."

Then I got a call from Bea, a shock in itself: she could not afford a phone. "What's this I see in the paper? Why is your name in this story?"

"I tried to help her, sissy. I didn't know she was in so much danger."

"You should have turned her in. You know that."

"Yes, I know that."

"Do you know it could have been you?"

I hadn't stopped thinking about that since it happened.

"Come home, Janie. You had your fun, but it didn't work out. You can get a job here, easy."

"I have a really good job now, cuz. Shirley is like a sister to me."

"Is that so. So you need a sister now?"

I could detect the note of jealousy in her voice.

"Yes, I do, Bea, because you're not here."

"That story wasn't on the level, was it."

"No, it wasn't."

"So what really happened?"

"I wasn't mixed up in it, I promise. I had no idea — "

"Well, you'd better get an idea. There's a lot more going on here than you know, and you'd better get wise to it now."

I had been sending modest cheques to Bea to try to pay back her small loans. Then they started coming back. It hurt.

I had been trying to help her and her family in my own way, and I felt slapped in the face. But she was right: there was much more going on here than anyone knew.

I kept trying to coax Shirley to explain to me what had happened. I remembered how she'd said she had Don Bishop (editor-in-chief of the infamous Hollywood Tattler) "in her back pocket". One day, Shirley told me what it meant.

"I told you about Don, right? Well, there's a lot more to it than that. Don knows things, and certain people know that he knows. It's like ammunition he can use against people, but most of the time he doesn't."

"Why not?" In such a muck-raking town, one would think he would need to use it every day.

"Because he doesn't have to. Threats are usually enough. And mentioning his lawyer, who's crooked as a dog's hind leg but famous for getting people convicted."

"So . . ." I still wasn't sure about the connection.

"Have you ever heard of William Harvey Benedict?"

It took a second to register. "Oh, the newspaper man."

"Newspaper man! More like newspaper emperor or sultan. Now *there's* power. But you wanna know something? That kind of power can collapse like a house of cards.

"So I got ahold of Don and I said, 'Listen, Don, I'd like to ask you a little favor.' And he listened to me, isn't that remarkable?"

This is how their conversation went, more or less:

Shirley: There's a story going to run, and there's no truth to it. It has to be corrected.

Don: So what can I do for you, doll?

Shirley: Don, you know a little bit about Harve Benedict, right?

Don: Enough to send him over Niagara Falls in a barrel.

Shirley: Do you think you can, you know, call him up and remind him of certain things?

145

Don: Oh, it'd be my pleasure.

"As it turns out," Shirley continued, "the 'little bit' he knew about was a broad, name of Malvina Barnes. A floozy, really, but she had a sort of career as a singer. Bad singer, but what can I say, Harve sort of set it up for her, he has lots of hand. And he liked her, I guess that's obvious, she was his bit on the side.

"Then all of a sudden she's dead. Just like that! A blood clot in her neck, I think it was, some hereditary condition, her sister died of it too. And that was supposed to be that. But as usual, Don was sitting on a secret, the kind of whopper that can bring down the most powerful man in the country.

"So here's the deal. Before she died, Malvina got a little careless, or else Harve did, I don't know. They say it wasn't even his baby. But something had to be done about it. And something *was* done, all right. That little "mistake" was undone, and she got hustled out of town. All of a sudden, it was as if she'd never existed in the first place."

"Wait a minute, Shirley. This sounds like a seedy novel."

"Well, where do you think seedy novels come from? So here's where Don Bishop comes in. Don has a great sense of timing, see? So he sent a message to Harve Benedict that he had photos of Malvina's dead body lying on the floor of a public washroom in a pool of blood. Obviously the victim of some backstreet butcher. But he'd sell the negatives to him if he did *one* thing."

"Change the story!"

"Yes! That's how the story of Alice was rewritten. It happens all the time in this town. All of a sudden she's sixteen, she lives with her sister, and you were the saint looking out for her. So nobody has to turn nobody in. Takes care of quite a number of problems, don't you think? Anyway, the revised version ran in every major paper in the country. Leaving you practically a heroine."

"Which I'm not."

"Enjoy it. It could've gone the other way."

"But what about those photos? Did he really have them?"

"Some things Don never reveals. Not even to me."

But that was not the end of the story — not quite. Many years later, a young Hollywood maverick named Randolph Hodge made a movie called *The Baron Jack*. Written, produced and directed by this "boy genius", it was later considered by many film critics to be the most brilliantly original movie ever made.

The Baron Jack was a fictionalized account of the rise and fall of William Harvey Benedict. Hodge's brilliant performance as the corrupt newspaper mogul (renamed John Franklin Evans, known for his crooked mining deals as "Diamond Jack") was shut out for an Oscar. Imagine, implying that William Harvey Benedict was involved in some sort of awful scandal! It didn't bear thinking about, especially not in a community where show biz and the press were so intertwined that the fourth estate was sometimes known as the "fourth escape".

As if the movie were cursed, *The Baron Jack's* stars all came to a bad end, dying of alcoholism, accident and suicide. Hodge never equalled his performance, spending the rest of his short life trading on his rich baritone voice on the radio. After Hiroshima, he had the nation in a mass panic when he read a fictional "news report" on the air about a nuclear attack on New York. Forced into an early retirement and branded a Communist, he ate and drank himself to death at the age of forty-five.

Alice's parents settled with the Hal Roach Studios out of court. The killer was never found.

⁂

The horror of Alice's murder did not let me go for a long time. Just when I felt I was breaking the surface, another hideous dream would pull me under. I would hear screams, see the dark shape of a man moving in the woods. I wondered if I would ever laugh again, or be able to enjoy life at all.

The first time I did laugh, it shocked me.

I did not realize then that in each of us there is a natural core of health, both physical and mental, that magnetically draws us back from the extremes of illness or despair. No matter how wretched we are, health wants us back, and it will pull on us relentlessly until we come home.

My relief at settling back into my sane, predictable job waiting tables at Chez Louise didn't last forever. Before long the urge to write began to itch in my fingers again. I looked back at my wretched history of failure, wondered if anyone would ever take me seriously again, and — began to write.

All these years later, I can see that my real motivation was to get close to Harold again. For my script was definitely about Harold. In fact, it had echoes of my last failed attempt: there were two of them, a "good Harold" and a "bad Harold", a bank robber and a policeman. The idea had lots of scope for gags. I could see it in my mind. This time it would work!

I screwed up my courage and sent it to Hal Roach. No aliases this time, I would sign my own name to it. He had put in a good word for me when I was in such desperate trouble. Surely he would take me seriously.

He phoned me, asked me to meet him at a tawdry diner/ dance club called *Hot Feet!* But the moment I saw his face, I could tell my idea had fallen flat.

"Muriel, as much as I'd like to take this story, I just can't do it. It isn't that it's no good. For your age and level of experience, it's really not bad. But you're getting ahead of yourself here. In ten or fifteen years you'll be writing novels, mark my words."

He might as well have said a hundred.

"But it isn't just that, Muriel. You may be old enough to write well, and I must say I've never seen a little girl write as well as this. But there's so much more to it. You have to be able to protect yourself. This town can be dirty and cruel. I think you've had a taste of that. People twice your age have been destroyed by it. And you can get swindled, just like that. Ever heard of plagiarism?"

"I think I know what it means."

"I figured. Listen, that was a nice little piece you sent us about the identity switch, it had possibilities."

I was astonished that he knew. "What happened to it?"

"Harold put the kibosh on it, I'm afraid. He said, 'Don't give her any encouragement.'"

"*What?*"

"He's doing you a favour, Muriel. You're not ready for all this. And it wouldn't be good for you to work with him again."

"Nothing happened, I swear."

"Yes it did. Remember the rainstorm?"

"But we were only — "

"Would you do that with me? Be honest."

"Of course not."

"And why wouldn't you?"

I thought about it for a second. Then it seemed completely obvious.

"Because it would be totally unprofessional."

"And dangerous. Men are men."

"But I didn't — "

"You didn't stop him either. Look, I know you're crazy about Harold. Almost all the girls are, except for the Chaplin fanatics, and they're in a class by themselves. But you're different. You think about him day and night. I can see it in you. But let me tell you, he isn't what you think. Harold is charming and good-looking and funny as hell. He's my discovery and I'm damn proud of that. But he's a boy. He hasn't grown up past the age of fifteen. And you can't have him, which makes him that much more desirable."

Hal Roach, the stolid, seemingly dull Hal Roach, had seen through me like glass.

"This *isn't* bad news, Muriel. A major studio has taken notice of you, out of all those thousands of hopefuls. That's something to be proud of. Keep writing, but keep your straight job too. Every writer does that. And Shirley's the real deal, a great dame. She'll protect you like a tiger. Meanwhile you'll be learning something about the ins and outs. Not to mention your craft."

"You mean racket," I said it with a kind of sarcastic hopelessness, wondering if the tough words would impress him.

"You're a writer, sweetheart, no mistaking it. Talent will out. And determination. There's no stopping you, Muriel."

He handed my sheaf of paper, my dream, back to me. I had no idea how I was supposed to feel.

Why Worry?

Time without Harold should have dragged unbearably, but as the shadow of Alice gradually began to fade, my life once again moved swiftly forward. Months passed, accumulated and added up, along with tips. I moved out of the smoke-stinking horror of my old one-room digs into a bright and airy, if small and sparsely-furnished apartment (one table, two chairs, bureau and bed). Shirley gently steered clothing my way that had been previously but lightly worn. I would find them hanging on the coat rack fresh from the dry cleaner.

Without formally breaking up, Tony and I stopped seeing each other. I missed our easy camaraderie, and his gentle and respectful treatment of me. Part of me screamed: *marry him!* Don't let him get away. But I was still very young, the needle not yet tickling nineteen, and he was almost twenty-six. I could feel his frustration building; because of the ironclad morality that had been driven into me, I could not "give myself" to him, as the quaint saying went, but I understood his need to have a girl to cherish, marry and have children with.

Eventually it came back to me that he had a girl. I had an odd mixture of feelings about this: relief that I no longer had to feel guilty about not seeing him any more; genuine happiness for him; curiosity about what she looked like; jealousy. This last one proved to me why such an elaborate code of deportment still needed to exist between men and women: relations between them are, more often than not, entirely irrational.

One day Shirley came into the kitchen and saw me standing in the corner scribbling on a pad.

"Not taking an order, are you, darling," she said.

I jumped, hid the pad in the pocket of my uniform.

"Relax, kiddo, I know all about your scribbles. Confidentially, Muriel, I think you're bored here. And no wonder. You're the smartest girl we've ever had, too smart to work as a waitress. You've saved up your tips, you're in a nicer place now, and wearing nicer clothes, more like you deserve. So I think you deserve a better job, too."

My heart jumped. With all her elaborate connections, Shirley might have pulled a string for me.

"Remember Don Bishop?"

"Of course." Everyone knew he was the new editor-in-chief of *Spotlight on the Stars*, but very few people knew why. William Harvey Benedict had been so grateful for Don's coverup of his little indiscretion with Malvina Barnes that he had somehow managed to "retire" the old editor and slot Don in.

Don Bishop's long experience with the *Hollywood Tattler* had given him an instinct for what the bloodthirsty public liked to see. Soon Spotlight had boomed in circulation, while keeping at least a degree of its reputation for well-written interviews and quality photography. ("It's the NEW *Spotlight* for the Smart, Savvy Fan!") Scandal could be hinted at, but not spelled out, and the photos were taken by real photographers, not private detectives or men selling French postcards under their coats.

Shirley blew out a long blast of smoke, reminding me of a dragon. "Don would like to talk to you."

"Really?" I tried to act nonchalant, and it was a complete failure.

"Yeah, seems he has a little opening, a position for a girl reporter. Somebody with a nose for news, as they say. And a few Hollywood connections."

"Oh but Shirley, I've only been in one movie."

"Yeah, well, that's one more than most of the girls in this town. But you sold them a story, whether they used it or not. And remember that newspaper article about you."

"But it was a pack of lies!"

"Not in my book. The things they said about you, Muriel, I think they were true. Well, most of them were true. Frankie had to kind of forget you ever worked for him. But Don remembers how you weathered that storm and came out on top."

"I came out on top because he twisted somebody's arm."

"So what? One hand washes the other."

"When do I see him?"

"Today. He's coming in here to interview you after your shift."

Today! Panic seized me. I had worn the most ordinary-looking outfit I owned. I wasn't even wearing nail polish. At least my shoes were good. (I still remembered my mother's advice about shoes.) I ran around in a panic while the other girls threw accessories at me to try to spiff me up.

In the end, it was fast, easy and direct. He asked me a lot of questions about who was on top in Hollywood, not just the stars but the men behind the scenes. He fired them at me fast, and I didn't miss a beat.

"I like you, Muriel," Don Bishop said. "You're hired."

And just like that, I was in.

❧❧❧

The role of Girl Reporter, exciting as it sounded, was completely foreign to me, and more than a little intimidating. I wondered what I should look like, sound like. I knew my neat but conservative wardrobe would need expanding and polishing into a look of professionalism. Unless I looked like I meant business, I knew no one would pay the slightest attention to me. To get the story, I had to be noticed.

It thrilled me that I would be interviewing movie stars. Oh, perhaps the minor ones at first: J. Warren Kerrigan wasn't exactly burning up the screen, nor was Blanche Sweet. Stars even slightly past their prime were like day-old bread, and the public knew it.

After my bizarre experience with Don and William Harvey Benedict, I wondered how much I was required to fabricate. If a has-been actor let loose with a bitter tirade against the business, should I discard the interview or try to "fix" it? And how much? I was going to have to find my way by sheer intuition.

And there weren't any other girl reporters, though they told me there was a young fellow, a cub reporter named Danny Hoolihan. It puzzled me a little that he could dress that well on a junior reporter's salary, but maybe he just wore his clothes well, like certain other men I knew. I wondered if I should meet him, try to befriend him. Would there be talk? Would he be helpful, or would he try to trip me up, to "scoop" me? There was so much to learn, it made me dizzy.

But there was nothing else to do except plunge in. I knew my limited wardrobe would never do for *Spotlight*: I had to look the part. I went shopping with Susan, the only friend I had left from my days at Frankie's, and we spent a whole day giggling and trying on the most unsuitable things to make each other scream with laughter. I even put on a fake diamond tiara and a feather boa and threatened to wear them on my first day.

I had an uneasy feeling that Shirley wanted to pay for my new wardrobe, and I was prepared to firmly turn it down. Sue and I were in Chaston's, a nice store with affordable clothes (many of them convincing knock-offs of more expensive items), when I remarked to her that everything I tried on looked unusually flattering. The clerk seemed to know my personal taste without being told, and handed me just the right things. I picked up skirts and blouses and jackets, and even a *faux* leather handbag that reminded me of Shirley's crocodile purse with the head left on.

I carried the heap of clothing to the till, while Sue squealed, "You're gonna look just peachy, girl!" Then came the surprise. The sales clerk told me, "These are all taken care of, Miss Ashford. You have a credit here."

A credit. This could mean only one thing. If Shirley couldn't get me one way, she'd get me another.

However, I *did* need the clothes, very badly, and the things I was buying would just about clean me out except for rent money.

I phoned her. "Shirley, something very strange happened to me today when I was shopping."

"What, honey?"

"Well, I went into Chaston's to buy some things, and it turned out I had a credit with them."

"Is that so."

"You wouldn't happen to know why, would you?"

"Not sure. But do you know what I think? I think wherever it came from, you've worked hard enough to deserve it."

"But Shirley . . . "

"The going rate for my waitresses ain't so hot, honey. And I was afraid to pay you more than the rest of them. It gets around. Even if you were head and shoulders above the rest, which you were, the others would be jealous and say it was unfair. I want you to think of this store credit as a bonus, one that you've earned a dozen times over."

"Please, I can't take this."

"Yes you can. You're starting out fresh and you need some glad rags. And let me tell you a little something, darling. Do you want to know the nicest thing you can do for someone?"

I thought. "Do them a favor? Or a kindness?"

"That's what most people think. But it's the other way around. The nicest thing you can do is let *them* do something good for *you*. It makes them feel better than getting something, y'know what I mean? It gives them a warm glow. People fight it so much, out of pride, and it's too bad. Better to let the goodwill flow. Sometimes it goes this way, and sometimes it goes that way. But it all works out in the end."

Though it sounded a little idealistic, I relented and allowed Shirley to help me, at least until I could save up enough to pay her back. I knew it would give her a warm glow, and that was more valuable than anything else I could offer her.

∾∾∾

For the first few weeks, I wasn't allowed to do much except sharpen pencils. I fetched coffee, I took down shorthand (*shorthand?* I made up my own version, indecipherable to anyone else), I filled in when the receptionist was sick. I even pretended over the phone to be an obscure old movie actress named Marella DuPuy, though it was a little embarrassing to find out later that she was dead.

Though there were other girls around, they weren't reporters. There was a sort of secretarial pool of women who all looked the same. Their figures were almost identical, busty and voluptuous, and they were all blondes. Though *Spotlight* was a lot more high-class than the *Tattler,* Don hadn't lost his taste for a particular type of girl.

I had so far escaped this sort of unwanted attention, since I was officially in a different category and didn't look the part. But for weeks, I felt like I was drifting. I wondered why they had hired me at all.

I had not yet seen the fabled cub reporter Danny Hoolihan, and wondered why he never came into the office. Apparently he was out in "the field", chasing after interviews with elusive, reluctant stars. Then one dull afternoon, he blew in — almost literally blew in, with a gust of sultry California air behind him.

Oh, Danny.

I didn't know another man could have such heartbreaking blue eyes, lustrous black hair, a smile like . . . no, his smile wasn't really like Harold's at all. I must be mad, I told myself. But he was dashing. Yes, *dashing*, and I'd never seen that quality in anybody else.

"Say, you must be the new girl."

"Muriel. Ashford."

He treated me to half the smile.

"So where've you been, doll face?"

"I'm not sure I — "

"I mean, where's Bishop been sending you?"

"Sending me? Nowhere."

"Geez. What a dumb bunny, not even using his sweet new girl reporter. Doesn't know what he's sitting on. I'll have to chew him out. Hey, you know Harold Lloyd, don't you?"

It was almost unbearable to hear his name. I was about to say, no, I don't actually know him, I was only a bit player in one of his movies, but then . . . I remembered that night at Frankie's, the intoxicating fox trot, his lips on my throat. Standing in the teeming rain with him, trembling in his arms. Not *know* him? How could I say I didn't know him?

"Yes, we've worked together." It seemed I was beginning to catch on.

"So why'd you bail on the picture business and land in this dump?"

"Long story."

"You're a firecracker, you know that? I can see it. Lady on the outside, baby vamp within. I'll bet you could get an interview with Lloyd in two shakes. I'm going to go into Bishop's office and work him over."

"Please don't."

"Relax, I just mean I'll pull some strings for you. There's no reason why you should be gathering dust like this. Lloyd's shooting a new one now, just started it. Has his new leading lady in it. He finally busted away from Hal Roach, and about time, too. This would be the perfect time for you to do an in-depth profile."

Yes: and to rip open the barely-healed tissues of my heart.

"So, are you in?" Then I saw the smile full-force.

"I'm in."

~~~

Don called me into his office the next day.

"You know Harold Lloyd, don't you, missy?"

I swallowed the usual response of, "Oh, no, I hardly know him at all."

"Yes, we worked together on a picture. *Mind your Manners.* I had a scene with Mildred Davis. Contributed to the story, as well."

"Did you know he's started a new one? A different sort of picture. Set in some sort of a tropical island somewhere. It's about this rich hypochondriac, and he goes away on a holiday for his health, except there's a revolution going on around him. Meanwhile, his nurse . . . "

"Mildred Davis?"

"No, he has a new leading lady now. I forget her name, it's sort of odd. Nobody can pronounce it. Anyway, she's supposed to be sexier. And this is his first project away from Roach. They finally broke up."

"You make it sound like a marriage."

Fortunately, he laughed.

"I'd like to send you to the set, just to observe everything. Since you know Harold, I don't think he'd object if you interviewed him. You know, to get the fans curious, perk up interest in advance."

"What's the title of it?" (*Trouble in Paradise? Lovesick?*)

"I think it's called *Why Worry?*"

"But that doesn't make sense."

"Harold will make it make sense."

It felt strange to walk onto a movie set again fter what seemed like an eternity. The atmosphere was different, more charged. Everything seemed to have accelerated. The old make-it-up-as-we-go-along method had been scrapped. Now there was an actual story, and the gags had been carefully worked out in advance. Everyone seemed to know what was expected of them, and worked together with grace and speed.

But I knew there was a tightly-wound mainspring at the core of all this frenetic energy.

When I contemplated coming face-to-face with Harold again, I was expecting one (or perhaps two) of the following responses:

He wouldn't recognize me.

He would, but would only acknowledge me with a frosty nod.

He would behave professionally towards me, but that's all.

But there was a fourth possibility I had not allowed myself to consider. When he saw me, did a cartoonish little jump, grinned wildly, then ran over and fairly hurled himself at me. He jumped around and giggled and exclaimed "*Muriel!*", before sweeping me up in his arms and giving me a lung-deflating squeeze.

So much for professional behaviour.

Though his delirious greeting wasn't what I expected, my reaction was. He was in his shirtsleeves, the weather was hot, and beneath the clean pressed shirt-smell and faint masculine trace of bay rum, I detected the dear familiar scent of his sweat. Dear God, I reprimanded myself: are you nothing but an animal, scenting out its prey?

He was amazed and proud of my success: "Imagine that! Our Muriel, working for Spotlight, the one everybody reads. Especially producers and directors. You're a girl reporter now, just look at you. Say, you look sensational. Did I tell you that yet?"

I certainly looked different. Like so many women of my time, I gritted my teeth and had my hair bobbed, and was immediately surprised at how much it changed my appearance. It added a few years, which for a nearly nineteen-year-old was not a bad thing. My head immediately felt lighter, which somehow improved my posture. I had to tame the fluffy curls that were released from captivity, but suddenly the colour seemed lighter and the texture almost silky.

I began to wear lipstick. (Why not?) And a bit of scent. And heels, but no more than two inches. The clothing credit at Chaston's had given me a chance to develop a sense of taste with just a hint of glamour.

Today I had chosen a shimmering turquoise-and-gold scarf to highlight a rather conservative navy skirt and blue silk blouse. (Shirley was one of those rare women who knew what to do with a scarf.) The gleaming gold earrings Tony had given me for my eighteenth birthday provided just the right note to finish my look. "Tasteful, honey," Shirley would have said, "but with a hint of pizzazz."

I looked like a woman. And Harold obviously approved.

Warming to his almost ridiculous *joie de vivre*, I asked him what was new in his life.

"Oh, I forgot to tell you. I got married!" He let go with one of his ridiculous giggles. Another railroad spike driven into my heart, but then, what could one expect from Hurricane Harold?

"Congratulations. Is it — ?"

"Yes. It's Mildred. We kept it all very quiet, so don't put it in the magazine yet. I convinced her to give up acting." He glanced around the set, which was not just busy but fairly vibrating with excitement. "This is really no place for a woman."

"So who's your new — ?"

"Oh, wait 'til you meet her. Jobyna Ralston. She's a sensation. She has so much talent, and we work so well together, it's as if she can read my mind."

So a movie set was "no place for a woman"? This was Harold's usual convoluted logic. How soon until . . . but that was none of my business. Writing the piece was. Not drowning in him. Head above water — or else.

"Come on, Muriel, I want you to see what we're doing today. We'll be shooting every scene maybe five or six times. But you remember that from last time, don't you? You just have to meet my new supporting player, he's the biggest thing in show business. A complete original."

When I saw him, I jumped. He was an original, all right. He must have been seven feet tall. Though dressed and made up to look sinister, there was something rather sweet about him.

"John, this is my old friend Muriel."

"Pleased to meet you, miss," he said, offering a huge hand. I was shocked to hear a gentle and almost boyish voice, completely at odds with his massive bulk.

"We have a whole string of gags with John. Some of the best we've ever done. He has a bad tooth and needs to have it pulled out. So I have to do all these outlandish things to help him."

I loved the gags, no matter how many times they had to reshoot them, and laughed at every take. I was seeing it fresh, right out of Harold's spinningly brilliant brain:

He hooks one end of a rope to the tooth, the other looped on a horse's saddle. The horse gallops off, the rope uncoils and uncoils and finally runs out and falls to the ground. .

He ties the rope around his waist, then runs like crazy, but nothing happens. He looks back and sees the giant running behind him.

He tries it again with the giant standing still, runs until he reaches the end of the rope and is yanked over backwards, falling with his legs high in the air.

Then comes one of his best sight gags ever: Harold scales the giant with the rope as if he were climbing an Alp. This was a bit of pure Harold genius, every bit as inspired and surreal as his famous dangle from the hands of the clock.

These gags were run again and again, and I wondered how the actors maintained their stamina and kept it fresh. It might be the tenth or the fifteenth take that Harold decided to keep, but it was always the right one, with just the right touch of quirkiness to be true to the enigmatic Glass Character.

Harold called for a break. Everyone was sweating, and a herd of extras was milling around finding floppy straw hats and bandannas and other bits of wardrobe for the revolution scene. A striking young woman came toward us, swinging her hips. With her cascade of lush dark hair and flashing eyes, she radiated intelligence as well as sexuality. I could only surmise that this was Harold's new leading lady.

Mildred Davis, she was not.

It was as if she owned the piece of ground she was standing on. There was banked-down fire in her, and a sort of unspoken challenge to Harold's crackling brain. Her densely-reddened lips had exactly the same kewpie-doll shape. This was a woman who would be able to express practically anything, I thought, with no need for a single word.

"Joby," Harold said in an odd voice. Then, "Oh, Jobyna, this is Mildred, my best friend. I mean Muriel. Sorry, Muriel." He seemed completely muddled.

"Hello, Muriel." I would remember the measured voice and cool handshake years later when I interviewed Gloria Swanson.

"This is so exciting! I'm so glad to be here," I babbled, wondering why I couldn't think of anything more appropriate to say, and puzzling over why Harold had called me his "best friend".

"Mostly it's just hard work. But, yes, every once in a while it's exciting."

I noticed Harold's eyes were glued to her, and hoped I was wrong about what I saw.

As the days of shooting unfolded, I saw more than a hint of a spark between them. She played gorgeous nurse to his pill-popping hypochondriac, a man so preoccupied with his imaginary illnesses that he barely sees her. In a scene that almost embarrassed me with its innuendo, she trips and falls into his lap, and stays there for a suspicious length of time while a slightly lecherous smile slowly develops on his face. Then, realizing with alarm that he is straining his heart, he dumps her on the ground and takes another pill.

There were several such scenes, in which he seems vaguely aware that he is physically attracted to her, but still oblivious to her hopeless love for him. This was odd for a Harold Lloyd movie, in which his character usually pines for an unattainable girl. His Glass Character had never developed emotionally or sexually beyond the age of about fifteen, mooning over girls who were beautiful and completely unattainable. This was what allowed him to play a college freshman or a daydreamy farm boy when he was well into his thirties.

But in *Why Worry?*, the situation is completely different. There is a tension between the two of them from the beginning, and more than once he forgets himself and becomes just a man yearning for a woman — this woman in particular. Even with this reversal, and Harold's essentially obnoxious character, audiences loved this movie, enchanted by its oddball charm. It would go on to become my personal favourite.

The final clinch, repeated an astonishing number of times, frankly shocked and titillated me. Harold flies into a rage and begins to rant against her, irrationally asking her, "Why didn't you tell me I loved you?" Dressed in a ridiculous disguise to look like a boy, she smirks at him, taunts him, swiveling her hips. Then he does something completely uncharacteristic: he grabs her by the shoulders, pulls her violently towards him and kisses her with tremendous passion.

Jobyna being the superb actress she is, she reacts in several ways: first stiffening in resistance, then going limp in his arms, reaching up tentatively as if to touch his head — fighting the impulse at first, then melting into surrender. As the scene fades, she bends her knee slightly in a subtle hint of submission. Their bodies are touching all the way down. The camera moves away for a few seconds, then comes back to the couple, still locked in a powerful, sexual embrace.

What made Harold decide to turn his character upside-down like that? Was it just a particularly good story, or did he feel a certain weariness with his perpetually virginal role? Unfortunately, he never did it again. He would extend his chaste boy image well into his forties, and as time went on it became increasingly implausible.

A young man in his twenties might be relatively innocent of sexual matters (though it certainly wasn't true of Harold himself). But a middle-aged man who has never gone beyond a kiss only provokes discomfort. The audience might see him as a case of arrested development and wonder what was wrong with him. Add the perpetually youthful voice to the mix, and you almost have a recipe for failure. The fact he did as well as he did after the sound revolution was a tribute not to his adaptability (which had never been his strong suit), but his overwhelming determination to succeed.

∾∾∾

I had looked forward to the interview with Harold almost feverishly, hoping he would somehow convey the force of his dynamism and charm on the page. But it was dreadfully anticlimactic. Because he didn't smoke or drink, we sat on two chairs facing each other while I tried to draw him out.

Even after a relatively short time, he looked different to me. The white makeup on his face wasn't so stark anymore, toned down for improved camera lenses so that he no longer looked like the ivory man-doll I had fallen in love with. I noticed his furrowed brow, and — though I didn't want to see this at all — a slightly receding hairline.

He spent an inordinately long time telling me about his boyhood, especially emphasizing his beginnings as a "classical" actor. I had no doubt he had a serious theatrical background, but in the small Midwestern towns he grew up in it couldn't have been a particularly grand one. He told me about how he and Roach broke in to the business, taking tiny roles in pictures that now seemed ridiculously primitive. I hoped *Spotlight* readers would find all this interesting, but I sensed they had read it all before, and kept trying to intercept his practiced monologues to get something fresh out of him.

"Tell us a little bit about Jobyna."

Again, Harold acted strangely. "Oh, she's a serious actress, started when she was knee-high, you know? So she knows the ropes. I don't even need to tell her anything, she just has it straight away. It's remarkable. I've never seen this before. Even Chaplin has to break in his — "

"How does an actress accomplish this?"

"Acting in pictures is all about your body posture and your face. That's where comedy comes from. You have to have an instinctive knowledge, though of course your skills can be honed and improved with experience."

"You wanted to be a stage actor. So why did you get into pictures in the first place, Harold?"

"Oh, it seemed like easy money, I guess." I was shocked at his answer: such artistry stemming from a way to make a fast buck? The legend of the fate-sealing coin-toss and months of living on sugar doughnuts wasn't far away.

I waited for it. "Once I was down to my last nickel, and — "

"Yes, and then you tossed the coin."

"To see if I'd go east or west, New York or Hollywood! I'm surprised you know that story."

Before he had a chance to talk about the doughnuts, I cut him off. "Harold, look. I know you're giving me good solid information. But it's the same things you've said to a hundred different magazines. It reveals nothing about you. I think our readers would like to know a little more about what motivates you as an artist."

"Artist?" He made a scornful sound. "Look, I know my business. There's no point in putting on false modesty. I come to work, and I apply myself. I work hard. Sometimes I'm pleased with the results, and sometimes I'm not. So I keep working at it."

It was as if Michelangelo were telling me that he paints by the numbers.

"What about the inner man?"

He looked at me, baffled.

"Do you have a private self who . . . "

His face changed to a look of irritation. "Of course I have a private self, yes. And it's private." That ended the conversation.

He seemed to feel a bit contrite as I packed up my things.

"Muriel, I still think you have me all wrong. I'm not some kind of highfalutin' hero. If you want to know what I worry about, it's the fact that I'm pretty sure my work will fall out of fashion. It has to happen some time. Whether it comes around again is anybody's guess, but I have a feeling it won't be in my time. And if it does, I won't be there to see it."

"So what's the reward?"

He thought a minute.

"You know when I came to the end of the rope and — " He mimed a snapping motion.

"Yes, that was very funny."

"Why?"

"What do you mean?"

"*Why* was it funny?"

"Because I didn't expect it."

"Didn't you?"

"Oh, well, I . . . yes, you're right, I did! I saw something funny coming, and I waited for it, and it came and I laughed."

"Do you know why *I* thought it was good?"

"No, why?"

"Because at the end of the rope, I hit my mark exactly, and managed the Brodie the way I wanted it."

"What's a Brodie?"

"It's an old expression. Means a kind of pratfall where you don't just fall but kind of throw yourself. Named after Steve Brodie, the famous bridge-jumper, who performed the granddaddy of them all by leaping off the Brooklyn Bridge and surviving to tell the tale. Or so he claimed."

"So that's what made it funny?"

"No. That's what made it *right*."

"So what is it that tells you it's right, when you can't even see yourself?"

"My back."

"Your — "

"I've just crash-landed in the dirt, but it's not just any patch of dirt. I've already seen and felt the contours of this particular space. That's where I want to land. So I time it and I pace it and then . . . "

"Then comes the Brodie. And it's not like anyone else's, am I right?"

"I have to tell you about the Brodie. And please don't put this in the article. Every comedian has to have a distinctive way to fall. Have you seen Keaton? His is alarming. He falls down, spins around on his back several times and jumps back up again. I doubt if another human being could manage that. I'm jealous of it, if you want to know.

"I worked with Sennett for a while when Hal and I were on the outs. Cheap so-and-so wouldn't pay me the ten bucks I asked for, so I walked out. It was an experience, I'll tell you. The pacing was unbelievable. I was just learning my craft then, and in that scrambling pack of fools I had to try to carve out a distinctive personality.

"One of the pack — I won't give you a name — he was brilliant, but drank so much we practically had to wash him out every day to get him to work. I kept my eye on this fellow. Thought he could teach me a thing or two just by example. Then one day they found him in the morning, dead as a doornail."

"From the alcohol?"

"From a bullet in the head."

I did not write this on my pad.

"I always loved the way he took a fall — landed on his neck, then threw his legs up in the air and almost over backwards. So I started practicing it. It didn't win me popularity points with the Sennett crowd. But soon it became my Brodie."

"Stolen from a dead man."

"Yes, you might say that."

"Harold, that isn't true, is it?"

He looked away from me, irritable. "What's the difference if it's true or not? It's all smoke and mirrors around here, and you'd better invent a version of yourself that will hold up and not collapse under the weight of people's expectations."

In future years, I was to see the development of that particular Harold, a rather sad Harold, surrounded by a sort of edifice he had built to protect his tremendous need for privacy. He had forfeited most of his privacy for world fame long ago, before such massive acclaim even seemed possible, but hung on to whatever bits of it were left to him.

I left out the Brodie story. I knew no one would believe it anyway.

∽∾∽∾

The interview experience left me feeling flat and a little depressed. I would have to use all my writing skills to make my notes interesting. While it was true I had thoroughly enjoyed watching the pratfalls and the sizzling kiss, the heady excitement of two years ago just wasn't there any more. Had Harold changed, or had I?

I was sitting at my desk, scribbling, crossing out and rewriting (for I wasn't going to waste typewriter paper until this mess was more coherent), when Danny Hoolihan strolled in, beaming. I had the strange thought that he reminded me not of Harold, but Jobyna: that utter self-confidence was positively solar, something so radiant you could tan yourself on it.

He sat on the corner of my desk as if he belonged there.

"Say, Mimi," he said.

"That's not my name, Danny."

"It is now. This is just between you and me, doll. So how'd it go with Mr. Wonderful?

I wondered how much he knew. *Knew?* There was nothing to know!

"It went fine. Except that it was a little dull."

"Harold Lloyd isn't a very good interview, Mimi. He sticks to facts most of the time."

"Well, I was struck by his professionalism and his — "

"Did he tell the Brodie story?"

"*What?*"

"Oh, nothing. It's just the best-kept secret in Hollywood. Stealing a pratfall from a dead man." He rolled his eyes in mock horror.

"I wasn't going to use it anyway," I said, irritated.

"Are you still stuck on him?"

"Danny, will you please stop?"

"I thought you could maybe get some good stories out of him. Use the, you know, personal angle. You didn't dress right, though. You're going to have to learn to — "

"For heaven's sake, I'm not a call girl."

"No, I mean just a little shorter on the hemline, a little tighter in the blouse."

"Danny." I horrified myself by giggling and blushing. Though I was furious with myself, I was loving every minute of this, his cavalier criticisms, his outrageousness.

"Call girl, chorus girl, actress, waitress, model. Harold loves them all."

"So that means I'm going to have to look like a hussy."

"It would help."

"Danny, tell me one thing. Can you even imagine me as a hussy?"

He shocked me by leaning forward and thrusting his hand into my hair. His face was inches from mine, and I could feel the heat of his skin. His eyes were so blue they were slightly exotic, like a husky's or a wolf's. *Oh for God's sake, Muriel, stop it.*

"Hussy, no. Maybe more of a wood nymph."

This time I didn't just turn colour. Something else was happening that was even more mortifying. For the thousandth time, I was grateful that sexual arousal didn't show on a woman.

"Would you mind, oh, say, kissing me? I mean, right now."

"Danny!"

"You have very kissable lips, Mimi. You need to bring that out a little more. Use a darker lipstick. And when you smile, you sort of duck your head — just a little — like you're shy. It's adorable."

"You are no gentleman."

"That's not in question. But I *do* have a question. Do you like me?"

No one ever said that, and it caught me completely off-guard. It was something a child might ask on the playground.

"I guess I do."

"Then we should go out. You're about ready to bust out of yourself. I think you keep yourself on a pretty short leash."

"Are you calling me a dog, Danny? I mean — a *lady* dog?"

"Oh, Mimi, that's too funny! No, I don't think you're a bitch. You're sweet. But you only let about half of yourself show."

"I should say so."

"No, I mean — look, you *know* what I mean."

And with all the blonde secretaries tapping away around us, with Don Bishop dashing from room to room, Danny Hoolihan leaned towards me and let his lips barely touch mine.

He stayed that way for the longest time. I thought I would go mad. I wondered if he had gone to the Harold Lloyd school of seduction.

Then he kissed me, really kissed me. It was completely unacceptable. I had no idea who else he was seeing, if he was married or had a social disease. But I had the feeling I would throw myself away just for the sake of being with him, in the best way or the worst.

～～～

He was taking me to the Jazz Bird, one of the hottest spots in town (but what did I know about hot spots? My one brush with glamour had ended in disaster.) But it wasn't until next week. It was agony trying to decide what to wear. My work wardrobe, appropriate for sitting behind a desk or interviewing minor stars, would not do: I didn't have anything remotely glamorous, and couldn't afford a dress I would probably wear once. It looked as if I would once more have to appear in borrowed robes.

After racking my brains, I consulted with Marigold Martin (a.k.a. Gertie Pye), a girl from the secretarial pool and part-time dancer in a group called Dizzy Doreen and her Peachy Chorines, a group that gave ostrich plumes a bad name. She took me to her tiny apartment, and when I opened the door I was flabbergasted.

I felt as if I had stepped into a doll house. I had no idea where a girl on such a limited salary had found furniture like this, flouncy and ruffly, all done up in various shades of pink. The draperies were even more fantastic, rose-tinted gossamer.

"This is so beautiful, Goldie. Did you do this yourself?"

"Listen, every stick of this furniture is from the Goodwill. The seat covers I ran up myself, you know? Made them out of an old bedspread. Curtains from the five and dime, with a packet of dye. The rest is just paint."

"It's wonderful."

Buoyed up by the bubbly Valentine pinks of the apartment, I happily auditioned dresses for what seemed like hours. I should have been bored, but felt giggly and light-headed. This feeling was enhanced by a bottle of illicit champagne.

I told her I wanted to look glamorous, but not cheap.

"Then you'll be walking a fine line, sweetie," she said, stepping around me and sucking the end of a pencil. "You need some height, for one thing. How tall is your date?"

I had no idea. He seemed about ten feet tall.

"All right, let's do a three-inch heel."

"Oh no. I couldn't walk in those, let alone dance."

"Learn. You're not a woman unless you know how to walk in heels. And for the dress — "

"I can't afford a dress."

"You can afford one of mine. All designed by the legendary Saint Vincent de Paul! You know" (she began to sing in a quavering voice): " . . . 'Second hand clothes, I'm wearing second-hand clothes, that's why they call me Second-Hand Rose . . . ' " I looked at her full, bosomy body and thought: anything of hers will bag on me like elephant skin.

Then I realized that Marigold always wore her dresses tight as snakeskin. Somehow she got away with it. Might we find one that worked on me? If we did, it would be nothing short of a miracle of couture.

One dress followed another, swaths of colour and texture such as I'd never seen before. My eyes must have been huge. Marigold was a most unlikely fairy godmother, but in this case she'd have to suffice.

"You never had a chance to be a girl, did you, ducky."

"No, I didn't." Tears pricked my eyes: I had never thought about this before.

"Well, it's time you did. Here, this is the one." I lifted my arms. She dropped it over my head, and it sighed into place. Petal pink, it draped on me subtly and flattered my hair and skin. As I gawked in her full-length mirror, she stood behind me and looped a long string of pearls over my head, then fluffed my hair. Champagne-colored open-toed shoes completed the look.

"And a clutch purse — here — and oh yeah, you'll need a wrap. I have one that should do." She rummaged in her closet and came up with ... *fur!*

I didn't know what kind of fur it was, except that it was white, reminding me of Shirley's beloved fox stole. When she laid it on my shoulders, I stood in shock: I barely knew myself.

"Oh Goldie," I said. "It's too much."

"No, sweetums," she said. "It's just enough. Now *go get 'im.*"

∽∽∽

But my Jazz Bird debut was detoured by a minor tempest in the office.

At first all I heard were buzzings among the secretaries, bits of gossip, all of it wildly conflicting. I couldn't get anything out of Danny, who was distracted and distant.

Then Don dropped something on my desk. "See what you can make of this," he said.

I wondered if it were connected to Harold in some way, if it would help my perception of him. My first draft hadn't been stellar, and we both knew it. I had tried hard to spark up the interview, to make it more interesting. Finally Don called me in and said, "Muriel, one of the things I hired you for was your integrity."

Here it comes, I thought: lose the integrity, or lose the job.

"But there are certain cases in which we may have to supplement a piece with some — well, colorful details to — look, Muriel, what I'm saying here is we gotta jazz this thing up, it's got no color. No — *sizzle*, you know what I mean? Look, everybody knows Lloyd doesn't give good interviews. Doesn't mean anything, just that he puts it all into his work. But the public wants to read something exciting about him. So: quick, without thinking, what do they want to know about?"

"His sex life."

"Good one, but tricky. They still have to like him. Next?"

"The accident."

"Pretty good, but too long ago, and nobody's supposed to know about his hand."

"How much he earns in a year compared to Chaplin and Keaton. And a popularity chart."

"Muriel, I think we've corrupted you."

"How about getting married? It brought Mildred Davis' career to a permanent halt. Can we touch that one?"

"It's a pretty good angle. I don't see how they can call us on that, seeing as how it's all true."

"And Jobyna. I can get plenty of good copy out of that one."

"Careful there. I know Jobyna's people, and they show no mercy."

"What about Greenacres?"

"What's Greenacres?"

Oh my. That meant I really did have something. On the set, I had overheard Harold in an animated discussion with one of the crew members. I came up and talked to him afterwards.

It seems that Harold was planning the sort of groaningly large monument to fame that Douglas Fairbanks and Mary Pickford were already famous for. Typical of Harold, everything would be on a huge scale. The foundation would be carved out of solid rock, and there would be dozens of rooms, a multitude of bathrooms, a tennis court, a golf course, massive gardens, and an Olympic-size swimming pool.

"How much can you find out about this Greenacres?"

"I don't know, but I remember the fellow Harold talked to. He was in *Mind your Manners*."

"Yes, but you see, that's the thing. This fellow doesn't want to lose his job, does he? I wonder who else would be willing to talk."

I racked my brains.

A thought formed in my head, so insane that I thought it might work.

"Mildred Davis. I could talk to her."

"By God, Muriel, you're a genius. You've met her before, haven't you? Played a scene with her? Two girls giggling together . . . "

"Well, we weren't like that exactly. She may not even remember me."

"Your worst trait, girl, is underestimating yourself. Drop it. Drop it now, if you want to get anywhere. Look, I didn't exactly make my name by being above-board. But I really don't see the harm in having a little piece about 'wifey' on the side."

"He doesn't even want me to write about his career, let alone his marriage."

"Ask *her*, then. What girl doesn't want to talk about her wedding?"

He was right. Mildred Davis was more than forthcoming: she was bubbling over, bursting to talk to anyone about their massive new project. Greenacres seemed more like a resort than a home, with a capacity for hundreds. She walked me through the property, most of it barely started and still ripped up by machinery. It was difficult to keep up with her endless chattering, but I did my best. This would work perfectly: the grandeur of Harold's estate, everything larger than life, built on a foundation of hard work and perseverance. The small-town boy from Nebraska makes good!

It almost worked. Just as I was about to make my getaway, I saw him. There was nothing I could do. There was no puppy-dog greeting this time. He looked weary.

"Hello, Muriel. I see you caught up with me after all."

"Boss's orders."

"Tell Don Bishop he's full of it."

"Harold, do you really feel that badly? I could always — "

"Oh, go ahead. Everyone's going to find out sooner or later. But why don't you write about this: I have no life of my own now. I belong to all this" (he gestured widely, taking in all the ugly holes in the ground). "I don't even know how it happened. I guess I wanted it, but now that I have it — "

"I won't write about that."

"I can't believe you're one of them."

"I thought you were proud of me."

"Yes, I am. But working for that gossip-monger — "

It was an awkward ending to an exciting interview, and I had to go back and rework practically everything.

So the odd-looking handwritten document Don dumped on my desk seemed unrelated to anything I was doing.

I was wrong.

Dear Don Bishop, I rember you sonofabitch didn't come through for me like you say and dont think I forget it. I have a story here noone else know and if you had it, make a milion. I hav e pictures and everyting and can see that he is his baby. This Harolld Lloyd treats women like garbadge and leafe them to hole the baby alone. He promise to take care of it. This is the big story and will give you al detail but I need five hunderd dollars. Yo know the deal if yo ever did keep up your end which I doubt. I want the money or I tell them all abot you and that croked deal yo did under the table with Benedict, yo know that would be the end of everthing. Ignorre me if you dare. Signed, Miss Betty Clayton. Enclosed, a photo of Baby Harold.

❧❧❧

I sat with Don for over an hour, trying to make sense of the letter.

"We get this sort of thing all the time," he said (but I didn't quite believe him). "It's extortion, plain and simple. This picture could be anybody's baby. People have been accusing Harold of this stuff for years — hell, they accuse any major star, but they can never prove anything. The best thing to do is ignore it."

"Could she really go through with revealing her — information — about you?"

"I don't know who would listen to it."

"Maybe the *Hollywood Tattler*?"

"I don't know. Maybe." I was amazed he let it pass. "Maybe this is my comeuppance, who knows. Or the *Tattler* has sent her over to make it hard for me. But the more attention we give this, the more power we give her, and the worse it will be."

"So does she get the $500?"

"Not yet she doesn't. And I hope she never does. It depends on how crazy she is, how far she goes. People make threats all the time. Everybody has a skeleton somewhere." He looked uneasy, as if he wished he believed what he was saying. "Anyway, kid, I like your piece. You really sparked it up with the Mildred angle. She has some problems with having to give up her career, and I know people will find that interesting. But you presented it in a way they can't object to."

"How did I do that?"

"By being respectful. Look, Muriel, no one knows better than I do what sort of background I have. It's not the classiest. A lot of people objected to my becoming editor here. All right, maybe they have a point. Meantime, *Spotlight* has had a twenty-five percent increase in circulation since I came here, and I don't think we're printing smut. But we've had to toss out most of that snooty stuff they used to run. If they criticized something, it stuck like cement because they were considered 'authorities'. Somehow, I don't know how, they made the picture business dull. But I think we've beaten that already."

"All right, Don, so what about this letter? It gives me a bad feeling."

"File it for now. Keep an eye open, be attentive to crank phone calls and the like. Let's hope it comes to nothing, like ninety-five per cent of these things."

It wasn't very reassuring. But I had my big date with Danny to distract me. This was something like a discount version of my starlit evening with Harold, though it also held the promise of a better ending.

As I dressed myself, I had the distinct feeling I was costuming myself for a play. Or maybe it was more like dressing up a doll. This just wasn't me: this rosy-cheeked, fluffy-haired, kissy-lipped little strumpet. I looked like the blonde on the candy-box, not quite real. I sprayed perfume in the air and walked through the cloud, like Goldie said I should, suddenly laughing at the absurdity of it all. If Danny really liked me, would he even recognize me in this absurd finery from the Goodwill?

I stood at the foot of the stairway in the dark downstairs hall, my high-heeled shoes hurting my feet more every minute. But I did not want to sit down on the stairs and crease my dress. He was late. I hated lateness, hated it with a passion, the rudeness of it. Fifteen minutes went by, then twenty. The awful feeling of being ditched began to sink like a deadweight in my chest. I kept peering out the window, feeling like a complete idiot.

Then I saw a car pull up — heavens, what sort of car was that? It wasn't new. Wasn't exactly dashing either, but at least it looked serviceable.

"Got held up in traffic," he said, out of breath. (Traffic, at 10:00 PM?) Then he looked at me.

I remembered Harold appraising me with a *"whew"*. But Danny didn't do that.

Instead, he picked me up off the ground and whirled me around as if I were a ballerina.

"I wish you could see yourself, doll. All lit up like Broadway."

Clichés like that, silly as they were, frankly thrilled me. I had waited all my life for them. Sometimes I wondered if I had dreamed Danny, or if he was just a giant bucket of whitewash to erase Harold once and for all.

"I have to warn you, Danny. I don't dance."

"Don't, or can't? Or are you afraid to?"

"That's too many questions."

"So what's the holdup?"

"I can't seem to get my feet to do the right things."

"I have the solution. Take your shoes off."

"What?"

"Pop 'em off, darling. That's right." He took his off and threw them in the corner.

"Now, come closer . . . hold my hand . . . and stand on my feet."

I shook my head in amazement.

"Stand on your *feet?*"

"You heard me. Now, just follow what I do. Yah, yah, *dum-da-dum-da-dum* . . . "

I couldn't help but follow. It was totally ridiculous, like something you would do with a small child. He took it slowly at first, then picked up the pace. I began to enjoy myself.

We ended the dance, flushed and happy. "Congratulations," he said. "You have just mastered the Baltimore."

"But Danny, I can't take my shoes off at the club."

"No, but I think you get the gist of it. The closer the better."

We lurched to the club in his jalopy, Danny singing unfamiliar tunes and not watching the road. I had never been in this part of town, and though it wasn't classy, the coloured lights throbbed with energy.

We came to a huge sign of an absurd cartoon bird flashing on and off. "This is it, baby," Danny said. Not a speakeasy choked with smoke (though the smoke was there), but a lively supper club filled with people laughing, talking, dancing.

Danny wanted to check my wrap, but somehow I couldn't let go of it. "You can't dance in this," he said. "And if you leave it on your chair, it'll be gone for sure."

"But it isn't mine." I suddenly blushed furiously. Why had I given myself away?

"Well, the car isn't mine either. Do you think I can afford wheels on what that old geezer pays me? Relax, you look great in it, probably better than Goldie. Oops, I mean the girl it belongs to."

We found a table, Danny introduced me to some people who took no interest in me at all, and then the floor show began.

A row of six young women in brief fringed costumes with feathery tails hopped onto the stage on one foot and began to execute an awkward bouncing step, extending the other leg and grasping it at the thigh as if they had hurt themselves. This wasn't the Peachy Chorines, but it was pretty close.

The band was working itself up to a song. For some reason, Danny was looking at me intently.

"Jazz birds, jazz birds, we're nothin' but jazz birds
We dance and sing all night, we'll give you such a fright
'cause we're jazz birds, jazz birds
So frisky and free
Won't you come and chase us out of our tree!

(The pace of the dance accelerated, with arms and legs flying in every direction.)

Jazz girls, jazz girls, we're nothin' but jazz girls
We flirt and drink champagne, we love to play the game
'cause we're jazz girls, jazz girls
How sweet can it be?
Won't you come and sing and dance with us
Won't you come and sing and dance with us
Won't you come and sing . . . with . . . me!"

In spite of the awkward performance, there were shouts and applause. Bootleg booze went a long way towards boosting audience enthusiasm. The girls went into their next number, a sort of mockery of the Charleston (for the Charleston was dead as a doornail now, taken over by even more bizarre and jerky steps.) Danny was strangely quiet. I looked at him.

"What is it?"

"I was just wondering what you thought."

"Thought? They're a middling bunch of chorus girls who can't sing."

"Ouch."

"What?"

Then it hit me: he must have had something to do with this number. Choreography; costume?

"I wrote it."

This was the save of all time, and I had to make it fast.

"Danny, that's great!"

"No, it's not 'great' if you didn't like it."

"It's just not my style of music. When did you take up songwriting?"

"Well, you see, that's the thing. I work here."

"Oh!"

As if to prove it, a spangle-wrapped Clara Bow type swooped down to hook her arm around Danny's neck. "We missed you, baby! Where have you been?"

"Get lost, Bonita."

"Who's the girl? She's pretty! Not your type at all."

He unhooked her arm and shot her a glance of such fierceness that it frightened me a little.

"All right, baby. But lay off the sauce." She waved a toodle-oo and trotted off to the next table.

"What did she mean, Danny?"

"About the sauce?" He looked down at his muddy cocktail.

"No. About working here."

"It's called moonlighting. Tonight's my night off, but they'll probably want me up there anyway."

"But you work ten-hour days at *Spotlight*. How long do you — "

"Nine 'til three, most nights. And it pays lousy, but it's what I love to do."

"Do you sing?"

"Not hardly! We have a girl singer, plus a few others. Oh, I sing once in a while."

"Do you play in the band?"

"Piano. And saxophone."

"Danny, this is amazing! You never told me you were so talented."

"Yes, but you hated my song."

"I have a feeling you've written more."

"Lots. But none published."

"When do you sleep?"

"I don't. Much."

"How do you keep yourself awake?"

"Oh, I have a little trick. But it's harmless."

What trick? My ignorance of stimulants knew no bounds (I honestly thought he meant coffee), but I did know that some people dabbled in something far more dangerous.

"C'mon, angel, let's dance."

"But it won't be the Baltimore. And I can't take my shoes off."

"You're funny. And you're sweet." He leaned over and kissed my collarbone, softly, lingeringly.

I knew that I would dance with him, any step he wanted, even to the edge of the abyss.

❧❧❧

If there was one thing in the world more stimulating and exciting than having sex, it was not having sex. Not having sex technically, at least, though I was close enough to Danny to feel his heart beating. With my embarrassing involuntary talent for picking up scent, I immediately noted the difference between Danny and Harold: mostly that Danny smoked and drank (the odor never quite left his clothes), and that he probably had hair on his chest, making his male scent stronger, a little more animal. Harold always had such a pristine smell, as if he showered three times a day, and his faint bay rum scent reminded me of ginger cookies.

Did smelling a man like an animal qualify as sex? Would I ever actually experience it, or would it always be just past my fingertips?

Thank God I refused champagne that night, for I was drunk enough on the atmosphere. I was dancing with the best-looking man in the room — and a musician, to boot — an *artist*! The floor was so crowded that I hoped no one noticed my relative clumsiness.

"I'm awful at this," I murmured, hardly able to look him in the eye.

"Mimi, there's something I can do that I think will help."

"What?"

"Push you around."

"What?"

"If I put my arm around your waist, so — " He tightened his grip. "Then, with my left hand,

I'll — "

He applied a subtle but firm pressure. I remembered Harold's ironic comment: "There needs to be a bit of tension between us."

No, don't think of Harold.

"Don't worry, I won't throw you around. This isn't an Apache dance, though I'd love to try it with you. (I had no idea what he meant: some tribal dance, perhaps?) I'm just — steering you."

"I appreciate it." And I did notice a difference right away. It was as if I could tell what he was going to do, half a beat before he did it. My confidence began to rise.

Then someone put a dent in it. A drunk-looking man slapped Danny on the back: "So, Danny Boy! Who's this little number?"

"Get stuffed. This happens to be my girl, Mimi. And she's a lady."

"Guess you needed some variety. Hey, they want you up front."

"Well, I'm not going. This is my night off and I want to spend time with my date."

"Aww, wouldn't your girl like to see you up there? He's so romantical, sweetheart."

To be honest, I *did* want to see him up there. What girl could resist the charms of a musician?

"Okay, one song. One *only*. Then I'm done."

"Great!"

The dance band stopped their predictable wash of music, and the bandleader, Duke Sterling (as in "the Silver Sounds of . . . ") made an announcement.

"Ladies and gentlemen, I don't play favourites in this band, but I have to tell you, the audience goes crazy for this fellow every time he gets up here. It's his night off and he's brought his girl, who by the way looks lovely as a spring rose. So he's doing this on his own time. Let's give a special hand for our master songwriter, Mr. Danny Russell!"

I felt a moment of shock and disorientation, before I realized this was show business and no one (including me) used their real name. Hoolihan did, after all, sound a bit like hooligan.

"Thanks, everyone. I always did appreciate working overtime." Hoots of laughter from the audience. "It'd be even better if I got paid. But when my boss talks, I listen.

"I'd like to do a little number and dedicate it to my girl, Mimi. She's sweet and smart and warm as a day in June. It's called *Let's Talk*." A minor cheer went up from the audience. They seemed to recognize this one.

He sat down at the piano. The room fell into a hush.

"So much of life is taken up with things we don't want to do
With boredom and chores and locked-up doors
And people that irritate you
I don't want to chase you, distract or embrace you
But wouldn't it be a delight
To sit next to you, admiring the view
And just shoot the breeze half the night

Let's talk
I'm tired of games and complications
Just chat
Spend time in sparkling conversation
Let's talk
We won't need highballs to get high
Forgive me if I accidentally
Breathe a sigh

I know what you think about politics, it isn't worth
anyone's while
I know what makes you furious, and I know what makes
you smile
But I don't know what you think of me — it's none of my
business, I know
So let's just sit and visit a while, and take things very slow

Let's talk
Your smile's a source of inspiration
Just chat
Without the heart's manipulation
Let's talk

We won't need moonlight to get high
Forgive me if I lose my head and
Breathe . . . a sigh."

Thunderous applause. Danny was sweating and looked a little pale, as if it had been an effort. He took a sketchy bow and came back to me.

"Oh Danny, that was wonderful. And I really, really mean it." I had lapsed into ridiculous schoolgirl prattle, and suddenly felt embarrassed.

"It ain't Rodgers and Hart."

"Maybe not. But the lyrics are so — "

"What?"

"Oh — graceful, sophisticated — I can't put it into words. You should be writing musicals."

"Do you know what it takes to get published in this town?"

I had some idea.

"Some day, someone will be sitting in the audience — "

"That never happens. At least, not to me. But let's not think about that. Excuse me, I need to go to the little boy's room."

Left adrift, I felt a little lost. I had stood up to watch Danny, and in the meantime someone had stolen my chair. With my basic shyness, it was hard for me to just walk up to someone and start a conversation. I stood there self-consciously, wondering where I could hide. Then I felt something, a hand creeping up the back of my thigh.

"Say, why don't you dance with me, little lady?" It was the drunk who had slapped Danny on the back.

"Get your hands off me."

"You should know your business. You're a walking advertisement."

I knew I should slap his face, but didn't want to create a scene. Everyone in the crowd was edging away from me.

Danny came back from the men's room just in time, took one look at the drunken slob and ignited. He grabbed him by the collar and whacked him across the face with the back of his hand. "Want some more, shithead?" he said.

"Sure, you fucking pansy."

He got more. Danny seemed hesitant to punch him outright, and later it occurred to me that he probably wanted to save his hands. But hard smacks sufficed. The crowd buzzed a bit, but they seemed to be used to this sort of thing. A big man appeared, probably the manager, and jerked Danny by the back of his collar.

"Hoolihan, your days are numbered here. Keep your hands to yourself."

"He molested my girl."

"I'll have him thrown out. But next time, it's you." Two big goons appeared and escorted the drunk away.

This was a novel experience: men were fighting over me, and I was enjoying it! No one knew better than I how flawed I was, how far from the ideals I expected of myself. But this was a new low, and it filled me with dizzy delight. On the way home, rocking and reeling in his rickety old car, Danny and I giggled and whooped. He seemed supercharged with energy, a complete change from his mood after the performance.

Then he parked it in a shadowy place, nowhere near where I lived.

"You're a wild child," he said, speaking low.

"Danny, I'm not."

"Yes you are, under that prim exterior. You just smolder."

"Are you telling me I should go to bed with you?"

A look of hope dawned on his face.

"That's up to you. But I think you're incredibly beautiful. An ungathered rose, dewy as the virgin dawn." I burst out laughing again. It was so absurd, but he seemed to mean it. "I'd like to make love to you, Mimi, but I want it to be good for you. You have to be ready."

"I don't think I'll ever be ready."

Then he said something that floored me.

"You're still in love with Harold Lloyd."

"*What?*"

"I can feel it. You've got to get away from him, Mimi, he's bad news. Especially for you. He's seduced a hundred women, ninety-eight of them virgins."

"Danny, for heaven's sake! People don't say things like that."

"*This* people does. Because I think to . . . " He seeemed to have lost his train of thought. "Anyway, it's important you know what you're getting into."

"So what are we — "

"Have you considered the possibility? "

"Do you mean, with you?"

That galled him a little.

"Yes, *me*. Who else?"

"Danny, we hardly know each other. I like you. Can't we leave it at that?"

"Have you ever had a serious boyfriend? I mean, apart from Mr. Spectacular."

"Don't call him that."

"Because it wasn't a real relationship. Even if something had happened, it would have gone nowhere."

"So with you, it's supposed to go somewhere?"

"I don't know. We'd be taking a chance."

"Look, Danny, I don't know what I think about all this. But I do know that this is our first date, and we've gone about as far as we're going to go."

"Sorry about the dust-up."

"Don't worry, it livened things up."

"Will you think about what I said?"

"I guess so."

"You don't sound very sure."

"All right, I will."

Swiftly, he grabbed my shoulders. As if he had seen *Why Worry?* (which wasn't in release yet), he kissed me with the same sort of savage intensity. I wanted to go limp in his arms like Jobyna, but couldn't allow myself.

"Good night, Danny," I said.

And closed the door, my skin almost tearing as I pulled myself away from him.

∽∽∽

I was certain that my successful interview with Harold and Mildred would rocket me to the position of top reporter at *Spotlight*. But it didn't happen.

"Muriel, we really need this spot on Fontaine La Rue."

"Fontaine La *What*?"

"No, seriously, she's one of the bigger minor stars."

I sat there trying to figure out the meaning of "bigger minor". But I was to find out, in the coming weeks and months, just how many of them there were.

Miss Fontaine was gracious but jittery, speaking a mile a minute and eager to list the pictures in which she had minor roles, and even more eager to convince me that her hobby was astronomy. I tried to imagine the gossamer-draped debutante gazing at galaxies through a telescope, but all I could think of was spying on the neighbors.

My interview with Baby Bonnie Barlow was almost surreal. Yes, Bonnie was quite popular, getting her start in a series of low-budget "dog comedies", an appalling form of entertainment which must have been brutal for the dignity of the dogs. But when I met Bonnie, a forerunner to the brilliant, precocious Shirley Temple, I was shocked to realize she was only four years old.

This fact was trumpeted as a miracle by her handlers, especially her mother, whose vicarious need wafted from her like poisonous fumes. Little Bonnie was an automaton, having been conditioned to be cute on cue, her eyes shining with God knew what sort of anxiety and confusion. She had had her childhood stolen from her, so was trying to live without it, in some sort of vacuum that would probably haunt her for the rest of her life. In the end I could only talk to her mother, then slam down the copy on Don's desk, saying, "I refuse to put my name on this."

"So what would you rather say? That the child is being exploited, that the public is feasting on the innocence of a little girl who can barely defend herself?"

"Yes. And more."

"How are you going to say all that without offending Bonnie's mother?"

"Could I say she's . . . well-meaning?"

"But you know she's not."

"That it should be Bonnie's own decision to enter show business?"

"Her mother insists it is. At eighteen months."

"How about . . . a day in the life of Baby Bonnie."

"Close. Keep going."

"How about . . . it's written in first person, in Bonnie's voice."

"Hmmmm. Can you do that? I mean, without offending everyone in her camp?"

"I can try."

And I plunged in. The piece was both innocent and knowing: "Mama says I should always look right into the camera and smile my brightest smile when they take my picture. But goodness me, I don't always feel like smiling! So Mr. Director reminds me that I'm a professional actress, and I have to smile even when I'm not happy. So I have to think of something wonderful — like a puppy or a lollipop or Santa Claus.

"It's important not to let Mama down, or she'll be cross with me, and then I'll have to go to bed without my supper. Sometimes I wonder why Mama is so strict. But if I do my best, a lot of people will come to the picture, and everyone will be very happy. And Mama will be able to buy me lots of nice things to wear, like the diamond tiara I wore at the last premiere. But, oh, fiddlefaddle — I can't have a puppy of my own because they cost too much to keep, and I'm too young for an allowance. Mama says I wouldn't know how to spend it."

Don roared when he read it. "This is a masterpiece. You've said it without saying it."

"Oh Don, it was so awful. I wanted to grab her and hustle her out of there."

"I'm going to run it, and see what response we get."

I was lucky. Though some of our readers must have been in on the joke, it sailed over Mama's head. She even sent us a note of thanks, which we printed in a prominent place. It was important to her that Bonnie be presented as a hard-working, disciplined professional earning a good salary. She was, after all, supporting everyone else in her family, a real accomplishment for a four-year-old.

When not dealing with such grotesque extremes of the movie industry, I was trying to cope with the disturbing letters that kept coming in at regular intervals. Most of them were similar in content, in the same barely literate style, full of vague threats. I wondered when these would fall off, when this woman would tire of these futile attempts at getting attention.

"Don, what if it's true?"

"Say, what? Oh, you mean the Harold thing. Well, it happens once in a while. Usually doesn't go very far."

"Why not?"

"To tell you the truth, it's because the public really doesn't want to hear those things about their favourite stars."

"So how does the *Tattler* survive?"

"Their readers already know that most of it is fiction. So they play a guessing game of trying to figure out which stories are true."

"I never thought of it that way."

"If all the stories in the *Tattler* were true, the editor wouldn't survive six months. He'd be found at the bottom of the river with cement overshoes."

"How close did you come, Don?"

"Let's not get into that. Say, here's one. Hobart Bosworth. Do you know anything about him?"

"I have a feeling I'm going to."

✿✿✿

My telephone did not ring often, and never after 10:00 PM I saw Danny only sporadically, his hours taken up with two demanding jobs. When he took me out to dinner, he either looked distracted or elated to the point of euphoria, discussing his musical career or his favourite books at a dizzying pace.

I liked Danny, liked him a lot, felt attracted to him as a man, and especially drawn to the element of danger in his personality. But some deep survival instinct told me not to get too close.

I also had the sense that if I did not "give in" soon, he would dump me. I could hardly blame him for this. He was young, very good-looking, loved women, and certainly didn't believe in waiting for marriage. I sometimes wondered if I was the only one who did.

The call was disconcerting, coming after 11:00 PM, long after I had gone to bed.

"I want to talk to Muriel." The voice was coarse and slurred.

"Speaking." The hairs on the back of my neck were standing up.

"You know that prick that got me in trouble."

"Excuse me?"

"I read that rag of yours, the one that tries to be so highfalutin'. Well, it's nothing but filthy smut, like all the rest of them. Worse, because it tries to pretend it's classy."

"Who is this?"

"You know who I am. And you know about my baby, Harold Junior. Yes, that's his name, isn't that a hoot?"

"This is nothing but a prank call."

"Don't be so sure."

"So this is the lady who wants the money."

"Hey listen, I asked nicely, and there was no response. So now I'm asking not so nicely, and I've upped the ante."

"Why are you calling me?"

"I know that you know him. You did that piece in *Spotlight*. Seems obvious to me that you must've fucked him."

"How dare you say that."

"You were his mistress, darling, and everybody knows it."

"I have no idea what you're . . . "

"You mean to say you're going to deny what happened at Frankie's Place?"

Jesus, I thought. The transgression that never was. Would it follow me around forever?

"Nothing happened."

"And then that little girl who died. You were all mixed up in that, too."

"I wasn't. Besides, that's old news, and no one will listen to it."

"I want you to talk to Harold."

"I don't even know him." For some insane reason, I thought of Peter after the crucifixion, denying his Lord thrice.

"Talk to Harold. I haven't even started here. I can ruin both of you so fast that — "

"Why would you want to do such a thing? You have no grievance against me."

"We don't even have enough to eat, bitch. We live in a falling-down old place with no heat. My husband ran off a long time ago, and I'm saddled with this little bastard. How am I supposed to raise a child in these conditions? Lloyd could support me on the side and it wouldn't mean a thing to him. Like losing an eyelash."

"That would be an admission of guilt."

"You're so right."

"So what are you going to do if he won't cooperate?"

"I've had an offer, a good one. There's a shortage of babies, especially fathered by big stars. He already looks like Harold. He's the spitting image of him."

"I don't believe you."

"Why don't you come see him. Just take a look."

"What would that prove?"

"One, that he's Harold's son. Two, that I mean what I say about the place we're living in. All it would take is one phone call for your whole life to come tumbling down."

"That's a lie. Don trusts me."

"I didn't mean I'd call Don."

"Who else?"

"The police."

"Ridiculous! That whole situation with Alice was resolved."

"What about that other situation?"

"There isn't another situation."

"You've been seen around town with a dope fiend for months now."

I was incredulous. "Danny? He's a musician, for God's sake."

"Haven't you heard of happy dust? Just look at his upper lip. He has a funny-coloured moustache."

"You're not making any sense."

"Why does he have two jobs? Because his whole salary goes up his nose."

I felt a stab of realization. I had suspected something for weeks, but had talked myself out of believing it.

"Look, even if he does have a bad habit, that doesn't make him a criminal."

"You don't have a clue, do you, girl. You don't know what else he's mixed up in. And if he's mixed up in it, so are you. A gangster's moll."

"That's just plain stupid."

"Robbery. Extortion. Even prostitution, though he calls them 'escorts'. Escorts them to bed, more likely."

"I'm not supposed to believe all this, am I?"

"Yes. Believe it. I want you to come see me, to prove I'm telling the truth. I know you don't have $500, so bring $100."

"I don't have that either."

"Yes you do. Smart girl like you, you've been building up your savings for years. For what, I don't know. Maybe for when you get married, fat chance of that now that guys like this have had their paws on you."

"You're disgusting."

"Come see me. Bring the money. A down payment. Then we'll talk."

"And if I don't?"

"I'm getting tired of all the crying around here lately. And those people who say they want to adopt him — they might not come through. You might say I have a fallback plan."

"You wouldn't."

"Relax, I'm not going to let him die, just leave him on a doorstep. People do. At least there'd be one less mouth to feed."

"All right. Give me the address."

There were times, like this one, when I had no idea what to do. Though I winced at the thought (I hated to admit how much trouble I was in), I knew I would have to go talk to Shirley, who had always been the voice of sanity to me.

Over the clank of dishes after closing time, we sipped our Cinderellas and talked all around the subject.

"Okay, sweetheart. What is it?" (At least she didn't say "what is it this time?", though perhaps she was tempted.)

"I've been seeing a boy."

"So far so good. Maybe he'll get Mr. Wonderful out of your system."

"Everyone seems to think he's in some kind of trouble."

Her expression didn't change, but a little vertical line appeared between her eyebrows. "What kind of trouble?"

"Well, there's this ridiculous claim that he's — "

"What's his name, Muriel?"

"Danny. Danny Russell. He's a musician, works at the *Spotlight*."

"What's his real name?"

"Hoolihan."

She shook her head. "Don't you know what they call him on the street?"

I could guess. "Hooligan?"

"And worse. Muriel — you know all that, and you're still going out with him?"

"I didn't want to believe it. He seemed so nice. He came in the office and sat on my desk and kissed me."

"Smooth is what he is. I know about Danny Hoolihan. He's a real stinker. You should've come to me."

"I know."

"This could take some doing." She sat and thought. I had never known her to be floored by a problem before. "You need to break up with him. *Now.* This instant. Meaning, no phone calls, letters, flowers, anything. The only problem is, you've been seen in public together, so you're still in a certain amount of danger."

My head was spinning with panic. "There's something else."

"Jesus, Muriel, why did I ever let you out of my sight? Are you a magnet for trouble, or what?"

"This has to do with — "

"Oh geez. Mr. Wonderful again. What is it this time, a paternity suit?"

This jolted me. "Yes, as a matter of fact it is."

"What does that have to do with you? Stay out of his messes."

"I don't think it's a valid claim."

"There's no such thing as valid or invalid. It's all the same mess."

"So it doesn't even matter if there's a baby or not?"

"There's a baby, all right. But it might not cry and throw up and poop its diapers. It might just be the kind that dies of the croup before it gets born. So to speak. Either way, it makes Harold look like mud."

"Well, this woman called me."

"Don't take her calls. Hang up. Get away from her. Why did she call you, anyway?"

"I did that big piece on Harold."

"Okay."

"She says I was his mistress."

"She'll say anything for bucks. And to ruin him."

"Why?"

"She has her own reasons. Look, Muriel, I'd say you're in trouble on two counts. Watch your step."

"Why does this always happen to me? I didn't do anything bad." Humiliating tears rushed into my eyes. I must have sounded like a little girl.

"You're never in the centre of these things. You're always somewhere around the edges. But sooner or later you get pulled in. It's like a tornado. If you let your guard down — "

"So I need to get hard as nails."

"You need to work on your judgement, sweetheart. So Danny swept in and sat on your desk and kissed you. Very romantic, but he didn't even know you. And you thought that was wonderful. It made you feel special. And it drowned out that not-so-little voice inside your head that tells you you *aren't* special, that you aren't worth anything at all."

Now I was really sobbing, and glad that no one else was in the restaurant. Shirley handed me a clean handkerchief, and I blew my nose.

"It's all true," I said. "That voice never stops, not even for a minute."

"Well, it isn't your fault. You had to run for your life to come here. You never had any guidance, and hardly any love. How's a person supposed to launch a life on that? You've achieved a much higher level of success than most people around here, much faster, and that's because you're smart and have talent and ambition. But the cost of all that is, you're more exposed. You may think you're seasoned and have been here a long time, but you're not even twenty! Congratulate yourself on how well you've done."

"Shirley."

"No, I mean it. Right now."

"I can't."

"You *can't*? Okay. That means you can't get a part in a picture with a major star, you can't write and sell original stories, you can't get a job with the best magazine in town and interview your idol. What else can't you do?"

"Find a boyfriend?"

"You did that too. Except he's a son-of-a-bitch."

I laughed through the mess of tears.

"The hardest thing for anyone to do is to lay low. Do nothing. Tell Danny you're not available. Don't explain. And don't, for heaven's sake, get involved with this woman. The baby is probably a Pekingese pup or something. These people feed on other people's fear. It's like a bad habit — sometimes you just need to starve it out."

"I'm lonely." I was mortified at how blubbery I sounded, but somehow I couldn't help it.

"Listen close, pet. The good Lord has someone in mind for you, and he's out there right now. But the two of you haven't met yet, and do you want to know why? Because you're not ready. If you met now, it wouldn't work. You wouldn't even recognize each other. So you're going to have to wait. Oh sure, you can have other boyfriends, but they're just for fun."

"Should I do a background check with you first?"

Shirley burst out laughing. "I like your style, kid. Just watch out for men who kiss you within thirty seconds of meeting you. Sure, it's flattering, but a real gentleman wouldn't jump the gun like that. And you deserve a gentleman."

Stupidly, my mind went to Harold. But then, my mind always went to Harold. I hadn't stopped thinking about him ever since I had heard about the accusation. I ached to see him again, wondered if I could somehow wangle a conversation.

Shirley's advice had been wonderful, sensible, perfect. And I was just about to blow it all into little pieces.

❧❧❧

Though I thought of myself as a timid and even weak person, I was drawn to risk and danger in a way that was completely irrational. Against all the sane and sensible advice Shirley had just given me, my desire to meet this woman and satisfy my curiosity was overwhelming. I had no idea why she would want to drag me into this mess, except that I still loved Harold and would do just about anything to protect his reputation.

I thought about what Don had said: that even if she did sell her story to the *Tattler*, readers would assume it was merely concocted as a form of entertainment (something like throwing the Christians to the lions). But I had trouble believing it. Scandal did drag stars down, often permanently. Clara Bow would fall, and Roscoe Arbuckle, and even the innocent-looking Mary Miles Minter. Actors lived the "fast life" in Hollywood, fuelled with illicit glasses of bubbly and shimmering clouds of happy dust.

Then I thought about Harold: oh, how straight he seemed beside those others. It was a curious twist in his personality, one of many. He built his life on the solid bedrock of Midwestern values, departing from them only in the area of sexual fidelity. In this, his beliefs were Victorian. There were two kinds of women, good wives and whores, and the wall between the two could never be breached.

I was never quite clear where he filed me, and perhaps this explained the slight confusion he seemed to feel when we were together. He had briefly tried for a sexual connection; one way or another, it hadn't worked. He clearly admired me, my achievements and my ambition, but was reluctant to offer me opportunities because of a vague sense that it just wasn't right.

Against every good and pure instinct I had ever had, I set up a meeting with Betty Clayton for the following week. I withdrew $100 out of my precious savings and put them in an envelope, realizing that she would never be silenced by such a ridiculously paltry sum.

And I waited, my nerves stretched tight. I worked on my usual mundane pieces, saw Danny come and go, brushed off his vague promises to take me out again. I wondered if he had another girl, which seemed likely. I watched him carefully for signs of cocaine frenzy, and saw none.

It was long past 11:00, and my sleep was as fragmentary as ever. My mind turned and turned, obsessing about the uncanny way I seemed to get enmeshed in trouble. I heard a heavy knock downstairs in the hallway. That door was kept locked at night, and no one was to open it unless it was a police matter.

I pulled on a long coat and felt my way down the stairs, afraid to turn a light on. The pounding hadn't stopped. I peeped out the window, and shook my head. My worst fears had come true.

"Open up, dream girl," Danny said in a seductive tone (hard to maintain when bellowing). "I need shelter from the storm."

"Not here you don't. Go to a hotel."

"I need to talk to you, Mimi. Just for a second."

"Then come back tomorrow when you're sober."

"I'm lonely. I just want some companionship."

"You want money."

"How can you say that, sweet thing? You've stabbed me to the heart."

"Listen, Danny, I don't have any money, and I don't want to harbour someone with a drug habit. It's dangerous."

"I won't stay long."

"You shouldn't even be here. You're waking up the neighbors. Don't you know how bad your reputation is? Everyone I talk to knows who you really are."

"Hey, I'm famous, isn't that great?"

"No, it's horrible. Go away."

"I won't. I want to kiss you, just once, then I'll leave."

This kissing "once" seemed to be a sort of male disease. I wondered if any of them really believed it.

Then, in an act of pure and utter insanity, I opened the door.

He didn't exactly lunge at me, but he tried to take me up the stairs with him, and I insisted, "No. We stay here."

"Somebody might come down."

"That's the whole idea. Listen, Danny, I can't see you any more, ever. We're breaking up, right here and right now. I keep hearing terrible things about you. Your life is out of control."

"You mean you believe those things?"

"Yes, I do. I've heard them from people I trust with my life."

"If I wasn't in this kind of trouble . . . "

"But you are."

"You like me, Mimi. You're attracted to me. Admit it."

"So what? Does that mean I should go to bed with you?"

"Why not?"

"You are completely insane."

"But you want me. Why wait any longer? You can't stay a maiden forever. Someone has to gather this rosebud."

I burst out laughing. "That's ridiculous," I said.

"Come on."

He began to walk up the stairs.

"Come on."

"Danny."

"Come *on,* Mimi."

He reached out his hand to me, I grabbed it, and he pulled me up. It was at that moment that I felt my sane and rational mind slip over the edge.

❧❧❧

I knew what a girl's "first time" was supposed to be like.

Though no one ever spoke of it (except, perhaps, your mother on the eve of your wedding), it was understood that it would take place within the bonds of marriage.

It was also understood that there would be little or no pleasure for the bride, whose main job up to now had been keeping her fiancé at bay. Her duty within marriage would be enduring the act for the sake of becoming pregnant, which no one talked about either.

In fact, no one talked about it at all until the baby was born, after which everyone ran around handing out cigars and congratulating the father (as if the mother had little or nothing to do with it).

If a girl "gave herself" to a man outside of marriage, she was either an innocent victim, seduced by some heartless bounder, or a slut. Sluts had very little chance of redeeming themselves, and either became unmarriageable maiden aunts or drifted into prostitution.

I could not fit the experience I had with Danny into any of those categories. It seemed almost idiotic, but it was a force of nature, as if it knew how to happen. He slid his hands up my body, lifting my nightgown over my head like a gauzy curtain. Then he startled me by falling on his knees in front of me. He wrapped his arms around my legs, lifted me up and slung me over his shoulder like some primitive prize or trophy, but with such care that I grew limp and passive as a doll.

Naked, my entire body in contact with his, I felt a subtle but powerful escalation, an inexorable rising, defying the usual bounds of decent repression. My mind kept screaming at me: stop it, Muriel, stop it *right now,* he's a dope fiend! You don't even love him! — while my body was buoyed up by one surging wave after another.

And I did not want it to stop.

At first he murmured his usual sweet, silly endearments to me, then stopped, because he was too embroiled in kissing me, kissing my entire body. I was stunned and awed by the things he was doing, things I didn't think existed or even could exist. Idiotically, I kept thinking of the inane phrase I had attributed to Harold: *ladies first.*

It wasn't as if I had never experienced those feelings before, but they were furtive, even frightening, and I had always taken my hands off myself in time. Danny looked at me and said, "This is your first time, isn't it?"

"Was there ever any doubt?"

"I want it to be beautiful for you." Surely he had rehearsed that line, his point of entry.

But in that moment, I wondered how it could be beautiful, or even possible. His big muscular body was covered with black hair, and he smelled strongly of tobacco and musk. His erection (and up to now, erections had been so unspeakable they officially didn't exist) looked enormous to me, almost threatening, in stark contrast to the shiveringly pleasurable waves that were escalating, growing inexorably stronger until they seemed to be tossing me violently into the air. Did God make us so hopelessly different from each other in order to torture us, or to bring together two wildly-different halves of a whole?

His hand was on me, and I was going crazy with pleasure, then his mouth was on me (which should have horrified me, but didn't), and then something just let go, and I went up and over the threshold. There were no words to describe the feeling, and all that came into my head were ridiculous and inadequate clichés: a ferris wheel spinning into space, the giddy lurch of a rollercoaster, a spouting geyser . . . and the sounds I was making were not in my voice at all.

So this was why people pursued sex with such fervor, even to the point of lunacy: it blasted away all the natterings and neurosis of the mind and stripped bare the mystery, the stark, staggering awe of being alive. That it could be Danny who revealed all this to me was almost beyond my comprehension.

"Jane," he gasped, shocking me by calling me by my real name, stripped bare of all the silly nicknames. He was breathing as hard as a long-distance runner. I lay flat, unable to speak. I smelled ocean, and the waves went on and on, surging hard. I both anticipated and dreaded what would come next: he put my hands on his penis, a throbbing column of flesh that I could not believe could fit into such a tiny, tender opening.

And I wondered once again why nature had designed us so cruelly. A woman's first taste of bliss had to be accompanied by pain and bleeding: it was simply the order of things.

Though he tried to be gentle with me, there was not much he could do to avoid the inevitable rupture of an intact hymen. I tried to hold on to the oceanic pleasure of my first orgasm while my flesh ripped and bled. This time I cried out for different reasons, while Danny apologized: but should a man have to apologize for doing what he was designed to do? I could not expect him to hold back, and in fact I did not want him to.

"I'm sorry, angel cake."

"You couldn't help it."

"At least there's no doubt now. Not that there was any before."

Then I sat up, already alarmed.

"God, Danny, I might be pregnant!"

He burst out laughing. "Listen, Jane, no one can work that fast."

I couldn't help stifling a giggle. Then I felt a shock.

"Say, how do you know my real name?"

"I looked up your file at work."

"Danny! That's terrible. Snooping."

"But I already knew we were going to be lovers."

"Is that what we are? Lovers?" My voice was tinged with sarcasm and disbelief.

He stared down at me. "How do you feel right now?"

"Like I'm melting. Like every sane thought I ever had has just dissolved."

"Don't you think that makes us lovers?"

"No."

"But you said you liked me."

"For God's sake, Danny, would I have done — well — *this* — if I didn't like you?"

"I guess not."

"I must be insane. I know you're in some sort of trouble, and I can't be seen with you."

"We'll just have to be careful."

"I can't sneak around like this. It's too dangerous."

"Don't you trust me?"

I looked into his face, shook my head in exasperation. "No. I've heard too many bad things about you."

"Then why are you in bed with me?"

"Wasn't it your idea?"

"I'd say it was both of us."

"All right. I had a weak moment. But this can't go on. You're going to have to take responsibility for whatever you've done."

"That's too bad. Because I really hoped you'd be willing to help me."

This was sheer brass, even for Danny. "Help you how?"

"Stand up for me."

"You mean in court? Good God, *no*!"

"Because, you see, Jane . . . I really need your help. And if I don't get it one way, I'll have to . . . well, try it from another angle."

"I don't know what you're talking about."

"You know how you got the job at *Spotlight*. In a sense, you actually benefited from that poor girl's death. Your file mentions William Harvey Benedict several times."

"*What?*"

"That whole story never really got resolved. People are still talking about it."

"So you're going to blackmail *me*? Forget it, Danny. I don't even have any money."

"But you can defend me in print. What would it cost you? You've already admitted you like me."

"Why should I? And defend you for what? You won't even tell me what you're mixed up in."

It was as if we had experienced the shortest love affair in human history. Somehow the whole earth-shattering experience had suddenly turned to dust.

"I won't defend you, Danny. I can't. It would go against everything I stand for."

"Then you won't last long in this business."

"Good! If you're any example, I hate this business already. Now get out of my apartment before I call the police."

I watched him dress, miserably, hating him. Wondering how my luck could turn so fast, and fearful that this mess was far from over. He turned to me one last time, beseeching, and I waved him away, trying not to cry.

There were cold spots on my sheets, disgusting bloody stains, and I wondered why this act that everyone rhapsodized about had to leave such an odious trail, like a particularly repulsive form of spit. Then it suddenly occurred to me that I was no longer a virgin: and not only had I not waited for marriage, I had willingly had sex with a criminal, perhaps even a felon. If I turned out to be pregnant, I vowed then and there that I would kill myself.

When I reached over to set my alarm clock on the nightstand, the drawer was slightly open. A stab of instinct made me open it.

The envelope with the $100 in it was gone.

By this time I was clear that Hollywood worked on a certain principle: everyone had something on everyone else, and it kept everyone in a state of paranoia and fear. Fear of exposure, mostly, and of losing face, losing one's reputation. Never mind that reputations in this town were fragile as eggshell, and probably false to begin with: they had to be maintained at all costs, or the result would be an Arbuckle, a tumble far more damaging than any mere Brodie.

I argued with myself about whether to tell Don I was going to see Betty Clayton. He would likely tell me to stay out of it, and I wasn't even sure why I was doing it. Shirley had never steered me wrong, and yet I was defying all her advice

Without the hundred dollars, I wondered if this Betty would give me the time of day. When I found her apartment, I was shocked: not because it was so terrible and run-down, but because it was relatively neat and well-appointed. She had furniture, if threadbare, more furniture than I did in fact, and an indoor bathroom. At first I had the impression of a hundred children in the place, but finally counted five, descending in age like stairsteps. I wondered how many fathers were responsible.

Betty was still in her twenties, shockingly young for a woman who had had six children. I saw the remnants of a pretty face and a nice figure, distorted by cheap booze and too many pregnancies.

To my surprise, she took me by the hand and practically dragged me inside. She practically pushed me down to sit on the threadbare sofa, setting a cup of coffee in front of me. The strange gesture of hospitality confused me, and for a moment I thought she was trying to drug me.

"So youse is Muriel."

"Yes, Miss Clayton."

"Drop that shit, will you? Call me Betty or nothing."

"All right, Betty. I have to tell you up front that I don't have any money."

She narrowed her eyes at me, and seemed to be calculating something in her head.

"But you do know Harold Lloyd."

"Only slightly."

She made a noise of disgust. "Only slightly. When he was screaming at you and eating your face off in a speakeasy."

"That was a long time ago."

"So you admit it?"

"Look, we never really had a relationship."

"He didn't fuck you?"

I sat with my mouth open.

"No, he didn't."

"But you know Don, all right. That whole fix with Harve Benedict — "

"Why don't people just let that go?"

"Because it was crooked. And it's on your record."

"So blackmailing Harold Lloyd *isn't* crooked?"

"I only want child support. I've got other mouths to feed. As you can see."

"Are you married?"

"That's none of your business. Oh, okay. I have a man, and he's good to me, but what he earns just won't stretch far enough. I don't see him very often. He's in the joint right now, but only for six months this time, breaking and entering. So I have my hands full here. Look, my place isn't a dump, and I'm trying as hard as I can to keep things going. But babies are expensive, and I sold the crib and the playpen and everything else after Arthur was born because I needed the money. It's a hell of a thing keeping your son in a cardboard box."

"Can I see him?"

"That's what you're here for."

It had been a long time since I had held a baby. He was a few months old, and still had that moist, slightly yeasty smell, fat little hands with rows of dimples, and jet-black hair. I looked at his hairline, how it went straight across like Harold's. I looked at his eyes, the shape of his face. I had seen a photo in a magazine of f Harold as a small boy. But I was grasping. There was nothing here.

"Pretty close match, eh?"

"I can't really tell."

"Muriel, I'm not asking for much. I just want Harold to do right by me."

"And if he doesn't?"

"I'm going to have to go public."

I found to my consternation that I didn't want to give him back. He was such a blameless, self-contained little bundle, mixed up in a situation he would never be able to comprehend.

"Tell me what you want me to do about it."

"Go talk to Mildred."

"Oh, Betty, *no!*"

"You have an in with her. She likes you, I read that piece in the magazine. She told you all sorts of private things. She'll make sure he ponies up."

"I can't do that. It's a lie anyway."

"The *Tattler* is just about ready to break this story. It's all set. They'll get the truth out of her, one way or another."

"Let them try, then. Harold Lloyd and his family are not going to get involved in this kind of slanderous filth."

"Something else is all set, too. I'm going to tell Don Bishop you've got yourself mixed up in all this. And that's not all. Sweet Danny Boy, too. Lord, girl, you're in a lot of trouble. He'll let you go for sure."

"Fine, then. I'll find another job."

"Yes. Mopping floors and cleaning toilets. With a great reference letter."

"I never should have come here. Just leave that family alone!"

"As soon as I get what's coming to me."

I felt contaminated. Even after I left, I wanted to brush the dirt off my clothes. The worst of it was, I still wasn't sure if it was Harold's baby. Did I want it to be, or not?

Idiotically, my mind flashed to a scenario: I would take him home with me, raise him, have some small part of Harold with me all the time. It was obvious to me that I had gone completely mad.

∽∾∽∾

As I dressed for work on Monday, I felt sickened by confusion and doubt. Shirley had told me, rightly, to stay out of all this, but now I felt snagged in several different places. I had not yet learned to navigate the shark-swarming waters of this business, and I had no idea what to do next.

I put on my favourite skirt and realized with a shock how loose it was. I must have dropped ten pounds from anxiety. But I felt a huge amount of relief that I couldn't be pregnant (God wouldn't do *that* to me, would he?). But I wondered. I doubted that this Betty Clayton had decided to be a prostitute when she was in grade school. No one did. But life had hardened her, and now she cared about nothing but her own gain.

Still, I could not help but feel some sympathy: that horde of children, all looking more-or-less cared for under impossible circumstances. No doubt they were fathered by different men, and it seemed doubtful that any of them had been movie stars. But her "suggestion" that I talk to Mildred sickened me. I could not even imagine it: Mildred had such a sweetness about her, a girlish innocence, and I had always thought she was enchanting on-screen.

Feeling sick, I dragged myself in to work and shuffled through the pile of assignments on my desk. I jumped when Don opened his office door and said, "Muriel."

It was a summons, and I knew it.

"Sit down. Muriel, I thought I'd better tell you that I've had to let Danny go."

"Oh, that's — "

"No, it's not too bad, it's the only thing I can do. It was getting around that he was mingling with the wrong element."

Then I remembered Betty's words, which had seemed ridiculous at the time.

"I want to know how much you know."

It was a strange question, like something out of a police interrogation.

"I don't know much of anything, Don, except that everyone seems to think he's a gangster."

"Have you ever heard of embezzlement?"

I prickled with the insult, but hid it. "I'm familiar with the term."

"He tried it with us and was caught. He's not a very good criminal, I'll say that in his defense. And he's already in trouble at the jazz club, and a couple of other places. He's in debt up to the eyebrows, and to the wrong people."

"I never thought of him as a thief."

"It all goes up his nose. In his arm, too. And some of it goes on girls. Chippies, I mean. He sort of manages them. Calls them "escorts". And he's invested some of it, just like it's an inheritance from Uncle Charlie or something."

I felt a little dizzy. I wondered how I could have been so naïve.

"How well do you know him?"

"Don, I am *not* an accessory to the crime!"

"I never said you were. But you could be questioned."

It seemed to be my fate to be dragged into things that weren't my fault. What was I supposed to say: that I'd had my first sexual experience with him, that I had lost my virginity to a common criminal?

"It was a shock when I found out. I wasn't involved in any of it, Don, I swear."

"I believe you. But someone saw him go to your apartment, late at night."

"*What?*"

"Not a cop. A private dick. The owner of the Jazz Bird is so sick of this guy, the way he's been lying to them and bleeding them, he decided to have him followed. Danny's a very busy boy, Muriel. You don't want any part of the things he's mixed up in."

I sat there dumbstruck, my feelings numb.

"Muriel, you're one of our best employees. We really think you're going places. But I'm going to have to put you on suspension until this thing blows over. This is for your own protection, so you can lay low. I want you kept out of this, because whatever sort of relationship you had with Danny, I don't think it has anything to do with the drugs and the extortion and all the other crap he's into."

I had to think of my survival. "Will I still be paid?"

"For two weeks. That's the best I can do."

"How am I supposed to live on that?"

"It's all we can afford if you're not turning in any work."

"Don, is this the best you can do for me? I trusted you."

"Muriel, look at me. No, *look*. I trusted you, too. And you slept with him, even with all your suspicions. That looks bad. Worse than bad."

"So it's all over town, then."

"Not exactly. But Danny has swindled more than one person he's worked for, and we have to present a united front in pulling him down."

"And I take the fall, as they say."

"No. You don't. This is temporary, and I want you back when all this is over."

"Oh, Don, nothing is ever over. Not even the mess with Alice."

"I know. That's why we have to be so careful."

My mind clicked the pieces together with such a sense of shock that my scalp prickled.

"So did everyone ignore all those articles that supposedly cleared me?"

"No, but I saw something."

"What?"

"I don't want to hurt you, Muriel."

"It can't be any worse than this, can it?" It was the kind of thing you should never say.

Don yanked his desk drawer open and rummaged in the chaotic mess, pulling out a folded piece of newspaper. Not the *Midnight Star* or some other smut rag, but the *Beacon*, a legitimate paper.

He showed me a cartoon that made very little sense to me. There was an old man sitting in a sinking ship called the S. S. Hot Water. From his sour expression and the moneybags beside him, I guessed it must be William Harvey Benedict. Somebody was bailing out the boat, a man dressed up in what looked like a cardinal's gown.

"Who in God's name is — "

"Get it? *Bishop.*"

"As in Don. But what's this?"

Harold Lloyd (it couldn't be anyone else!) smiled smugly in a lifeboat called the Home Free.

Hitched to it was a tiny boat with a young girl sitting in it — good God, who was that supposed to be?

The caption was, "It pays to have friends in high places."

I stared at it. It made very little sense to me.

"Don, I don't understand this."

"Wasn't Harold in a lot of trouble? Over the murder, I mean."

"He might have been. But I was in worse trouble."

"That's why you're both Home Free."

"So everybody knows you blackmailed Benedict?"

"I wouldn't call it blackmail. I just got Harve out of hot water. So to speak."

"So who's that little girl?"

"Who knows. Don't let your imagination run away with you."

"Everyone is crooked in this town. It's nasty."

"Have you ever considered the alternative? Do you know what would have happened if I hadn't done it?"

"I would have been thrown in jail for failing to protect a little girl who was murdered."

"Maybe not that far. But you wouldn't have this job now, and you might have had a hard time finding a job anywhere."

"So, back to the old homestead." I knew I sounded bitter, but my head was whirling with shock.

"I need to talk to you about something else."

"Can you put the gloves back on, Don?"

"Muriel. You're starting to sound pretty hardened."

"Well, what the hell else am I supposed to do? I've taken about as many blows as I can stand."

"I'm afraid this is for your own good. This Betty Clayton, I'm pretty sure she's completely bogus, but she called me and said you promised her she'd get the money."

I could not even speak.

"She's pretty close to blowing the story wide open."

"Oh yes, in those magazines that nobody reads! Or if they do, they only believe what they want to."

"We're going to have to give her what she wants. The *Tattler* isn't too fond of me, Muriel, not after that promotion Benedict fixed up for me. We're rivals, after all." He lit a cigarette, fumbling around with it for a moment so he wouldn't have to look me in the eye., "And one more thing. There's something nobody knows about."

"I can't imagine how it could get any worse."

"Remember how Benedict ousted the managing editor here to make me the boss? Did you ever wonder what happened to him?"

"Don, don't tell me. I can't stand any more."

"No, he didn't join the *Tattler*. It's worse than that. He started something called *Stars by Night*. Sounds innocent enough, but it's a smut rag, and for some reason they've got it in for Harold Lloyd."

"And I suppose you think it's *my* fault?"

"No, but it means you have to watch your step with this woman, whether she's lying or not. She's set and ready to tell them her 'story'. I want you to deliver that money in person. She wants you. It's the only way to keep her quiet."

"That baby could be anyone's. I think she lost track a long time ago. How am I supposed to know if she's telling the truth or not?"

"Muriel. Just look at her name."

"What?"

My God. *Clayton*. It was Harold's middle name. She had been playing with us all along.

"So should I just throw myself off a bridge now?"

"Please don't be dramatic. I was telling the truth when I said you were one of our best. But you're still young, still learning the ropes. It's almost impossible to stay out of scandal around here. You've had a rough shake from the start, but so far you've handled it. Don't blow it now. Don't get into the booze or all that other stuff, it sinks too many people with talent."

"Like Danny."

"Were you in love with him?"

"No. Thank God. But I liked him. It seems that even liking a man is enough to land me in disaster."

"Do you have anybody to stay with? I don't think you should be alone right now."

I dreaded seeing Shirley, after completely ignoring her wisdom. I refused to go back home (if it could be called a home), to be swallowed up by the dust and the scorpions.

"Maybe I can ask Goldie. She loaned me a dress once." It seemed like the thinnest possible premise for a friendship. But I remembered how the fabric had fluttered down my body like a dusty pink butterfly.

"Give her a call," Don said, showing me the door.

By this time, I expected everything I tried to do to be difficult, if not impossible. It seemed crazy even to approach Goldie, whose life apart from typing seemed to consist of giggling with her girl friends and doing her nails. Sometimes I envied her easy way with the others, who often glanced at me in a way that seemed cool and dismissive.

"Excuse me, Goldie — "

"Oh, hi, Muriel! How'd it go on that date?"

"Oh, okay I guess. But he turned out not to be my type."

"Smart girl, to figure that out so fast." She studied a cuticle with deep concentration. "Say, what do you think about Danny being fired?"

"I'm not sure. Maybe he just wasn't the right person for the job, you know?"

"Yeah, you're probably right."

"Listen, I have a big favour to ask you, and you can say no if you want to."

"How can I say no when you haven't even asked me yet?" She giggled adorably.

"Don thinks I need a little time off. I had a family situation that really upset me, and he thinks it's affecting my work."

"D'you think? I've seen your work. It's the best we've ever had."

"I'm — just not feeling well." Tears flooded into my eyes — why couldn't I turn off the waterworks these days? — making me want to run back to my desk, or, better still, out the door.

"Hey, sweetie, what's wrong? Maybe you just need a little rest. Everybody in my family's had at least one nervous breakdown. I've got plenty of cures."

"Could I stay with you for a couple of weeks? Oh Goldie — "

She jumped out of her chair and hugged me — no, squeezed me tight, letting out little squeaks of joy.

"You can stay with me as long as you like. It'll be fun! I have a little hen party in my place every Friday. Oh, you don't have to come if you don't want to. I got one of them Murphy beds that folds down out of the wall, you know? And nobody's used it yet. You'd be breaking it in for me.

"Oh Muriel, I've always wanted to know you better. You keep so much to yourself, it must be lonely. The other girls say you're stuck-up, but I know better. You're just shy. And smarter than the rest of us put together. And being the only girl reporter, you must feel like a fish out of water sometimes. You're so pretty, but you're not making the most of it. I can do your nails for you. French manicure! What do you say?"

Now *she* was asking *me*. It was all so odd. I said yes, barely knowing what I was getting into. Before I knew it, I was packing my suitcases. I had such a need for privacy that I wondered how I would keep from going mad.

"Look at this." The Murphy bed, covered in pink satin, flopped down out of the wall as if by magic, then flopped back up again.

"And look over there, Muriel, here's a little place you can have a cup of coffee or write a letter or something." I was astonished to see a tiny room with a desk, and a typewriter.

I remembered my buried desire to write stories, and wondered if I could unearth it.

"This is perfect, Goldie. I don't know how to thank you."

"Get happy again," she said, with such guileless honesty that I could have hugged her.

But she beat me to it.

 riariaria

My stay with Goldie went far beyond the two weeks my salary would hold. Though I called Don more than once just to "catch up", I could tell by his vagueness and excuses (and at one point, wishing me luck) that my services were no longer required at *Spotlight*. In spite of his reassurance, he floor had given way under me for reasons that made no sense. Guilt by association seemed to be my fate.

The only blessing that came out of this disaster was the fact that Betty Clayton suddenly withdrew her demand for the $500. Apparently she'd had a better offer from the smut rag *Stars by Night*, who refused to let her associate with *Spotlight* ever again.

Then a curious thing happened: the story never appeared. It had been killed, by Hal Roach, Harold or someone else entirely. It was as if Betty's scandal was available to the highest bidder.

Goldie was generous and wonderful, but about as sensible as an intoxicated butterfly. Her little pink-icing apartment was all a-twitter with a constant whirl of little parties with girl friends and gentlemen callers. These looked like they were cut out of magazine ads for smart men's clothing, not quite real, but they were certainly preferable to the kind of skunk I had been mixed up with.

I was still plied with questions about Harold Lloyd. I was beginning to think of him as a lingering disease, like malaria. Every once in a while I thought about going to see him. Then the sane part of my mind said, "*No.*" There was nothing to be gained. I would only embarrass him, and myself.

How many bridges had I burned? Though I could not exactly say why, I couldn't bring myself to talk to Shirley. How much of this did she know about? . Probably a lot, with those long antennae of hers. Maybe everything.

I was feeling particularly morose about all this as I once more trudged through the employment ads in the newspaper, when there was a buzz at the door.

"Miss Ashford?"

It nearly caught me behind the knees. *Chorney*, I wanted to say. I don't deserve the name Ashford.

"Yes, that's me."

"Special delivery." He handed me something, not the usual long white box that would hold a bouquet of roses, but a squarish one, unexpectedly heavy. I was completely puzzled.

I ripped the layers of brown paper off it.It was a huge cactus garden in an earthenware pot: every sort of variety, tall and squat, furry and branchy, some with exotic colorful blooms. It was decorated with little ceramic horned toads. My jaw dropped.

It could only be from one person. I could not get to the phone fast enough.

"Oh Shirley, I don't know what to say, I just love it."

"That's us, kid. We ain't roses. But they're nice, aren't they? They'll last a long time. And they can look out for themselves."

"Shirley, I'm in such a mess."

"Oh, I wouldn't say that. You have a nice little place to stay, friends, a break from your job. I'd say the worst is behind you."

"I don't have a job. I feel like I have a criminal record, and I haven't even done anything."

"Listen, sweetie, you can come back here. Any time."

We both knew I couldn't do that.

"Can I give you a little bit of advice?"

Oh God, please.

"Find yourself a nice straight job, not as a waitress mind you, but a hostess, because that's what you really were here. But I'd spend every spare minute working on those stories. Try to work them into scripts. You don't even realize the contacts you've made in the business."

"Yes, but all of them are bad."

"Well, you gotta break a few eggs. And you've weathered it. I can name a couple of names of people, right off the top, who'd help you get noticed. Such as Hal Roach. You were all broken up when he handed back your script, but do you remember what he said?"

"Come back in ten years."

"Not exactly. But he *did* say come back. Whatever ideas you have, no matter how outlandish they seem, work on them, and keep working on them."

"Do you really think it will do any good?"

"Would I tell you to do this if it wouldn't?"

She had me there.

"You know the difference between you and everybody else around here?"

"I attract danger."

She chuckled. "Well, that too. No, I meant that you follow through with things. Hardly anybody does that. They sit there in bars and blather on about how they're going to write the great American novel. Real writers just keep writing. Opportunities will come or they won't, but if they finally do, you'll be ready."

"And until then, I . . . "

"You go on over to the Moonglow. I mean today. They have an opening — in fact they're desperate for someone. Their hostess just fell off a ladder and broke her ankle."

"Or you're pulling my leg."

"That doesn't matter. They really do need someone, and that someone is you. Get Goldie to fix your hair."

"If I borrow any more of her clothes — "

"Don't borrow. Go to Chaston's. Remember, turquoise and magenta, but not together. Spiff it up a little, you need bright colours. Lipstick, but not too dark. And earrings, God, don't forget the earrings! You know what earrings do? They draw attention to your lovely face. But they also add a couple of years, meaning you'll look closer to twenty. Maybe you should borrow some. I'd like real gold on you, but whatever you do, *not* hoops."

Then she said something that astonished me.

"You're going to have to practice that smile, too."

"What smile?"

"You don't even realize you're doing it. It's — well, it's a little bold, and bright like a sunbeam, but it's over in a couple of seconds. Learn to keep it going a little longer. It's to your advantage."

Even my face was being managed. It was a bit of a shock.

"So, head up, shoulders back, skirt swirling — remember what I told you, make sure it's cut on the bias so it flares out when you turn. I can see it now, kid. I think I'd even hire you myself."

It had been a long time since I had really laughed. It was like warm water poured over all my wounds.

As always, Shirley was true to her word. Taking a huge breath, I walked into the Moonglow, decked out in my finest (or so I hoped: I had to trust Goldie and the good folks at Chaston's). I aimed for a look of businesslike sophistication, whatever that meant. I was interviewed by a man, which was a shock: I must have naively assumed good restaurants were all run by women.

When it came to recounting my experience, I erased Frankie's Place (at the same time suspecting that the whole town knew about it) and concentrated on Chez Louise, which was respected by nearly everyone. The manager, Howard Bronson, kept making notes on a clipboard, which was nerve-wracking. Obviously there were many other candidates for this position. What did I have that the others did not?

Then it hit like lightning.

"Oh, and I worked with Harold Lloyd on *Mind your Manners*. I did extra work and appeared in a scene with Mildred Davis." I decided to withhold the suggestions I'd made for the story, not wanting to come across as an outright freak.

"So tell me, Miss Ashford, why didn't you pursue a career in acting?"

God, God, *please* tell me what to say.

"I discovered that the people I worked with saw potential in me as a dramatic actress. These sorts of roles are much harder to come by, and I don't want to jump at the first thing that comes along. To be honest, I've been advised to wait for the right role."

From the look on his face, he either bought it, or thought I was as brazen as a streetwalker. Whether due to Shirley's coaching or my own increasing ability to lie my way in, I got the job.

She'd been right: this was not like waitressing. Not at all. I had to keep track of an elaborate set of reservations, escort people to their tables while keeping up bright, gracious chatter, field questions about the menu, hire and fire staff (Howard actually made the decisions, and I broke the news to them, good or bad), deal with irate customers, delicately remove the overly intoxicated, and generally keep the operation running as smoothly as possible.

The most bizarre aspect of this job, something I absolutely did not expect, were the questions from tourists about Hollywood, the stars and the directors, their upcoming projects, and whatever good gossip I could dig up. I did my best to come up with answers– I had a certain facility for sounding like I knew a lot about a subject — but I had to resist the temptation to invent things outright. How would they ever know? But with my uncannily rotten luck, some chance remark could come back on me and land me in trouble again.

It was hard work — I never got to sit down — and it required a hard head. Though most people were polite or at least civil, I was sworn at, patronized, flirted with, groped. In other words, in spite of a dramatic raise in salary, certain things hadn't changed since my unfortunate stint at Frankie's. I had to keep steady even when an earthquake hit: one night, Douglas Fairbanks and Mary Pickford casually walked in, and my heart dropped like a broken elevator.

I was required to greet them wearing my carefully-rehearsed smile: "Good evening, Miss Pickford, Mr. Fairbanks, and welcome to the Moonglow. Where would you prefer to dine with us tonight?"

"Oh . . . " Mary, who was impossibly tiny and barely resembled her screen persona, gazed up at her swain.

"What do you think, Dougie? Over there, by the window? It looks private."

"We'd better. Don't want to start a riot, toots."

It was Saturday evening, our busiest time, and they hadn't bothered with a reservation, so there was absolutely nothing left, let alone a window table. They had already cut to the head of a long, disgruntled lineup; stardom automatically conferred entitlement. I had a mad thought of overturning one of the tables and shooing the customers out, but that wouldn't do. Where to put them? Where to put them?

I couldn't exactly ask them to wait. They were the lord and lady of Pickfair, after all: the closest thing we had to royalty. Even if Mary's voice reminded me of a fishwife's, even though Douglas looked a little puffy and paunchy from booze, they were Hollywood elegance at its finest, and it was imperative that I meet their needs. And quickly.

The prime table, the pearl in the oyster, was a little nook in the far corner, where they would have both privacy and a window view from two sides. An elderly couple celebrating their fiftieth anniversary had been drinking tea and picking at cream pie for what seemed to be an eternity. Finish, *finish!* Panic seized me as Mary levelled a hard look at me. *Come on, girl.*

There was nothing else to do. I excused myself, walked up to the corner table wearing the smile, and announced, "Good evening, Mr. and Mrs. Hudson." (Thank God I remembered their names!) "I'd just like to tell you wonderful people how much we've enjoyed your company tonight. And I have a surprise for you: we have some special guests who've just arrived. If you'll take a look by the entrance . . . "

"Oh, my!"

"It couldn't be."

"But it is. Martha! It's *Little Mary!*"

"Since you've been such wonderful customers, I'd like to give you an opportunity to do these great stars a little favour. This is entirely my fault, but I'm afraid we don't have a table for them just at the moment. Now, if you'd like to sit a little while longer, that's perfectly all right, but if you would be so generous as to allow them to have your table where they can have some privacy, I think they'd be most grateful."

"Oh Martha — just think — Douglas Fairbanks sitting where I just sat!"

"They'll never believe it. They'll never believe Little Mary sat at *our* table!"

On their way out, they stood there, fish-mouthed, in the way the two legends knew all too well.

I had to jump in once again: "Mr. and Mrs. Fairbanks, I'd like to introduce you to to our most loyal customers, Mr. and Mrs. Hudson. (I couldn't say "favourite" or Mary would have burned me down with her eyes.) They were just dining over there at the corner table."

"Oh Mary — I mean Miss Pickford — we're such huge fans — we're — we're — "

I handed Mary a menu and a pen. Her eyes flicked sideways at me.

"Oh, *would* you?" Mrs. Hudson was almost completely undone.

And thus, the power of stardom once again worked as a magical Open Sesame to the best table in town.

~~~

I didn't get to sit down for five years.

The problem was that I was too good at my job: which meant I became mired in it, and unable to take any of the leaps necessary to succeed in "the business". Producers may have flirted with me, but none of them asked me to audition for parts. I saw D. W. Griffith and Tom Mix and (even) Ramon Novarro, and my heart quickened, but they turned out to be ordinary people after all, eating and burping and fighting over the cheque.

When I signed on for the job, I had no idea the Moonglow was so popular with industry types. Was the rabble kept out by some subtle code? Howard the manager would go down the reservation list and cross certain names off. I'd have to call them and apologize. Usually they were put off so many times that they gave up and didn't get in at all, or were only allowed a table by the swinging kitchen door at 4:30 PM

And though I told myself I wouldn't, I did see Harold. His fame had crested with *Safety Last!*, though of course he didn't know it (nor did anyone else). He had the gleamingly anxious air of a man who assumed he'd be famous forever, with fear lurking just below the surface.

He was with Mildred, who looked gorgeous in a cream beaded gown and white fur, and he took a solicitous air with her, murmuring into her hair in a way that seemed to speak of real intimacy. But it was impossible to tell. Harold could do intimacy if he wanted to.

It was difficult for me to switch on the smile that night, as the scar tissue from my disastrous relationship with him remained. For some reason I hoped Howard would look after them as he sometimes did, reminding everyone that he was in charge of the place. I should have been happy to see them, but as usual with the really big stars, I didn't know what to do with them.

"Ah, it's our girl Muriel! They told me you worked here." (My idiot brain piped up: is *that* why he came here?).

"Hi, sweetie pie," Mildred cooed. "Don't you look fetching."

"Fetching" was no word for how they looked. The air around them shimmered with motes of silver and gold.

"Oh hello, Mildred, Harold. It's so good to see you again!" To call them by their first names still thrilled me. Harold swept his intense gaze across the room, then pointed with his good hand.

"That one, sweetheart."

"Are you sure? If you'll wait just a couple of minutes — "

"That's our favourite table. It's right in the middle of things. Hide in plain sight."

Harold should know something about that. It worked, of course; in most of these matters, he was seldom wrong.

While developing my hostess deportment and enduring at least two more Harold visitations, I listened to Shirley's advice and plugged at the writing, submitted it, endured rejection after rejection. I went to movies, even took notes, tried to discern what "worked" in the industry, but it all fell flat. Even the ploy of using a man's name wasn't working.

I started a novel, threw it away, started another one. One night at the Moonglow, completely preoccupied with another failed story, I stepped on Charlie Chaplin's toe in high heels, and he glared at me in a way that made my neck hair prickle. So much for the beloved Little Tramp.

Then, feeling a burst of mad inspiration, I began a novel/ memoir about the experiences of a young girl in Hollywood. It would never make it — *I* would never make it — but with my wretched, compulsive tenacity, I had to keep trying.

One night when the Moonglow wasn't very busy, I spoke to a man who sat by himself. I can't explain this, but his gaze seemed to enter me, to comprehend what was inside me, even appreciate me. My strangeness, my lack of a place in the world resonated with his.

This was the most transparent device in the world, showing up for lunch or coffee and "incidentally" talking to me. And of course our conversations remained frustratingly superficial. But I began to look forward to seeing him come in. Like Danny, like Harold, like all the men I had ever been drawn to, he was impossibly good-looking. His name was Robinson, Ray Robinson. A defense attorney, he told me, which sounded impressive. I wondered with a sickening lurch if he had been involved with the Alice murder and the ensuing coverup. But if he had, he said nothing.

I wasn't supposed to date customers: this was an absolute, hidebound rule. I knew I would be jeopardizing my job. And when he asked me out, I said yes. No movies this time, by Harold Lloyd or anyone else, but the ballet: *Romeo and Juliet* by Prokofiev.

I had never seen or heard anything like this. There was nothing like it in Santa Fe, nor even any awareness of it. The only music I had ever listened to was popular, mostly on dreadfully scratched records. The music, overpowering, melancholy and sweet, washed over me and took possession of me, and the dancers seemed to defy gravity. By the end of it, the ovation that went on and on and sang in my ears, embarrassing tears spilling down my face (and, as always, I had no handkerchief with me).

Surely Ray would see me as an unseasoned hick, someone who didn't even know how to deal with culture and keep it at arm's length. But somehow or other, it must have been the right response. As we rode home in the back of a cab, sitting very close together in the dark, he saw my pensive mood and lifted my chin to look in my face.

"What happened tonight?"

It was a strange question. "What do you mean?"

"You looked as if you'd found something you had been looking for your whole life."

"Oh, Ray, that's — that's kind of ridiculous, isn't it?"

"Maybe not. You've only been living half a life."

It insulted me, but I still wanted him to keep talking.

"You mean you can take me away from all this."

"As a matter of fact, I can."

It spoke volumes about me that at that particular moment, I was convinced Ray was my last chance. For what, I could not spell out: was it security, a real home, children? But shouldn't you love the man you marry? I loved Harold, and look where it got me.

It was just at that moment that the axe fell. When a girl gets serious with someone, especially a customer, it's time to cut her loose. Howard invited me into his office, offered me severance pay, and wished me luck. Meanwhile Ray worked fast: sensing my feeling that the floor was dropping out from under me, he proposed.

. For the second time in my life, I took a deep breath, and plunged. I told myself it had to work this time: I was grown up now, nineteen years old with three solid years of working experience behind me. I was not the naïve girl who had climbed on the bus in Santa Fe. This was different, a new kind of adventure with a man who wouldn't manipulate and elude me. I told myself it was a fresh start: a new love, a new city (New York, a hive of constant excitement which terrified me with its unfamiliarity). Since I had never had any writing success that counted, it seemed liked a small sacrifice to leave it behind.

If it had been difficult to ride out the lurching waves of show business, adapting to being a lawyer's wife was infinitely worse. Ray kept convincing me in the sweetest way possible that I was doing everything wrong.

"You're wearing that?'

"This colour is flattering on me."

"Look, honey, there's nothing wrong with it, if you're working for a magazine. This is an opening night."

"All right, I'll talk to Carolyn about it."

"Carolyn! Why do you take advice from the staff?"

It was clear that my choice of friends wasn't acceptable either, though I continued to talk to Carolyn when Ray wasn't home. I had more in common with the maid than with his high-powered associates and their sophisticated wives.

It did not take me long to realize I had made a terrible mistake. I felt expectations pressing down on me: Ray's opinions were my opinions; I wore my hair for him; I dressed for him; I tried to give him the kind of sex he wanted (pretending I hated it like a proper woman, when I longed to experience the pleasure I'd known with Danny), until one night I exploded in a shrill diatribe.

He looked at me wearily. "So what is it this time?"

"Do you think it's easy for me to be alone in this apartment while you're off being the big-time lawyer all day?"

"If you're alone all day it's your own fault." He lit a cigarette and blew smoke angrily.

"So what am I supposed to do, get a dog and walk it?" I was dismayed at my own complaining, fretful tone.

"At least go out and make a few friends."

I wondered how I was supposed to do that.

"Ray, I want to get a job."

"Not on your life! I won't be shown up by having a wife who works. And what are you fit to do, anyway, besides wait tables?"

It was a stinging remark, and not even true, but it devastated me, and from then on I avoided arguing with him. I decided to get out of the prison on Park Avenue and spent a lot of time trying to keep myself occupied. I went to the movies, art galleries, restaurants, always alone, wondering if I could sneak in a part-time waitressing job just to kill time. The fact that I was always walking around by myself sometimes drew disapproving stares.

One afternoon while I was walking in Central Park, I became aware that I was being followed. Someone was "tailing" me, ducking behind trees, blending into crowds and emerging again. An irrational, almost insane thought popped into my head: this was about the Alice murder! Someone had caught up with me, maybe a detective. I began to run on high heels, looking ridiculous, stumbling and nearly falling.

"Slow down, sister! You're going to hurt yourself." I turned around and saw a man — a huge man, baby-faced, who for some reason looked oddly familiar to me.

"Someone's following me," I gasped.

"Who?"

I motioned behind me. The creep tried to hide behind a tree again, and my new friend — if that's what he was — literally picked him up by the back of his collar and hoisted him up off the ground."

"Going somewhere, bud?"

"Ah, nowhere in particular."

"Tell you what. If you go THAT way, I won't rearrange your face for you." He turned him around, set him down on the path and placed his foot on his backside.

He didn't even have to push. The would-be assailant ran off.

This was the strangest thing that had happened to me since I had moved to New York.

"Thanks a lot."

"No trouble."

"Sorry, but — who *are* you?"

He extended a large, warm hand to me. "Roy Brooks," he said, beaming. "At your service."

Suddenly, and very unexpectedly, I didn't feel alone any more. It seemed unorthodox and perhaps unsuitable to have a male friend, one I had made practically on the spot. But didn't I know Roy Brooks already? He had appeared in many of Harold's early pictures, back when the Glass Character was just beginning to evolve. A member of Harold's informal repertory company, he was happy to be slotted in wherever a large, amiable character was needed (with the odd villainous role thrown in). And oh, he was wonderful to look at, like the man in the moon: big and tall and cuddly, with a face that wore a genuine, sunny smile.

We would sit in a booth sipping milkshakes — like something out of a collegiate movie — just chatting away. He was so open and charming, so easy to talk to. I couldn't help but notice how much talk had been bottled up inside me, things I could never say to Ray's rarefied crowd because they sounded silly (or so I feared). Though I kept fighting the urge, I finally had to ask him about Harold.

"Oh, Harold! I'm not in the club any more — I mean, not in his pictures. But I'm still close to the family. I'm his secretary now."

"Secretary?"

"Don't be so surprised, Muriel. It's a man's job, make no mistake. I pretty much manage the estate now, all forty-four rooms of it."

"And Harold doesn't mind you working around Mildred?"

"Mildred and I went to school together. We're chums. Besides — you don't know about this, do you, Muriel? I'm of that other persuasion."

"That other — "

"Oh, there are lots of names for it. Such as pansy, nancy-boy, fairy, flit — "

"You're *never!*" My small-town background spontaneously popped out of me.

"As Harold says, I make no bones about it. If people know, they know. If they don't, that's fine too, though I'm not about to tell them."

I was all agog, having barely heard of such things, or at least not in too much detail. He seemed so comfortable with something that most people would probably die rather than reveal.

We fell into an easy friendship that I knew couldn't last. For one thing, I knew Roy would not be in New York for long. But I asked no questions. We strolled together on Park Avenue, looking in the shops and making outrageous comments. No longer was I stared at for being a woman alone, and many people recognized Roy from Harold's early pictures, to his obvious pleasure. But something sank in me when he gently told me he would soon return to California, though I suspect he extended his "business" in New York several times. I also came to realize, in later years, that he had likely been seeing someone.

It's only rarely that people use the term "lovely" to describe a man, but Roy Brooks was the loveliest of men, and during that desperate time he saved me from going mad from loneliness. We agreed to avoid awkward goodbyes, telling each other we would meet again (and against the odds, years later and to our mutual delight, we actually did). But I couldn't avoid falling into a depression that left me teary and irritable.

"What's bothering you now?"

"I — oh, it doesn't matter."

"Honey, I want you to be happy here. You seemed so — I don't know, for a while you were better, and now it's all falling apart again."

"I made a friend. A very special friend. But he had to leave, to go back to California."

"HE?"

I don't know what possessed me to admit that my special friend was a man. I told him who he was, I tried to explain, but it sent Ray into a cold sulk that he would not emerge from for a very long time. He *wanted* me to make friends, yes, to stop being so insular and frightened, but they had to be a certain kind of friend, within the bounds of propriety.This meant no letters, no phone calls, no contact at all. Roy Brooks was a man, a homosexual, and (perhaps worst of all) in show business! With those three deadly strikes, he was out.

∾∾∾

There is only one sure way to save a marriage which was a mistake from the very beginning, one way to cement the spreading cracks. It became our solution to everything.

I agonized about my capacity (or lack of it) to nurture a baby: how was I to give something I had never received? And I was dreadfully sick during the entire nine months. I was required to socialize with wives of lawyers during this time, and if I'd felt artificial at the Moonglow, I was an outright automaton now.

Even when I was certain that I was completely prepared to enter the fray, I would manage to make yet another social gaffe.

"Muriel."

"How are you, Mrs. Conrad?" *Damn!* Why am I so afraid to call her by name? Who am I, the hired help?

But the baby would be the saving bond between us.. When my daughter Arlene was born, I fell into a trance of love infinitely more profound than anything I had known with Harold. I surprised myself with the level of competence and even comfort I felt in taking care of her. Perhaps she wasn't rescuing the marriage, but she was doing a very good job of rescuing *me*.

It was heavenly to take Arlene out in her buggy and wheel her around Central Park, where I was often surrounded by elderly women who exclaimed about her beauty and compared her to their beloved grandchildren. Though it was rare, I sometimes struck up conversations with other mothers, though the talk always revolved around babies and their habits (specifically, sleeping, crying, feeding, burping, and bowel movements).

Then I made one of the most costly mistakes of my life. Ray had gone away on a four-day conference, one of many mysterious trips that had started to make me suspicious. Leaving Arlene with Carolyn, the only person I trusted to care for her, I decided to surprise him at his hotel.

It was a surprise, all right. In those days a wife could get into a husband's room without much difficulty. Feeling a strange sort of trepidation, I knocked briefly, opened the door and heard something.

Moans.

I shook my head, trying to get rid of the horrible certainty of what I was hearing.

Idiotically, I backed out the door again, closed it. For a moment I stood in total confusion: then rage surged up in me, my face flaming, my heart racing in fury.

The bastard. *The bastard.* While I stayed home like an idiot with the baby, he was rolling around with cheap women in expensive hotels. I charged through the door and into the bedroom, where the two of them lay naked.

"Muriel! For God's sake, what are you doing here?"

I realized with a sickening shock that *he* was blaming *me*. He probably felt entitled. Interrupting his little tryst was apparently very bad form.

"For God's sake, Ray, what the *hell* do you think you're doing? Who *is* this woman? Look at me, you hussy! Who *are* you? Secretary, chorus girl, common whore?"

"She's a dear friend of mine. We haven't seen each other since — "

"Since last night! Oh, I can guess. These little intimacies spring up out of nowhere."

"Muriel, you were never supposed to see this."

"Why? Why shouldn't I see it? I'm your *wife!* What else have you been doing that you can twist around to be my fault?"

The woman, a plump, not-very-bright-looking kewpie doll with large sagging breasts, was squirming around trying to pull the sheets up to her neck, until Ray ordered her to get dressed. Dressed, she was not much more dressed.

"Muriel, you know things haven't been good between us since Arlene was born. Look, I understand you need time and energy to look after the baby, but what about me? A man has needs."

"And a woman doesn't?"

"Not the same needs."

"What do you mean, then? The need to *screw*? Is that what you're saying, the need *to fuck someone blind?*"

Even the chippie looked shocked.

"*Muriel!* Stop that filthy language right now."

"Why? Haven't you heard those words before? Haven't you used them yourself a few times?"

"It's not suitable for a woman."

"Except for *this* woman." I astonished myself by landing her a hard kick in the calf with my best high heel. "Get out of here, you goddamn *slut*!"

Then I knew where that language was coming from. It was as if there were a virtual recording of my father's curses sleeping in my head, and all it took was this kind of rage and betrayal to switch it on.

"Muriel, if you keep on like this I'll have you arrested for assault."

"Oh, I see. And adultery is considered acceptable! It's breaking a commandment, Ray. But you're the legal type. Catching your husband in bed with another woman isn't a sin, is it? Well, *is* it?"

"You could have at least considered my feelings." All during this conversation he was motioning to the floozie to leave. But she stayed, transfixed by the personal drama unfolding in front of her.

"Do you *have* feelings, Ray? Answer me that. Do you have any sense of responsibility to me and your child?"

"I gave you an opportunity you never would have had without me. A chance to move up in the world."

"So what was I before? One of *these*?"

"No. But you were working in a restaurant, living in a one-room — "

"I see. So giving me a nice place to live and an allowance and fashionable clothes means you can just screw anyone you want."

"Muriel, *stop* it! Have you gone out of your mind?"

"The only crazy thing I ever did was marry *you*, Ray. I showed very poor judgement there."

"If you don't stop it, right now, you will lose custody of Arlene. You'll never see her again."

"Why? Because *you* had a tawdry little affair, probably the latest of many? Am I to be punished for being abandoned and betrayed?"

"Don't be so dramatic."

"Get this woman *out* of here!"

I was astonished when he pressed a wad of bills into her hand. She smiled vacantly, then tottered out on her heels.

"I could charge you with attacking her."

"She deserved it."

"Muriel — "

He looked at me in bewilderment and — to my surprise — shame. There was an awful, "what-have-we-done" moment, the last tattered remnant of the love we had shared. I was about to collapse in tears, so I got out of there fast. But I didn't go back to my room. I went downstairs to the bar. Hating alcohol, never coming near it because of what it did to my father, I ordered a double whisky and knocked it back. Fire roared through me, my head split and shattered, and for the moment, all my troubles went away.

⌘⌘⌘

We were separated, but still living in the same house, neither together nor apart. Ray would not let me move out, claiming he needed someone reliable (meaning "free") to look after Arlene. And because I had no income and depended on Ray for everything, I could not afford a place of my own.

Meanwhile, we started divorce procedings: I had to charge him with something, and both of us agreed it could not be adultery. So it was "alienation of affection", whatever that meant. The wheels would grind slowly over the next few months. Ray supposedly knew all about these things, even though he was a defense lawyer who advocated for murderers and thieves.

Why was my judgement about men so fatally wrong? I remembered what Shirley had told me, about my secret fear that in spite of all appearances, I was worthless. When I looked back logically, I had accomplished a great deal since running away from the horrors of home. But now it all added up to nothing.

For the next six months I trudged through an emotional wilderness, ashamed to write to Shirley or anyone else from home, reluctant to reveal what felt like my worst failure. Arlene was my only beacon, an adorable, bright baby who loved me without reservation. For the first time, someone looked up to me. And I gave her all the energy and care I had left.

Then she got sick. Diphtheria, the doctor said, assuring me it wouldn't be serious, that children pulled through this all the time. In spite of a 103-degree fever, the doctor would not admit her to the hospital. Babies got sick. It was a fact of life.

One night I came into her room, and all the fine hairs on my body stood on end. It wasn't the presence of something, but the absence: I stood rooted for a few seconds, not wanting to believe what I already knew.

I didn't scream when I felt her cold, waxen hands and realized it was too late. In fact I didn't do anything but stand there. For some strange reason Ray came in. He never did this. He stood behind me and said, "What is it?

"The baby's dead," I said in a remote voice I had never heard myself use before.

"*What?* What happened? Why didn't you take her to — "

"I did."

"This can't be." He leaned down, picked up her limp body, looked into her lifeless face, and did something absolutely unexpected: he burst into loud, raucous sobbing. Meanwhile I had somehow hardened into wax. I heard something inside me, the minute sound of very thin glass, perhaps a fragile old Christmas ornament, shattering into dust.

༄༅༄

For a brief, desperate time, Ray and I attempted a reconciliation. We clung to each other in heaving, freezing waters, attempting to make our grief bearable. He was, after all, the only other person in the world who knew how I felt.

The thought of having another child was too overwhelming, so Ray suggested adoption. I knew I couldn't go through with it: someone else's baby would never fill the void. I thought of the time I had held Betty Clayton's baby, Harold's "son", and ached to take him home with me. I was not quite in my right mind then and wondered if I could trace little Harold's whereabouts, find out what happened to him. But my embarrassing phone calls led nowhere. One day Ray found my scribbled notes and confronted me, asking me if I had gone completely insane.

Once more he was gone every night, no doubt seeking solace elsewhere. The divorce proceeded at an agonizingly slow pace. Unable to bear the empty apartment, I wandered aimlessly with nowhere to go. I must have looked like a madwoman. Meanwhile people told me I was "bearing up well", praised my stoicism and secretly felt sorry for me.

Then I overheard two women in the powder room of a fancy restaurant (I occasionally had "pity invitations" from the wives of Ray's colleagues) discussing the fact that Ray was divorcing me because of my emotional coldness.

"Well, you can hardly blame him."

"She is a queer little thing . . . "

"And it's obvious she feels no grief at all."

"A cold fish. And we know what that means, don't we?" (titters).

A nasty thought popped into my head: *Are you fucking him?* And though I would have been within my rights to pop out of the bathroom stall and confront them, I didn't. For some peculiar reason, I was the one who felt ashamed.

One kindly elderly woman, someone I liked and had talked to several times at those interminable parties, crushed me even more: she told me Arlene's death was "God's will", all part of "God's plan" for me and my family. I wondered why some people felt entitled to interpret the death of my baby with such utter certainty, even imposing their opinions on me as some sort of religious conviction.

So profound was my lassitude, depression and shame that I said nothing, did nothing, letting people's ignorant remarks stand. One day I realized there was nothing left for me in New York and packed my bags for California, a place that hardly seemed like home. But I had very little money, just my savings which wouldn't sustain me for long, and even less choice.

If it hadn't been for Shirley, I would have lost my last shred of hope. She put me up in a room in her sumptuous apartment and told me to stay there until I was on my feet again. She made me eat. She walked me, step by faltering step, through the routines of the day. It was understood we wouldn't talk about the baby or the divorce.

Then after all those months, the log jam suddenly broke. My supposed mental illness and inability to look after a child must have been considered grounds for divorce, at least for Ray. No mention was ever made of his "indiscretion". But to my astonishment, the settlement was more generous than I had ever expected. I could live on it quite comfortably for the rest of my life.

"After what he put you through.? It could've been more," Shirley grumbled.

"I don't care. Enough to live on, and more." I sat on her huge round bed picking at the fringe on the bedspread while she rummaged through her closet looking for a stray feather boa.

"Honey," she said, trying to catch my eye, " I know you'll have enough to live on, but you're going to have to give some thought as to what you're going to do. A woman like you can't just fritter her life away in salons. I know you can't believe this now, but one of these days you'll wake up and realize you want to live again. You have so much to give, sweetheart. Real talent. I've never seen so much in one person."

"And look where it got me."

"See, I don't like to hear you talk that way. Angry, yes. Heartbroken, well, of course. But what I hear is bitter. Bitter doesn't suit you. It hardens a person up. Nothing is ever any good any more. You feel hard-done-by, and other people aren't to be trusted."

"They aren't."

"Okay, you have your reasons to think that way. But you've had people watching over you all along. I know it doesn't seem like much, but I think of you as my own daughter."

I looked up at her, stunned.

"I think Hal Roach looked after you, though you might not have seen it at the time. Tony did for certain. He protected you when you really needed it. Maybe you think Goldie is a little silly, but she's a quality person. She opened her home to you, even gave you the clothes off her back. And Harold, if I may mention his name — "

"You may not."

"Fair enough. But I still think Harold is a decent guy. In way too deep, if you ask me. It's a long way from Pawnee County. But his heart is in the right place."

"So what do I do now?"

"It's going to come to you soon. You can't stay with me forever, and it's not me I'm worried about. Look, what you went through is just about the worst thing that can happen. But there's a lot of life left for you."

"And that's supposed to be a *good* thing?"

She turned my face up to hers.

"Yes, dear heart. A good thing."

Welcome Stranger

MY CAREER — MY LIFE — NEVER MOVED IN STRAIGHT lines. Double twists, switchbacks, and harrowing rollercoaster lurches seemed to be the norm.

For the first time in my life, I had some money. The first thing I did was vow to send a large monthly cheque to Bea, though I was astonished and hurt when she sent the first one back. The note attached to it wasn't mean, but it was still hurtful: "You need this more than we do, cuz. Thinking of you." This wasn't true — her family situation was perilously close to the bone — but pride, or estrangement, or some other mysterious factor made it impossible for her to receive it. I remembered Shirley saying that the best thing you can do for someone is let them do you a favor. In this case, Bea was cutting off all possibility of goodwill.

But Shirley was right: I needed to work. I ran into one of the *Mind your Manners* girls at a social function (I forced myself to go out, even though my smile was often pasted on), and she told me about an opportunity at Paragon Studios: a receptionist position that "might lead to more". She meant movie work, of course, but I immediately thought about writing scripts. Taking a deep breath, I walked in and asked to see the manager.

Not for nothing had I dabbled in acting: I had to summon up a confidence I didn't feel. But it worked, and I was given the position of receptionist in an office that looked uncannily like the one at *Spotlight*. It soon became evident that my main purpose was to get rid of people, either at my desk or on the phone, and look decorative while I was doing it.

My boss, Sid Frieberg, was so untidy I was constantly having to pick up after him, dump out cigar ashes and discard crumpled paper. One day I unearthed a tattered old script with scribbles all over it: *Merry Month of May*, or some such idiotic title. Surreptitiously, I slipped it into my bag.

It was then I realized how truly awful Hollywood scripts could be. The story was hackneyed and the titles idiotic ("At last, I've found you!" "No, dearest love — *I* have found *you!*"). I was completely disgusted with what I saw, so much so that I began to retype the thing from scratch. But what would I do with it? Would the two seasoned collaborators who had written it say, "Oh, wonderful, this little amateur has totally transformed our script"?

I was a coward: once I made my way through the thing, I placed the two copies side-by-side on Sid's desk, assuming it would be quickly buried under letters, memos, magazines, first drafts, discarded projects, and coffee cups. I had a sickly feeling in my stomach as I answered the phone and made bright chat with industry types as they came and went.

"Muriel, would you come in and talk to me?" I couldn't read Sid's voice: it seemed neutral. Anger might have been more reassuring.

"You didn't put your name on this." He waved the screenplay at me.

"No. That's because I didn't really write it."

"True. But I take it you wouldn't have done this unless you thought the original stunk."

I didn't know what to say.

"Listen, Muriel, I can't just take your version of it and use it. About all I can do is take some of your suggestions under consideration. Screenwriters are used to having their work changed, desecrated or however they think of it, but not by an unknown."

I wondered if I'd still get a credit, then thought: *are you mad?*

"Listen, girl, I'd like to give you a few tips here. Pull up a chair." I felt as if I was being called into the principal's office.

"There's some good stuff here, much more wit and humor than in the first one. Obviously you have the touch. But your titles are — well, it's like you've been reading too many novels. Never, *never* use words like "rather". Nobody says that except seventy-year-old university professors."

I was blushing hard, feeling anger and resentment rise, but trying to keep an open mind. "Another thing. Your version just doesn't *move.* Everybody's talking about pictures with sound, but we're not quite there yet. Give it another year or two, and we'll be in the soup. Actors still have to tell the story with their bodies, their gestures, their faces."

"Then how can I write — "

"This isn't bad, it's just more like a stage play than a movie. Maybe you should consider writing for the theatre."

"Thanks, Mr. Frieberg."

"Sid."

"Thanks, Sid." I wondered if being allowed to use this elite monosyllable represented some sort of minuscule promotion.

Like every other attempt to succeed I had ever made, this one had been neatly short-circuited by circumstance, not to mention my apparent shortcomings as a writer. I kept chopping away at my other projects, sometimes wretched with discouragement, at other times taken over by an even more heartbreaking hope.

But something was about to happen: the entire industry would be revolutionalized, and those unable to adapt to the change would quickly sink.

❧❧❧

We called them "talkers" at first, and the industry approached them with a mixture of heady excitement and sickening dread. Early experiments in synchronized sound recording were dreadful: tinny, noisy, with the actors completely static as they sat around a huge microphone hidden behind a potted palm. Cameras were placed in a suffocating glass box to minimize noise, with the cameraman forced to sweat and gasp inside them (until someone, I think it was Cecil B. DeMille, got the brilliant notion of putting just the *camera* in the box).

Everything had been dumped upside-down: stories once told through artful bodily gesture and facial expression now had to be talked out, and since the public was fascinated by any sound from a movie, dialogue went on seemingly forever. Everyone was coached to speak in a highfalutin', false English-sounding accent. No one's voice sounded good, but some were so dreadful their careers ended with a thud.

This transformation spanned a couple of years, and I was fascinated to follow its progress. Sid began to quietly leave bad scripts on my desk, presumably because I knew how to write dialogue. I did what I could with them: cleaned them up, gave them back, and never got a credit.

I was astonished when I heard that Harold had made his first "talker", a picture called *Welcome Danger*. Though critics were hard on it, most of them baffled by what he was trying to achieve, the public embraced it as his finest work: and all because they were so eager to hear him talk.

Harold had taken an unusual approach with this movie. He had finished shooting it as a silent feature in 1929, but had a revelatory experience that changed everything. Walking by a movie theatre, he heard uproarious laughter. Peeking in, he saw the audience watching a short feature: ice clinking in glasses, doors slamming, cars starting, and so on.

People were roaring with laughter (or at least they were in Harold's account) even at the most "punk" gags. In a panic, he assembled his boys and announced, "We have to make this picture over, some way." Then came the bizarre, torturous procedure of trying to make a soundtrack stick to a movie that was never intended to have one.

Bits of it were reshot with dialogue. Sound effects were awkwardly inserted. No one knew anything about dubbing then, so Harold and his boys were taking shots in the dark. In fact, one whole scene, a very long one, was played out in complete darkness, a gimmick that seemed to say, "See, I don't need pictures at all. I can do it all with sound."

The fact that the public accepted this clanger with enthusiasm was both intriguing and very sad. I went to see *Welcome Danger* with Goldie and two other girls from Paragon, and tried very hard to giggle and be pleased at what I was seeing. The main character, Harold Bledsoe, was a botanist who became embroiled in the shady underworld of Chinese opium dens, while at the same time getting entangled in a ludicrous romantic mixup in which a girl was mistaken for a boy.

I could not make myself like this picture. The plot was an unlikely muddle that had come unmoored from Harold's greatest strength: telling strong but simple stories about a seemingly-ordinary man facing extraordinary challenges. His character was arrogant and obnoxious, as offputting as his bizarre name. How could Harold's brilliant instincts as a moviemaker have misfired to this degree? Was sound really so intimidating to such a master?

Perhaps. Since I knew what his normal speaking voice sounded like, I was concerned: though it wasn't exactly high, it lacked resonance, and shot up irritatingly when he was excited or upset. The remnants of Burchard, Nebraska were still evident in a certain twang that came and went, as if he were trying to get rid of it. The clunky, primitive microphones of the day made everyone but Garbo sound muddy and artificial.

But Harold was completely different. He sounded like a cricket.

Oh, I tried to like his voice, tried very hard. The audience didn't seem to mind it at all: *Harold Lloyd speaks!*

The other girls chattered excitedly on their way out of the theatre, trying to unscramble the convoluted plot of the thing, marvelling at the primitive thuds and clangs that punctuated a movie that wasn't very strong to begin with. Noticing that I wasn't chiming in, Goldie finally turned to me and said, "You didn't like it very much, did you, Muriel."

"I'm afraid not."

"Well, he'll be a different Harold from now on."

I hated this new truth, cries and groans escaping from what was once a flicker of enchantment in the dark. When I got back to my cozy little apartment and went to bed, I pulled a big lace-edged pillow over my head and wept for the lost Harold, for all I remembered and all I had lost.

I often thought that the passage of time during those years could be charted by hair styles. Women's heavy masses of hair were lopped off in the '20s into short boyish bobs, freed from the constriction of tortoiseshell combs. Some were cut at geometrical angles around the face, à la Louise Brooks. Spit curls figured large. These "easy" styles weren't easy at all if you were interested in emulating Clara Bow, Bebe Daniels or all the other "good little bad girls" of the era.

My hair was wavy and even kinky, and trying to make it go smooth was nearly impossible. Pomades were smelly and messy. Clasps and barettes were uncomfortable. For a brief, desperate while, I wondered if I should resort to turbans like

Shirley (who, as it turned out, had limp, scanty hair that she didn't want to reveal to the world). Finally I gave up, fluffed it out and hoped for the best. It looked all right, but I secretly hated it: so my first perm was a revelation.

The Marcel Wave saved my life, matured me in the best possible way (and imagine a woman wanting to look older: but how else would I be taken seriously as a writer?). The hairdo was highly structured and hard to maintain, as were all the styles of the '30s. Clothing followed suit: dresses and skirts were cut closer to the body. No more low-waisted flapper gowns, no beaded bags or feather boas. This made my skinny body look almost curvaceous. For the first time in my life, I was actually pleased with my appearance.

Every woman is familiar with those rare, blessed days when everything falls into place: hair gleams, complexion glows, skirts fall just so. I sat at my desk on one of those days, accomplishing very little, feeling like a particularly elegant Siamese cat draped over a chair. More than one man quickly eyed me up and down as he hurried past (everyone hurried in that place). Instead of the usual annoyance, I felt smugly pleased. I was twenty-six years old, almost old for an unmarried woman of that era, and I had never looked better in my life.

Usually on these charmed days, nothing happens and no one comes near you. Then I saw someone from my vantage-point as the gatekeeper of the office. He was beautifully dressed, and there was something familiar about the shape of his head, the way he carried himself. Then he turned around, and I saw the dazzle of his smile as he talked to one of the girls.

Come here, come here, don't leave without talking to me!

I was no better now than I had been as a teenager. My suppressed passion for him sprang up like a jack-in-the-box. I wanted to jump out of my chair and run to him, but was glued down by inertia and embarrassment. I kept willing him to come to me, but he was leaving, probably forever. Almost out the door! And then —

It's sometimes true that we can feel someone's eyes on us, even though we can't see them. My gaze must have been burning into the back of his head.

He turned around. Looked puzzled for a second.

Then his eyes ignited. I braced myself: I was about to be knocked over again.

He came striding towards me, exuding the same old candle power, planting a big movie-star kiss on my cheek. Same smoothly-shaven face, with just a hint of bay rum aftershave: *did it ever end?*

"Muriel! Gosh, it's good to see you."

"Harold, you look wonderful." And he did. He had aged, but lightly, the fine lines around his eyes just adding to the boyish exuberance in his smile. He still had the clean jawline, fine profile and swept-back dark hair of a matinee idol, and his eyes were crystal blue. Avoiding drink, drugs and cigarettes had paid off. Though the styles of the '30s didn't flatter him quite as well (his trim body looked a little lost in all that bulk), his suit was beautifully tailored and the fabric expensive.

"So I hear you're a professional writer now." *Hear?* With my near-anonymity, I was amazed I had any reputation at all in this place.

"I try," I said. Why was I so pathetic?

"I've heard you do more than try. In fact, you may be just the person I'm looking for."

It was no secret in the industry that Harold had fallen on hard times since pictures began to talk. Unlike many of his silent film cohorts, he plunged ahead, refusing to give in to the anxiety that plagued every actor of the era. The runaway success of *Welcome Danger* in 1929 helped him wipe the sweat off his brow, but he knew he would need to release something within a year or be completely forgotten.

The script of *Die Laughing* seemed promising enough: a comic murder mystery in which Harold played a bumbling detective investigating the disappearance of an heiress. I expected him to show up in a double role somewhere, though fortunately it never happened. But the script had no flow: it stopped and started, with the actors either standing around talking, or performing stunts. Dialogue; action. Dialogue; action. The entire medium had experienced (or suffered) something beyond mere transformation: it was metamorphosis, the caterpillar dissolving into a formless blob before emerging as a completely different creature.

As in every crisis, some people rose to the top, ascending to prominence as if they hadn't existed before. Laurel and Hardy, W. C. Fields, the Marx Brothers: they bloomed with the advent of sound, and audiences quickly adapted to their fast banter and distinct comedic voices.

But what of those who had acted almost entirely with their faces, their bodies? It was all over for them. It was as if the industry suddenly demanded: *say something, Harold!* His delivery was as unnatural as almost everyone else's, but in his case it didn't quite come off.

People still came to his pictures. Critics were generous, noting the craftsmanship that had always been the foundation of every Harold Lloyd picture. But audiences didn't notice or care very much about such things. They wanted to jiggle in their seats with laughter. They wanted a Harold that could suddenly, miraculously talk like a ventriloquist's dummy. Harold stood behind Harold, petrified, trying to make his creation speak. He might as well have been made out of wood.

I went to see *Die Laughing*, but without any girlfriends along: I attended in the role of an anthropologist analyzing the picture scene by scene. It was not a bad movie, in spite of the flaws in the script. But I fervently wished the director had taken Harold aside and said: "Just speak in your normal voice." Whether it was because of his background as a juvenile stage actor or his unfamiliarity with the form, he sounded like he was trying too hard, attempting to compress a three-act stage comedy into a ninety-minute picture.

Harold just didn't have a memorable voice. It didn't drawl or simper or bellow; it had no ludicrous, phony foreign accent. It didn't trawl the bottom of the lake like Garbo's (and why in God's name would that voice catch on so well, when it was lower than the average man's?). Harold realized long ago that he needed a signature, a trademark of some kind, and in a stroke of genius had come up with the glasses. But when sound arrived, he had no such signature. It was as if he had lost his glasses somewhere, and couldn't get them back.

Having Harold back in my life, even in such a limited capacity, re-ignited my desperate desire to please him: every day I dressed for him, did my hair for him, walked through a cloud of atomized French perfume, while shaking my head in disgust. He was in and out of the office constantly, waving at me on the way by, slamming the door to Sid's office. I could hear them talking in there, their voices rising and falling. One day he was accompanied by someone I didn't know. Then I could hear three voices behind the door, and I couldn't tell if they were arguing or just sharing jokes. Big gusts of laughter boomed periodically. But then someone's voice shot up and went on and on in a sort of tirade.

That could mean only one thing. Harold wasn't pleased.

❧❧❧

At first it didn't seem like much, just another script plopped down on my desk for me to proofread for consistency and errors. I put the other three aside, on the hunch that this one was somehow a priority.

It wasn't as bad as some, but there were problems. As with so many movies of its time, it was too "talky", too full of long sweeps of dialogue punctuated by feverish activity. The stunts were difficult enough that they would require professionals, though they might pass for the characters in long shots from the back.

I began to mark it up. It was mostly tinkering, though I longed to cut certain scenes out entirely. The picture was sentimental, but old-fashioned melodrama and traditional romance was still popular in the early '30s: the smart, independent woman had yet to make her appearance.

Then the strangest thing happened: Harold appeared in front of my desk. He leaned on it with his hands and lifted both feet off the ground, like a little boy. Strange for anyone else, but not for Harold.

"Well, what do you think?"

"It's . . . it definitely shows some promise."

"Oh Muriel, cut it out, I know what that means. I need the straight truth from you. This is important."

"I think it would be fine, with a major rewrite. I mean, a complete overhaul."

"How would you like to do it?"

"*Me*? Harold, that's crazy! I'm just a proofreader. I don't have the skills to — "

"That's not what I heard."

"Sid would never approve it."

"He just did."

"Would I be — that is, would I — "

"Yes, you'd get the going rate. We don't expect you to do this for peanuts. It's going to be a lot of work." He leaned so far forward that I could sense the heat from him. "Listen, Muriel, I really need a hit." I saw a flicker of desperation in his eyes before he looked away. "I feel like the wind's gone out of my sails. I need a good strong updraft, and quickly. This is a departure from anything I've done before. I only threw in with Sid because he's had a couple of hits lately and seems to know what he's doing. But the character isn't even named Harold. We've decided to do away with him. I can keep the glasses, but everything else has to go."

"But why, Harold? People love your character."

"He's too old. Or I am. My reflexes have slowed down. I'm not a kid anymore. This new director I'm working with, this Sterling Prescott, he's nothing short of a miracle worker. He sat down with me and told me everything he knew about making pictures, and it knocked me from here to Sunday. I'm still stuck in my old ways, Muriel. Prescott's the newest thing, and he's willing to help me."

Don't sell out, Harold, I wanted to say, but dared not.

"Then I'll need his approval on the script, scene by scene."

"He wants to see a draft from you before he does that."

"What?" I quickly collected myself. "When?"

"By Monday." My scalp prickled: this was *Wednesday!* I'd have to work night and day to make the revisions. Then the entire thing would have to be re-typed, probably on my rickety old home model with the stuck keys.

"I notice it doesn't have a title," I said, trying to sound cool.

"We haven't named it yet. We've just been calling it the Circus Picture. At one point it was called *Top This!*, but I couldn't stand that. Look, Muriel, I've never done anything like this in my life before. I can't do any of the stunts, they're high-wire things that will have to be done with a double. Oh, I'll have a few flips and falls, standard clown stuff, but nothing too impressive. I'm going to have to juggle, and God knows how I'll manage that. And of course there will be a romance. We're trying to get Mariette Piercy."

I was impressed. Piercy was a tiny, exquisite young brunette with a striking French accent. When accents worked in sound film, they worked magically — or else they clanged so badly it was painful to hear.

"I won't keep you, Muriel, I know you have lots of work to do. And you're the one to do it." I prayed he'd kiss me, at least casually, but he didn't. I wondered if I had matured at all since that furtive kiss during the rain storm.

I opened the script, overwhelmed. Took up my red pencil, and got down to work.

∾∾∾

I had never worked under such pressure in my life. I gave it my undivided attention during the day, took it home with me at night, and worked until I couldn't focus my eyes any more. I prayed my draft was an improvement, but without any word from Prescott it was impossible to say.

After all that desperate effort I got it in on deadline, but Prescott merely snatched it out of my hands and dismissed me. Later I found out Harold had given him hell for it. The two of them were not getting along, and it wasn't a good omen.

As it turned out, being asked to leave was the longest communication I would receive from him, except for violent scribbles on the script as it passed back and forth between us. He obviously felt Harold had made a bad mistake in assigning this task to a mere girl (never mind that I'd just turned twenty-six and had been writing all my life). The process went on and on, a shuttlecock batted endlessly back and forth.

It had been a particularly trying afternoon, during which I worked hard to translate the stilted, near-hopeless script into something that lived and breathed. Though dialogue was my particular strength, and I would have enjoyed writing it under better conditions, the escalating pressure was making me anxious and even slowing the process down.

Harold always seemed to be in a bad mood anyway. He would hang around my desk, which I secretly loved, and sound forth on the disadvantages of dialogue: "This isn't a drawing-room comedy, this isn't a stage play, it's a *picture*, and people come to a picture to be entertained! Movies are called movies because they *move*. Talkies sound awful, and the only reason people go to them is novelty. It'll wear off soon enough, mark my words."

He desperately wanted his medium back, and felt it slipping through his fingers. Though the reviews of his first two sound pictures had been respectful, one critic remarked that his part could have been played just as well, or perhaps better, by a new talent more comfortable with sound.

Ironically, many decades later I heard his mature voice, and instead of wavering and growing higher like most older men's, a miracle happened: it dropped an octave, spread out, settled in, and took on the wide, generous sound of an old raconteur, a prosperous Nebraskan cattle-rancher speaking in tones that breathed Middle America. But by then, it would do him no good as anything other than an ageing legend.

"Muriel. Haven't you got that scene done yet? It's the most important one in the whole picture and we need it right away."

"It isn't finished, Harold."

"Isn't finished." I didn't like what I saw on his face, something like thunderheads gathering.

"I need another two hours." I knew that Harold required exactitude, boundaries, needed to know just how long he would have to wait.

"You're holding everything up. Do you realize that? You're holding up production with all this nonsense. You have to deliver your work *on time*."

"With all due respect, Harold — "

"Respect! What does this have to do with respect? How can you say you respect me if you're not doing your job? I hired you to get this done and deliver the goods when I need them. And I need them *right now!*"

I had witnessed his rages — we all had — but hoped I would never be the target. I took a deep breath, and decided I had to stand my ground. I wasn't about to weep or turn to jelly in the face of an infantile tantrum.

"The script will be ready in two hours."

"Two hours. I haven't *got* two hours! The clock is running, girl! Do you know how much two hours of wasted studio time costs us? I thought you were competent enough to handle this job!"

I looked levelly at him, refusing to show what I felt.

"I *am* competent. You hired me, so if I'm incompetent it shows poor judgement on your part." (I knew I was fired already, so why not say what I really thought?) "I won't hand in work that isn't up to my standards or yours. This script is very weak, and it needs a great deal of revision. That's why you hired me. You can have it fast, or you can have it right. Which way do you prefer?" I could not believe what I was saying, but I knew I had to say it.

There was a box of files sitting beside my desk. He levelled his eyes at it, wound himself up, then kicked it ferociously, tearing a big hole in it. Loose pages flew everywhere. They seemed to explode in the air like partridges flushed from a bush.

I refused to react. I would not show intimidation. I would not show fear.

He looked almost wild, like a crazy person. I had to last it out. It was only a Harold Lloyd tantrum, I told myself, everyone knew about them, just the price of working for him. He shot me a withering look, then strode away, slamming the office door so hard I could hear the frame crack.

I busied myself with useless tasks, wondering when I would be asked to clean out my desk. Nothing happened. I took up the script again, wanting to finish what I had started. I worked on that dialogue, all the long meandering pages of it, tightened it up, and (I hoped) made it sharper, wittier, more like Harold at his best. In an hour and a half, it was finished to the best of my ability. I would hand it in, then give my notice.

Gritting my teeth, I walked over to his office door. It was like entering the lion's den.

I tapped on the door. No answer. Then tapped again.

"Yes," I heard, not in an angry voice but a weary one. "Come in."

I came in. I carried the finished pages over to him and set them down carefully in front of him.

"I've finished this scene to the best of my ability."

"Muriel — "

"I assume you've talked to Sid about this." I tried as hard as I could to keep emotion out of my voice, my face.

"Muriel, I don't even know where to begin to ask for your forgiveness. I behaved abominably, and I am truly and deeply sorry." He pressed his fingertips into his eyes so hard, it was painful to watch. "If there is anything I can do to make this up to you, anything at all — "

Give me a raise, I thought, but that's not what I said.

"Are you firing me?" I wanted to keep as cool as possible, not fall into the miasma of his remorse.

"Oh no, no, Muriel, you're the best thing we've got. You're such a fine writer, and to be honest, we don't know what we're doing here. My first talkie was a disaster. People liked it, but they would've liked hearing me recite the alphabet. We didn't know anything about dialogue or dubbing or any of the rest of it, we just floundered. I feel like a beginner again. It's awful. But you're saving the situation."

I knew this wasn't true, even though it was generous of him to say it. However, it *was* true that the pages that had been handed to me were, by and large, far too weak to use. I'd discarded many of them, and rewritten whole swaths of story which I prayed would pass.

Then he did something astonishing. He got down in front of me on one knee, as if he wanted to marry me. It was a scene out of one of his movies, and he looked, eerily, like the glass character without his glasses. Ten years had fallen away in an instant. He had that ivory look, almost translucent, his eyes soft with emotion.

"Please forgive me, Muriel. Please. I'll do anything."

"Don't, Harold." I was both shocked and embarrassed for him. He looked beyond distraught, almost disturbed.

"Please. Just say it."

"Harold, get up right now. Don't do this."

"Not 'til you forgive me."

Was this what I needed, or what *he* needed? Surely it must be the latter. I wondered what would happen if I didn't, if I just said, "No, Harold, I won't forgive you, because what you said was totally demeaning and unfair." Would the tirade start again?

Or — what if I reached out my hand, put it on his dark head, and gently mussed his hair?

"I forgive you."

"*Mean* it, Muriel. Because I know you don't."

"I need more time."

"Of course." He got up again, looking dazed, even disoriented, as if he didn't quite know where he was.

"Please let me know if the work is satisfactory."

"Oh, Muriel, please, *please* don't be so cold to me, it's worse than anger. We've known each other a long time now, and I admire your talent. But that's not the point. I want to keep our friendship no matter what."

"Of course."

Then I turned (not quite on my heel, but almost) and left the office, shutting the door very quietly behind me.

Harold could not live on a normal scale, and his extravagance could be shocking. That evening as I knitted and half-listened to the radio, there came a tap on my door.

"Delivery for Miss Ashford."

It was a long, narrow white box. A heady scent wafted through it before I had even opened it.

A dewy mass of roses, dark red velvet anointed with a heavy sweetness. Not a bouquet but a *forest* of roses, lush with ferns, intoxicating. I could not tell how many dozen, perhaps three or four.

As I stuffed them in the biggest vase I had, a small white card came tumbling out:

oh please forgive me,
Harold

❧❧❧

I began to feel as if I were living inside this script. Prescott told me over and over again that he wanted sentiment, that audiences loved it, and that he wanted them to feel sorry for Punch, Harold's washed-up clown character.

On the surface of it, it was completely natural that Harold would play a clown: he had always been a sort of man-doll, white-faced, naturally comical, using his body more eloquently than anyone else. But he had always kept just this side of the fine line, refusing to let audiences pity him. I wondered how palatable Prescott's idea would be, not so much to the audience as to Harold.

Facing the stack of pages each day was intimidating. The plot was paper-thin: a Big Top thwarted romance, which seemed to borrow elements out of every circus movie ever made.

The Circus Picture (working title: Top This!)
Story synopsis:

A clown (Punchinello: Punch for short) is in love with a beautiful trapeze artist named Paloma, "the Dove". Punch specializes in pratfalls in which he falls over backwards, sprays seltzer, does back-flips (Prescott's note: *can we get a double for this?*), vaults over things, rides horses backwards, and generally causes mayhem. He won't tell anyone his real name, trying to preserve the idea that he was once a great aerialist who had taken a bad fall and had to retire. The rumour among the circus people is that he was a window washer who fell off the scaffolding and developed an extreme fear of heights.

Paloma already has a boyfriend, a muscle-bound fire-eater named Marco the Magnificent. (I winced at this, but Prescott insisted.) The circus's star juggler is a shy, charming French girl named Pierrette, who has been madly in love with Punch for years. He doesn't seem to notice her, treating her like a little girl or just another member of the troupe.

One day the ringmaster, concerned about sagging attendance, comes up with an idea. There will be a contest with a $1000 prize to see who can make it across the tightrope (Prescott: *with a safety net, I hope!)* Screwing up his courage, Punch decides he will enter the contest to prove his love for Paloma, He changes costume and puts on a mask so that he is completely unrecognizeable, forcing himself to master his greatest fear. *Ending*: he wins the contest/ Pierette's love. *Alternate ending:* he fails the contest and wins Pierette's love.

The cast called for a dwarf, and Harold just happened to know one: Pinky Reynolds, a circus performer who had popped up in many of his feature films. I tried to work Pinky's unique voice into his scenes as I wrote them.

Scene 12: Pierrette and Pinky have the following exchange:

"Little girl, you're wasting your time on that guy. His heart belongs to another."

"Yes, but she has no heart."

"Be that as it may. It's the dames he *can't* have that interest him."

"What really happened to Punch? I hear rumours about him. All sorts of stories."

"Well, the real story is, he started out with another circus where he was an aerialist. Tightrope, trapeze, the works. Used to be a headliner, The Great Punchinello or something like that. That's where he got his name.

"And the usual thing happened: he fell for a dame who wouldn't give him the time of day. His trapeze partner was a bigger guy, brawny, if you know what I mean, and very good-looking. And one day during a performance, he sort of forgot to catch Punch. Kind of cleared the romantic obstacles out of the way for him. Punch landed the wrong way, ended up in the hospital with a slipped disc and was told his career was over. And the dame never even sent him no flowers."

"That's terrible."

"Oh, it's a lovely story. And it'd be even lovelier if it was true."

"You don't believe Punch? But he's so sincere."

"I believe Punch is a clown. You know what clowns are like. There's more honour among thieves."

"Did he really get hurt that badly?"

"He didn't get hurt at all. He just has a fear of heights. It goes way back. Started when he was a baby and fell out of the high chair."

"So why won't he tell anyone his real name?"

"Who knows. We don't ask no questions in the circus. Just keep your head down and do your job."

"Pinky . . ."

"Oh boy, here it comes. No, I won't deliver your love letter, signed *From Your Secret Admirer*."

"That's not what I want. But I have something for him. Here." She hands him a small object wrapped up in tissue paper. "Just leave it in his dressing room."

"The things we do for love." He sighs, takes it and leaves the room.

∽∽∽

I had begun to vividly visualize the scenes as they unfolded: but it was still difficult to picture Harold as a downtrodden clown robbed of his former glory. The naive, virginal Glass Character he was famous for just wouldn't work any more. Could he play Punch as a world-weary figure who had almost given up, or would it cut too close to the bone?

Then I had an idea that excited me so much, my scalp prickled: instead of a seedy old failure hiding out in a circus, Punch would be a tragic artist, a poetic figure misunderstood by everyone — except Pierette. My brief but intense introduction to higher culture (particularly opera) made me wonder if Ray hadn't served some purpose in my life, after all.

Scene 17: Pinky knocks on Punch's dressing-room door.
"What are you whistling, champ? Sounds a little familiar."
"Vesti la Giubba."
"Vesti la *what*?"
"Means 'put on the motley'."
"Like in 'motley crew'?"
"Sort of. Clowns used to be treated like riff-raff and lived on the street. People used to throw stones at them."
"Some kind of applause. So what's this fancy song all about?"
"It's from an Italian opera. Pagliaccio's a clown who's in love with Colombina — "
"Funny name. Like Columbia, the Gem of the Ocean."
"Not quite. It means . . . well, it means dove."
"Say, isn't that the same as Pal — "

"Never mind.

"Oh, listen pal, don't get your hopes up on Paloma. She's the most selfish dame I ever knew. I hate to see you knockin' your head on the wall over her. You can do better than that."

"Well, don't worry, I won't do a Pagliaccio."

"What's that supposed to mean?"

"He kills them both. Then himself. Just a pile of bodies on the stage."

"Obviously one of your funnier-type clowns."

"How can I attract her attention, Pink?"

"What about . . . take *off* the motley. Let her see you as you really are."

"It'll never fly. I'll just disappear into the scenery."

"Ever occur to you that you might love those feathers and sequins more than the real girl?"

"Who *is* the real girl?"

"I have a better question, Champ. Who's the real Punch?"

"I think I lost track of him somewhere."

"What happened to you? I mean, what really happened.. Forget about all those stories."

"Oh, you mean — what sort of awful crime did I commit? I wasn't a trapeze artist when I started out. I was in pictures, a dramatic actor. Damn good one, too. Then something happened. Styles changed, they said I was old-fashioned. I was 'out'. So I had to start all over again. I went back to doing what I did when I was just starting out. Hell of a lot harder now, though."

"I'd say so. Every season you break a different bone."

"It wouldn't be a season without it." He smiles into the mirror, then turns away, oblivious to the tiny package Pinky leaves on the makeup table.

❧❧❧

Working on the script dragged out every insecurity I ever had about my craft. At the same time, there were moments of exhilaration so high and dizzy, I couldn't wait to come to work in the morning. I took the script home with me at night, which I knew Sid didn't approve of, and bit down hard every time Prescott snatched it out of my hands.

If only I could hear what they were saying behind those walls. I had the sinking feeling Harold was fighting for my contribution, which could only mean the other two were against it. Prescott drew a huge red slash across the Pagliacci references, but Harold insisted they be restored. Then one day the office door was left open a little. This is what I made out:

"The audience just won't get it, Lloyd."

"Do you think they're idiots?"

"They're (*something-something*) customers, and we have to give them what they want."

"Have you ever heard the word (*something*)?"

"Look me in the eye and tell me you never thought about what the audience wanted. You practically invented the (*something*)."

"Yes, yes, I did. But did the movie-going public vote for (*something*)? The whole thing was forced on them."

"Yes, and what a (*something*) that turned out to be! Get with the (*something*), Lloyd, you're lagging behind."

"I am *not* lagging behind. I care about the quality of this picture."

"And I don't?"

They were two old lions in the same unhappy den. Meanwhile, I felt tremendous pressure to deliver something that would make everyone happy. But Prescott's scribbled comments were growing like vines across my typed pages.

Story synopsis:

Punch enters the tightrope contest in mask and harlequin costume and faces his worst fear. Because of his clown agility and past experience he manages to get across the tightrope, with a few flips and tricks that leave the audience gasping. To their embarrassment, everyone in the troupe discovers that the window-washing story is false and Punch really had been a gifted aerialist. But when Paloma realizes who it is, it backfires: she is furious at the deception and refuses to speak to him. (*Doesn't all this come too soon? Why not save it 'til the last scene? S. P.*)

Paloma is doing increasingly risky manoeuvres to gain audience approval, and begins to work without a net, with predictable results. She falls, Punch tries to get to her, Marco pushes him out of the way, he insists and Marco punches him in the mouth and carries Paloma away. (*Note: please don't tell me she dies in his arms! S. P.*)

Scene 39. Punch is wallowing in self-pity and singing Vesti la Giubba very badly in his dressing room.

The circus manager, Dan Patch, comes in and shakes his head with disgust.

"C'mon, Punch, you can do better than that."

"Maybe not. Maybe I lost my chance when I was young and falling out of the high chair."

"Listen, we were wrong about that. We all owe you an apology."

"But I won't get it."

"Only because everyone's embarrassed."

"*They're* embarrassed. I got punched in the mouth in front of everybody."

"We don't always get what we want, Champ."

"Do we *ever* get what we want?"

"Can you believe that what we do get is better for us?"

"No. That sounds like Sunday School."

"Anyway, you have two hours to pull yourself together before the 2:00 o'clock matinee. Unless you want to do a drunken clown routine."

"I'll see what I can do."

"What's this?" He picks up the little figurine. *(For God's sake! S. P.)*

"Don't touch that! Put it down."

"All right, I was only looking at it. Where did it come from?"

"I'm not sure. I think it's some kind of clown."

"Well, *this* clown had better get his motley on and get out there." *(What's a motley? Signed, The Audience. S. P.)*

"Sure, boss."

Two hours later, he wakes up, hung over, and groans. Punch has to put on his makeup and costume and go on, even with a bloody nose. *Vesti la Giubba* is playing on the radio in the background. *(Groannn! S. P.)* Pierrette knocks on his dressing-room door.

"Hi, Sis. What'd you think of the disaster?"

"You were brilliant, Punch. We all owe you an apology for being so cruel."

"Oh, it doesn't bother me. I prefer being a clown anyway."

"Do you?" *(Yes, he does! S. P.)*

He tries to ignore the question. "So who's the little fellow there? I think I know who gave him to me."

"It's Pulcinella. He's one of the classic clowns from the *commedia dell'arte* in Italy. *(Jesus, Jesus, Jesus! S. P.)* He's your namesake, Punch. You might say . . . "

"He's who I really am?" *(Note to S. P.: he says this with self-mocking irony. Harold can pull it off. M.A.)*

"I wouldn't presume to tell you, Punch. But you are an artist. I believe that you were once an actor, a great one."

"Not so great. I was mostly an extra or a bit player. I had to do all sorts of . . . odd jobs . . . "

"There's no shame in that. Actors have to survive any way they can."

"I only had one major role." He takes his glasses off for the first time and faces her. *(Lloyd take off his glasses? He'd sooner take off his nose! S.P.).*

She looks astonished, but doesn't say a word.

He nods.

"But everyone loved you in that movie. They said you showed so much promise. Punch, what are you doing here?"

"It didn't work out. There was an accident on the set — "

"Yes. I heard about it."

"It left some scars. Bad ones. The kind that need lots of makeup to cover them up." *(You had me up to this point, doll, but this is just TOO corny. Art imitates life? Please! S. P.)*

"Punch — I mean, Pulcinella — have you ever thought of retiring from the cirus, maybe directing or writing scripts?"

"It's got to happen sometime. Probably soon. My body is going to retire me, and then I'll have no choice. I'm getting too old for this, it's kid stuff. But I don't know what use the world has for a washed-up clown."

"You can work on that novel." *(Double-Jesus with a purple sidecar! S. P.)*

"*What?* How did you . . . "

"I hear lots of things. But mostly, I see them. I've seen you scribbling things on little pieces of paper, so you won't forget them."

"So either I'm crazy, or . . . "

"Or you aspire to write."

"But I never finish anything, kiddo. That's the problem. Then I'd have to send it out, and I'd rather keep the illusion going that I'm an undiscovered genius."

"Would you let me read it? I mean, as a favour."

"I guess." He looks confused. Then looks at her directly.

"Pierrette, I've heard you have a crush on me."

"News travels fast in the circus."

"If it's true, then please don't. I'm not worth it."

"Isn't that for me to decide?"

(Affecting a 'tough' voice): "But I always fall for dames I can't have. That's what everyone says. 'Dames'. Somehow I don't think you're a dame, Pierrette."

"What am I, then?"

"An artist. I've seen you work, and it's amazing. *You're* amazing."

"And you also are an artist. Then don't we belong together? I mean, as friends."

"Or more than friends?"

"Maybe." She smiles at him (as only Mariette Piercy can smile). "After all . . . anything can happen in the circus." (Music swells, credits, end.)

(*Okay, girlie, that's all well and good, but the audience needs to see them* kiss *at the end. None of this "friendship" stuff. It won't play. S. P.*)

～～～

The subject of the script was a touchy one. Though it was plain Harold felt I had vastly improved it from the awkward, cornball original, he was a little wary of all the "classical" references, fearing they would be too high-toned for his audience: "If I still have one," he said.

"Harold, stop saying that."

"My last picture lost money. That never happened to me before, and I can't afford to have it happen again."

"Is money that important?"

He looked at me, incredulous. "Of course it is. Losing money means you're on the skids. It's the end of your career."

I realized he was right: in this industry, movies were a product, and if they didn't sell they were about as useful as stale popcorn.

This feeling of doubt hung over the project. He read his lines with his usual skill, but I had the feeling they were "lines" to him, artificial in his mouth. He knew he wasn't making anyone laugh with this, and was afraid he was begging for sympathy, something he had always refused to do.

"I just don't see how I can play this Pagliaccio character. It isn't me." He sat on the edge of my desk, a little boy whose feet didn't quite touch the floor.

"But Harold, you already have."

"When?"

"Remember in *Girl Shy*, when Harold's manuscript is rejected and he feels like a failure — "

He looked away from me, as if lost in thought. "Yes. And he tries to cut his rich girl friend loose because he thinks he isn't good enough for her — "

"And he sneers at all the sweet times they had together, and laughs in ridicule — "

"Cruelly." His eyes were beginning to spark.

"Cruel to *her*, yes. But he's not really cruel — he's trying to be kind. And dying inside."

"And what about *The Freshman*? There's that scene after the dance."

"I remember, Harold. Everyone is making brutal fun of him, and he's trying to convince his girl that he doesn't care. And he laughs — "

"And laughs — "

"Then collapses in tears."

He looked doubtful. "I always wondered about that one. It seemed like a good idea at the time. Now it feels a bit too sentimental."

"But it's the best scene in the picture."

"Okay, I guess I've done some of that crying on the inside stuff. But make a promise to me right now: don't let the audience feel sorry for me."

"All right, I promise."

Prescott wasn't convinced the costuming and makeup would work, so Harold had to audition it for him and make a test. He had never done this before and secretly found it humiliating. For some reason, he allowed me to sit in (though I wondered if I had anything to contribute). When he was fully costumed and made up, Harold looked more like a harlequin from the *Commedia dell'Arte* than a down-at-heels clown from a small-town circus. In fact, he looked almost medieval, and something about it was a little disturbing.

I looked him up and down. His eyes were asking for my approval. But the face —

It was a classic mask of tragedy. Almost every Pagliaccio in history had been made up that way, but I had never thought it made sense.

"Come on, Muriel, there's something here you don't like."

I tried a tactful approach. "Harold, what do you think of the makeup?"

"Frankly, I think I could have done it better myself." I knew of his artistry with making up faces; it was one of his instinctive gifts.

"So how would you change it?"

"Oh, spit it out, Muriel. Tell me what you don't like."

"Well, if this is a clown who's 'laughing on the outside' — "

The light came on. He looked at himself in the mirror.

"Then it's the wrong face."

"Exactly."

"We need a smile. But not a jolly one."

"More — sinister?"

"Or just artificial. Painted on. As if he's hiding something." He grabbed a jar of goo and a towel, and began to get rid of his face.

Prescott came in and stopped dead in his tracks.

"Harold! What are you doing? We shoot the test in about two minutes."

"That should be long enough," he said cheerfully, treating him to a particularly dazzling smile.

❧ ❧ ❧

Harold's world was a strangely tilted Wonderland I would never get used to. He was gone for barely ten minutes, then backed into the room (a strange gesture for anyone else). When he turned around to reveal his new clown face, I felt a thrill run through me: he had painted on a new personality, a mask both classic and modern, designed along the lines of his own features, but with a tinge of exaggeration that brought out a slightly wicked quality I had never seen in him before.

Harold didn't have soft features; they were almost aquiline, from the long and somewhat pointed nose to the clean jawline to the high forehead. The curve of the smile with its bow-shaped lips was sensual as a satyr's, the eyes intense. But it was a clown face nevertheless: and how could we ever be afraid of such jollity, such crazy eagerness to please, no matter what the cost? This was yet another incarnation of the Glass Character, Harold at the Big Top, pushed down again and again, discouraged, despairing, until that magic moment when his never-say-die courage makes him leap to his feet and win the day. I was absorbing all this (and by his expression, he was obviously pleased) when he did a suprising thing.

"So, Muriel. It's your turn now."

"*My* turn?"

"Of course. Can I make you up? You have such a lovely face, I'm sure you'll make a very pretty clown."

In his long history of strange behaviour, this was the strangest thing yet. Here was this slightly menacing Pierrot with a paintbrush, asking to turn me into a different person. His artistry was obvious, but I was a little uneasy about the results.

And yet I succumbed, sitting in the makeup chair which he turned away from the mirror. I began blushing almost instantly as he pulled my hair back and tied it. He did it so gently, almost tenderly, that I thought of a mother fixing her child's hair. But as he fastened it, bending so near, I felt his breath on my bare neck, a long, warm exhale.

Most of the men I knew had strong tobacco breath, which I had always hated. But here was this pure, soft stream from inside him. He was Harold, the sweet man I had always loved, but at the same time changed, not Harold at all, a painted figure bizarrely transformed.

He laid down a base coat of cold cream. Next came the clown white, which he spread on with deft fingers (using both his left and right hand, which he had learned to use with surprising dexterity). Then he began to work on me: his concentrated expression was fascinating to watch, as this was an area of mastery for him, a talent that even predated his movie career. All the while he didn't talk, didn't even look in my eyes, but whistled tunelessly in the most irritating manner possible.

A clown making up a clown. It was an idea too strange to entertain. Costumed, disguised, masked in gleaming white, he was an illicit figure, a fox, a hunter with a bow and arrow . . . a lover climbing through my window? *I've seen too many Fairbanks movies*, I thought, but there was no telling this to my body, its needs unchanged since the rainstorm, the fiery kisses my skin remembered and still craved.

As he drew lines and smudged them, touched my lips with carmine, created false lashes and brows, I realized with a shock that he was literally turning me into someone else. Why did he need to have such power over me — or was it merely a game? Did he want to touch me, was this the only acceptable way he knew, or was this just another area in which Harold shone, in which he was the best because he knew he had to be?

But I could not analyze myself out of my feelings. This was *Harold*, not some idiot circus jester! I wanted to surge forward in my chair, blur and smudge the white perfection of his face with a penetrating kiss that would ruin the work he had done on himself, changing the curving lips to a smear of blood.

He carefully applied a beauty mark, looked me over one last time, smiled. "Ready, Muriel?"

"I suppose so."

"Behold!" He turned me around so rapidly my head spun.

My stomach dropped. Harold had found me out — had looked inside my cringeing, vulnerable, childish soul, found all my mooning romanticism and false courage, my hopeless ambition and desperate loneliness — and somehow, he had painted them all over my face.

My eyes looked huge in the dead-white skin, full of fear and a strange kind of awe. They were pretty eyes, almost doe-like, but not timid. They had the glassy, faceted look of a doll's eyes with blinking eyelids. He restrained himself from painting on a single tear, but the effect was the same. And yet, there was also a desperate hope in them, a willingness, even an eagerness to go back for yet another round of pain and rejection.

Ye gods, Muriel: and you thought Harold didn't understand you? The problem is, he understands you too well!

"Look at us. Are we a pair?" he exclaimed with an antic grin.

"I suppose so. But I look pretty serious for a clown."

"Sad clowns remind us how precious happiness is."

"And happy clowns?"

He looked a bit confused. "You're half a mile ahead of me, as usual, Muriel. I'm a simple soul, just offer what I have and go home. I leave the analysis to others."

The strange thing was, it was largely true. Harold was a roll-up-your-sleeves type, and not easily daunted. He didn't sit up all night agonizing about his art. He wanted to make people laugh because that was his job, and he was very good at it. Just lately he had been faltering, or he thought he was, and it terrified him, though he was not about to admit it. There was nothing for it but to try again. There had to be a way — a way that worked — it was just that he hadn't found out what it was.

തതത

Sitting in on a movie set was a fascinating experience for me, observing while not taking part. Harold was a strange, unpredictable mixture of intense concentration and flaring irritability: most of the time he worked hard and spoke softly, but things could erupt without warning. One day he began tugging at his costume: he was dressed in a rather ridiculous harlequin suit with a stiff ruffle around his neck. He scratched and pulled at the collar, then ripped it away and threw it on the floor.

"*Off!* I want this off. This won't make anybody laugh. It's pathetic. Wardrobe! Somebody get me a real costume. And don't make me look like some sort of Shakespearian idiot. Go to the circus, why don't you, and find out what a real clown looks like." He stalked out, a black cloud over his head. Everyone looked at each other with a "*what do we do now?*" expression.

I felt responsible. After all, I was the one who had started the Pagliaccio theme, trying to make a drearily clichéd script a little more intriguing. But I didn't know what else to do with such a sow's ear.

Harold wasn't really a clown, not in the classic sense. He was a slightly surreal version of a man, representing everyone and no one. The whiteface and stylized body language were clownish, but his dress and persona were not, which made him accessible to his audience. It was impossible to imagine his Glass Character in the circus, so I was left with the daunting task of reworking the script once again.

One day he approached me, shyly, as if he was struggling with what to say.

"Muriel. You know that aria . . . "

"*Vesti la Giubba*."

"Yes, that one. Well, I have to confess, Muriel, I'm not much on opera. But I want to know what the fellow is saying. I mean, obviously he's in agony over something — "

"He is."

I didn't know how to tell him that I had known far less about opera than he did, until Ray had given me a crash education. I managed to find an English translation of the words, but they were so awkward I had to rewrite them, to keep at least some of the flavour of the music.

"This is my version, remember."

"Good, good! I want your version. No snooty stuff."

"It isn't snooty, but you'd have to call it a very loose translation."

Vesti la Giubba

Dear God — must I go on stage tonight?
When I'm sick with anguish,
When I'm out of my mind
with jealousy and hate!
Still I must face them all —
Yes, try a little harder.
Act like a man!
But you are not a man.
You are Pagliaccio!

Put on your costume
And paint on the whiteface
And hide the anguish
That's tearing your soul apart
Grieve for your love,
Your darling Columbina

Put on the motley
That hides your jealous heart.
And if your rival stole her from your arms,
Your life has ended, though you still must play the fool

Laugh, Pagliaccio
Though your love has betrayed you —
Laugh, though revenge
Will stain your hands with their blood!

He read it in silence, read it again. Looked up and smiled. As usual, I saw several layers, or perhaps veils of emotion. He was obviously pleased. Wasn't he? He was just a tiny bit in awe (for writing was certainly not his forte). And at the bottom of it all, he looked afraid.

"You did well," he said.

"Thank you, Harold."

"I didn't know it was quite so . . . "

"Bloody?"

"That's the word. But I guess, if it's an opera . . . "

"But the picture isn't opera. It's just . . . "

"*The Circus Picture*. We'll have to get a decent title for the thing. They're threatening to call it *Laugh, Clown, Laugh*."

"That's dreadful. I'll try to think of something else."

One morning I came on set with a few new pages, desperately rewritten the night before, and knocked on Harold's dressing room door.

Inside, I heard something.

Music.

I knocked again. "It's Muriel."

"Come on in. I need you to help me."

I stepped into a bizarre scenario. Harold was kneeling on the floor, his head pressed to the speaker of a massive cabinet record player.

A tenor was singing an aria: it was *Vesti la Giubba*. The recording was old and a bit distorted, but Caruso's heroic tones could not be obliterated by time.

When it finished, Harold methodically removed the record from the spindle and replaced it with another one.

"Can't pronounce this one. Sounds like giggly — "

"It's Gigli." Harold listened again, his concentration like a hum, as the tenor wrung pathos out of every note. Then Martinelli. Then . . .

"This is my favourite," Harold said. It was the first time he had looked up at me. He looked fascinated and eager, like an eight-year-old boy studying frogs.

Lauritz Melchior did violence to the piece, while Harold pressed his eardrum to the blaring speaker.

"I think I understand this now, Muriel. Everybody sees Pagliaccio as feeling sorry for himself, feeling hard-done-by or swearing vengeance. But there's so much more to it than that. He's the consummate professional. He'll go on no matter what, even if his heart is breaking. He has total commitment to his craft."

I had never heard that interpretation before, but it made sense to Harold, so I would try to use it. Wardrobe came up with a different costume, less classical, more clownish, and adjusted his makeup to something slightly more natural. But he had never done anything really outlandish to his face before, and wondered if his audience would know him.

"You're a clown. You're *supposed* to be in disguise. But people will know it's Harold Lloyd under all that makeup." I immediately wondered if I had spoken out of turn.

"Really." He looked at me with that slightly disquieting, penetrating expression. He didn't wear his razor intelligence on his sleeve, but it peeped out periodically and could be a little unsettling.

In the end, he won, or the glasses did. They were as much a part of his face as his eyes or his mouth. And they would have looked ridiculous on any other man, but not on Harold Lloyd. He had made his crippled hand work for fifteen years, hiding it in plain sight. And with the same determination and skill, he would sell the audience on the world's first clown with glasses.

∾∾∾

After two months of sweating hard work under broiling lights, endless rewriting and reshooting, adjusting costumes and makeup (which slowly evolved towards the frizzy hair and painted-on smiles of traditional Big Top clowns) and Paragon negotiating a higher salary for Mariette Piercy, the time came for the preview.

Previews were torture for actors and directors, who sat in the back row and sweated while the test audience in some anonymous picture palace reacted, or didn't react, to the movie. Then they filled out detailed questionnaires which were often painfully revealing. Sure-fire gags could fall completely flat, while relatively minor bits drew shrieks of laughter and even applause.

Harold strolled into the office the next day, his hands in his pockets, his face unreadable. He sat on the corner of my desk and leaned forward.

"Muriel."

"Oh Harold, wasn't that exciting last night?"

"Of course it was." This wasn't what I had hoped to hear from him. It was his let-her-down- gently voice.

"What was wrong with it, then?"

"Muriel, I'd never use a word like 'wrong'. It's a question of — "

"Of what?" I knew I sounded defensive.

"Of the audience not being familiar with it. Listen, I'm the first to say that more people should go to the opera — "

"*Should*"? This couldn't be a good thing. "So what's the problem? Is it over their heads?" I meant it as sarcasm.

"I'm afraid so." I caught my breath in shock. "Sterling and I have been talking it over. It looks like we're going to have to remove the references to Pagliaccio."

"Which ones?"

He looked at the ceiling, struggling for words. "All of them. It has to be one way or the other."

Scores of pages of dialogue, hammered out laboriously for months, blew up into the air and fluttered out the window.

"Why, Harold?"

"You were there. Nobody laughed. Or not enough. The picture somehow turned into a drama, Muriel, and I'm not a dramatic actor. Or at least, that's not what people expect of me."

"But it's a romance!"

"Yes, but . . . listen, when I started making pictures, I had to find my place, something that hadn't been done before. So we came up with a new thing. Romantic comedy. Yes, it has a romance *in* it, but the really important thing is the comedy."

"But can't you — I mean — branch out in a new direction?" I looked at his middle-aged face, the face that was as recognizable as Chaplin's all over the world, and realized that such a thing was not possible.

"Oh, you'll still get a writing credit, sweetheart." The phony endearment infuriated me. "You deserve to be paid for all that effort."

"So that means the picture is — "

"Pretty much the way it was at the beginning. We'll have to reshoot a lot of it. Sterling has found a new writer — no disrespect to you, Muriel, this was your first script and you did splendidly, but he needs someone with more experience."

Someone Prescott can manipulate and bend to his will?

"And Mariette, well . . . Mariette is Mariette, and she insists on more lines. And she's above the title now. Either that, or she's threatened to walk. But listen, Muriel, I've had to make changes like this with practically every picture I've ever made! It's not such a bad thing."

"It isn't?"

"No, not if it makes it funnier."

"They are NOT calling it *Top This*!"

"No, of course not. That's the bad title to end all bad titles. But Sterling insists that *A Fool for Love* is too romantic, and *Laugh, Clown, Laugh* is too melodramatic. We think we're going to call it *Big Top*."

He beamed at me. I wanted to punch him in the mouth.

Since I had no choice, I went to the wretched premiere, though at least this time I bought my own gown, making sure it was a stunner. I saw Harold in full evening dress, a headspinning sight. Never was a man more born to wear a tux. Mildred Davis, a diminutive porcelain doll, hung on to his arm, mermaid-like in a close-fitting designer gown. But I saw them only from a roped-off distance, the same as the rest of the crowd.

For emotional support and protection I went with Shirley, who kept up a hilarious and morale-boosting running commentary. During particularly funny or touching moments, she'd nudge me and whisper in my ear, "That's your stuff, right?"

But it wasn't true. Little or no dialogue remained from my amended script. They had indeed started all over again, except for some of Pinky's more sardonic quips.

But when the moment came that I had lived for, my heart dropped into my shoes. My name wasn't in the credits. Only Joseph R. Simpson and Wallace Ford were listed as writers.

That meant I couldn't even put this fiasco on my resumé.

Harold explained (his face tellingly red) that of course I'd be paid for my contribution, but since it wasn't used in the picture . . .

So I was demoted to a glorified receptionist again. I told Sid I was sick, got home just in time to burst into sobs, drank two shots of brandy, threw up, and spent the rest of the day in bed.

It seemed to be my fate that success would remain just beyond the tips of my fingers. I went on working at Paragon, prudently banking my modest fee for being a "script consultant" on Big Top. I was later to learn that women earned about a third the rate of male screenwriters, a fact that went unquestioned for decades.

I told myself for the millionth time to forget Harold. And for the most part, I was able to push him to one side, except for those rare, unannounced times when he would pop in, beaming at me as he walked briskly past my desk to Prescott's office. He didn't stop to talk. Months would go by, the wound would start to heal over — then he would appear again, with that silly comic grin that made me want to smack him.

On a particularly dismal day, when my morale was dragging and my body felt heavy as lead, the phone on my desk rang.

A casual friend from my speakeasy days told me that Shirley had had a heart attack and fallen dead on the floor at Chez Louise.

The fact of it wouldn't sink in, and I kept asking over and over again, who *is* this, why are you telling me this, why would you make up such a cruel lie? Then someone else came on the phone, and everything sank. It was Frankie, and he said in a gentle voice I had never heard him use before, "Muriel, I hate to tell you this, but I'm afraid it's true."

When I hung up the phone, there was an odd whistling noise in my ears. Everything turned slightly grey, as if I were looking through a fine screen. I stood up suddenly, stumbled forward, and dropped straight down.

I could hear shrieks, then nothing. Then, the oddest sensation of all: I felt as if someone were carrying me. I had not experienced that feeling since I was a baby, and it was very strange, but comforting. I was being gently laid down, and something was pulled over me. I heard murmuring. I felt something cool pressed to my forehead.

I opened my eyes, and looked deep into Harold's face.

Years later, when Harold was criticized for being too boyish, too extravagant, too competitive, too shallow, too exuberant, and any number of other too's, I wanted to scream at them: *you did not see him as I did.* You did not see him leaning over you, his face so close you could feel the heat of his skin, the air soft with his presence. On his face was anxious, inscrutable tenderness I had never seen before.

"Muriel, don't sit up, you hit your head quite badly and it's bleeding. You're going to need some stitches. I've called a doctor."

"What happened? Did I — "

"You went down like someone had cut your strings."

Then I remembered, and an involuntary moan escaped me.

"What happened, dear heart?"

"Shirley had a heart attack. She's dead."

"I'm so sorry. I know how much she meant to you."

"She saved my *life!* I might have gone to jail except for her. When I went through the divorce, she fed me and clothed me and put a roof over my head. She was *everything* to me!"

To my utter humiliation, I began to sob uncontrollably, as I couldn't do when I lost sweet Arlene. Then it got worse. I began to scream and scream. I felt hands holding me down as I thrashed. A doctor and a nurse suddenly appeared out of nowhere, the doctor holding a syringe.

I had been here before. The cold dead walls. I would not go back. *Could* not.

∾∾∾

When I opened my eyes, I experienced the surreal sight of Harold perched on the side of my bed. For a moment I wondered if I had died. This was not the way I had dreamed of Harold in my bedroom, but it was still remarkable.

"Say, she's awake! How's your head, kiddo?"

"Better." It hurt like hell, excruciating red-hot needles of pain accompanied by a dull thudding ache. My hand went up to touch the bandage, covering an unknown number of stitches.

"Listen, Muriel, I've arranged for a private nurse to stay with you. And I want you to take at least a month off work, more if you need it."

"Oh, that's ridiculous, Harold."

"No it's not. You have a concussion. You know what can happen with those."

"No, not really."

"Your brain can bleed. We have to watch you carefully over the next few days. And there's something else."

I couldn't imagine what.

"Your emotional state is — well, Muriel, to tell you the truth they wanted to put you in a different ward, but I told them you were in severe shock due to your friend's death and that we would look after you privately."

"A different ward."

"Yes. And I didn't think you'd want that."

"Thank you, Harold. No, I wouldn't have."

"But I wanted to make sure you're all right."

It was only much later that I found out I had been thrashing around so violently that they were about to commit me. Harold had held my wrists tightly so I wouldn't hurt myself, but the sight must have been alarming to everyone in the office.

"It was too much for you, Muriel."

"What?"

"Everything that happened to you. You just need a good long rest."

When the fog began to clear, I was shocked and humiliated to realize that there had never been a nurse and a doctor with a syringe. My mind had dredged up that particular horror from a sealed tomb of memory, my father's threat of "putting me away" when I was about to expose his savagery to the world.

"The nurse will be here in an hour. Please accept this help, Muriel. I think we both agree it's better than the alternative."

Which meant he had to leave. I ached for him to stay, to sleep beside me. I wanted his skin next to my skin, touching me all the way down. I knew he would make love to me; one could hardly expect a man like Harold to abstain.

Drug-addled, I could see something like a halo around him, a bright nimbus of warmth.

"There's so much beauty in you." I dared to touch his face, on the right side where the horrible burns had healed.

"Oh Muriel, I'm not beautiful. I'm very ordinary. I wish you could see that. I'm just a fellow from Pawnee County who made good. It was all hard work, not magic. I used to try to tell you, but it didn't sink in. I've done plenty that I'm not proud of. It would shock you if you knew. I'd hoped you would have grown out of this infatuation by now. I don't think it's good for you."

"It's *not* infatuation! I love you, Harold. I've loved you since I was a little girl and saw you on the screen. And I still love you. I love you *now*, this minute. I'd sacrifice my life for you."

"Muriel, I . . . " He had no idea what to say to this outburst of embarrassing melodrama. He did not want to hurt me when I was this fragile. He probably knew I was half out of my mind with morphine, sedatives and shock, the equivalent of gulping down four Scotches in a row.

"Hold me," I pleaded, sitting up and locking my arms around his neck. He did not have much choice but to hold me, but he did it carefully, as if I was a stranger.

"Let's not make a mistake." It was that low voice of his that meant dangerous emotions had been stirred.

"I *want* to make a mistake. I've been so careful all my life, and look where it got me. I watched my marriage die, I watched my baby die . . . "

"Oh, no, Muriel." It was the first time I had mentioned it to him, and his look of shocked, wide-open compassion set off another wave of sobs. The only way he could calm me was to hold me very tightly.

This was not the way I had envisioned intimacy between us, one of us in raw, intolerable pain, the other anxious and bewildered. Life pushed things on us, ugly things, and twisted our expectations, presenting us with bizarre travesties of our dreams which we had no choice but to accept.

To my amazement, he phoned and cancelled the nurse for the night, telling her he would keep watch. And he did. If he hadn't, I might have given up. Memories did not bubble up, they shot up under pressure as from a geyser. All of them were riddled with ugliness and despair. Once more I relived being beaten with the buckle end of my father's belt, being called a slut and a whore. I remembered running away, not so much ambitious as terrified, trying to fulfill a dream that now seemed completely hopeless.

I remembered the horror of Alice's death, and the responsibility and guilt I felt which would never leave me. The memory of Arlene in her tiny casket was so unbearable I had to push it away. I tried to drown the more intolerable aspects of the pain in Harold's miraculous presence. Still under the influence of heavy medication, I babbled and raved, no doubt disgracefully. Harold didn't say a word. At one point I touched his face, and it was shining wet.

"Muriel, you're a grown woman. If we keep on like this, you know what will happen. And I don't want to take advantage of you, especially not now. It wouldn't be right."

There was always something that "wasn't right", something that put a barrier between us, either my age, or his wife, or my vulnerability and situation.

"I know you're right, Harold. It's just that I . . . "

"You're in shock, dear. You don't really know what you're saying."

"I mean what I say! Don't you believe me?"

"We can't always get what we want."

"Do we *ever* get what we want?"

"Can you believe that what we do get is better for us?"

"No. That sounds like Sunday School." I couldn't remember if I had heard those words before, then realized with a shock that I had written them.

"Then how about this. What we get is what we get. But in times when we just can't bear it, we need other people to help us. Sometimes we give, and sometimes we receive. And it all works out in the end. Does that make sense to you?"

It sounded familiar, like a philosophy the Glass Character would follow. "When did you come up with that?"

"I think it was after the accident."

"Make love to me, Harold. I don't care what happens."

"No."

"*Goddamn* you!"

"You may never thank me for this, but it's the only thing that's right. Now try to get some sleep."

∞∞∞

I woke with no sense of time, and only a vague idea of place. I felt the tattered old crazy quilt on the bed, the one my mother had made for me years ago. I must be in my apartment. But what was that sickening throb on the side of my head?

I tried to sit up, then lay back in a hurry when nausea shot up my throat. Light splintered through my eyelids, and I was reminded of that old Irish term for a hangover: "whips and jingles". Broken shards of memory festered in my mind like fragments of glass.

I had an absurd, unbelievable memory of Harold in my bedroom, of Harold lying on my bed beside me. Perhaps I really had gone crazy. If any of it had actually happened, it would kill me with humiliation and shame.

"Muriel!" My bedroom door opened, and a cheerful face popped in. It was absolutely surreal: Harold was standing there with my baking apron on. A strong waft of coffee made me nauseated. "Would you like some eggs?"

"Oh, I don't think I can . . . "

"Then how about some pancakes. I make very good pancakes."

I tried to picture him in his forty-four-room mansion, the one with twenty-six bathrooms and two dozen staff, puttering around in the kitchen making pancakes.

"Harold, are you always this relentlessly cheerful?"

"Just about. Say, how's the head?" He came over to take a look. No one would ever know that only a few hours ago I had been in his arms, hysterical, suicidal, and ready to sacrifice myself to him completely.

"It's wretched, thanks."

"It's going to take some time to heal. And I want you to relax completely and let the nurse take care of you."

I don't want the nurse, I thought to myself. *I want you.*

Then the horrible truth forced its way in.

"Shirley . . . "

"Her memorial isn't till next week. You need total bed rest. You know, I had to fight to keep you out of the hospital."

"The psycho ward, you mean."

"I never would have allowed them to put you in a place like that, kiddo. No, it was a sanitorium, a very reputable one. But I still thought you would rather recover here at home."

Then, with a sudden shock (would they ever end?), I realized I was wearing my nightgown.

What had happened to my clothing?

It could only mean one thing. At some point, he must have undressed me.

He read my thoughts. "Don't worry, Muriel. You weren't even conscious, just dead on your feet."

Fate, God, kismet, bad luck, whatever the force was, it always insisted on ripping us apart just as we were about to come together. It was about as bearable as having all your hair torn out by the roots.

I knew it was hopeless. I had been naked as a little girl's doll in his hands, and he *still* hadn't made love to me. It was that wretched decency of his, something that didn't even go across the board, since I knew it could easily be breached for a naughty night with a chorus girl.

He touched my face. "I'll just leave you alone for a while, all right, Muriel? Bless your heart. I'll be right here."

He closed the door. In broad daylight, I lay in an utterly lonely twilight which seemed worse than death.

Larger than Life

Though it looked as if I would never rise again, something surprising happened after my breakdown: some sort of invisible wings caught an updraft, and I was lifted to sanity and health again. My small cadre of friends formed a tight circle around me, a nest to incubate the next phase of my life. I was undescribably moved, as I had never known people to care for me this deeply. What had I done to deserve such devotion?

My life and my work had fallen into a pattern which I was trying hard to accept: great leaps forward, then inexorable dragging pulls back to the beginning again. Or so it seemed. I didn't have Shirley to tell me I was selling myself short, not playing the cards I had been dealt (or stolen!) in the movie industry. But in spite of myself and my fear (and my weakness, and my perceived inadequacy), I kept on working.

Leaping from project to project, the writing was my only constant: I plugged away at novels and plays, and sold several screenplays (some of which were actually filmed!) to small studios. Watching them was hilarious, and a few times I had to leave the theatre during a dark drama to go into the ladies' room and laugh. Even in the darkest melodrama, the leading men they cast all seemed to look like Eddie Cantor.

When I landed a small speaking part in a Fred Astaire and Ginger Rogers movie, I thought my ship had finally come in. Just being on the set was lovely: the buzz, the bustle, the floaty costumes, directors yelling orders, stampedes of extras . . . I was allowed to watch rehearsals some days, and was astounded. Astaire seemed to have the same plugging, almost blinkered single-mindedness as . . . well, as someone else I knew. He drilled and drilled and drilled, so that every step would be perfect. Ginger gamely kept up, his charisma and power slowly pulling her into synch with his every move. Sometimes bits of her dresses, ostrich feathers or glass beads or sequins, came loose and drifted down as delicately as spring rain, so that the crew's footsteps crunched on the floor of the set.

When it was time for a take, it all melted together: they were thistledown, buoyed up by charm and grace and some other quality that doesn't have a name. By this time they were so well-rehearsed they didn't need a lot of retakes. Beaming at each other, they exuded a weightless joy, then when the cameras stopped they both looked down, hoping the sweat would somehow miss their costumes.

The days were long, but no one complained because if they did, Astaire would wither them with a look. I don't think he was unkind: perhaps just unnaturally talented, almost punished by his gift. His burden was such that no one else could ever quite keep up. He knew this, and knew that they could only try their best.

One day after an exhausting, hard pull, I noticed Ginger's face fell when she received no praise from him after mastering a particularly difficult step. He swept right past her, the implication being that if you weren't criticized, you were doing all right and didn't need reassurance. She made a mask of her face, pulled off her extravagant high heels and tossed them in a corner. I had the insane idea of stealing them, but suppressed it. When I walked past them on my way out, I saw they were stained with her blood.

As if Astaire and Rogers had worked some sort of mysterious charm, opportunities began to drop into my lap: somehow I found myself managing a restaurant, and while it wasn't Chez Louise, it provided steady work and decent pay while I toiled away at my scripts. Had I somehow inherited this position in the restaurant business from my mentor? How much had she told people? I would never know. Shirley had ways of quietly sowing seeds that blossomed later in all sorts of unexpected ways.

Men made overtures, and sometimes I was tempted. I dated a few, and acted interested, or at least interested enough to disguise my abject boredom. I studiously avoided actors. I did not see Harold; God had taken him out of my path, apparently, perhaps for good. No doubt he was still seducing the world, pursuing his thousand-and-one interests with an intensity that sometimes bordered on the frantic.

The few movies he did in the '30s were neither good nor bad. I tried not to see them, but some deplorable magnetic force pulled me into the theatre every time. I so wanted to like them. I wondered what had happened to him, but who could sustain something so remarkable? Chaplin never equalled the surreal charm of his Little Tramp, and recoiled from sound until well into the '30s. Keaton had to resort to low-budget educational films to keep working. Harold plugged on, though he must have wondered where his popularity had gone.

My favourite aspect of being so connected to the world of entertainment was rediscovering old friends. This could come at the strangest times and in the most unexpected places. I was standing in line to see The Movie, the one everyone had babbled about for literally years. It was 1939, an unprecedented year for blockbusters, but this one was the Ultimate, dubbed the greatest movie ever made (by the filmmakers).

As I stood there impatiently, smoking too many cigarettes (a dirty habit I had finally caved in to), I heard women up and down the line buzzing about the picture.

"Well, at least they got the leading man right."

"You're so right! Nobody else is handsome enough, even though he doesn't have a Southern accent."

"Bully for him. Leslie Howard talks like an Englishman!"

"Well, wait until we get a load of that actress. She's going to sound more English than Lawrence Olivier!"

"And nobody even knows who she is!"

They were soon going to know who she was. But when I was on the point of walking away from the endless line, I heard a booming voice, saw a man near the head of the line beckoning to me.

I threw my cigarette away and ran to him. In a bizarre re-enactment from one of Harold's movies (I think it was *Never Weaken*), I jumped up into his arms like a kitten.

Roy Brooks!

Not only did I get to cut to the head of the line. Roy knew more about this picture than almost anybody, with an insider's knowledge. We tried to keep it quiet, but several times audience members hissed at us as he whispered some bits of delectable gossip.

When Vivien Leigh began to flirt with the Tarleton twins, Roy buzzed, "Vivien spent all her weekends on the shoot with Larry."

"Larry?"

"You know. Sir Lawrence Olivier, her lover. They're both married to other people."

(*"Shhhhhhhhhh!"*)

"They're never!"

"Oh yes they are. And it's just boom-ba-da, boom-ba-da —"
(*"Shut up!"*)

Though the picture was touted as the greatest historical romance of all time, to Roy and me it was nothing short of the funniest romantic comedy we had ever seen.

I was delighted to re-connect with Roy, and we quickly fell into our old routine of malt shops and easy banter. But even this rich friendship wasn't quite enough. Then when I least expected it, someone phoned me, someone I didn't even know. This alarmed me: where had he found my number? He wanted to talk to me about a script. This was a bad idea, an extremely bad idea. For some reason, I agreed to meet him.

My first impression of Michael was of a teddy bear that has been a little overstuffed, so that the stuffing is just fuzzing out a bit on the sides. Not fat, mind. Not slovenly. Just. . . the sort of man you'd want to hold. He had a brown sweater on, and a slow smile, and yes, he smelled good, but he had a completely different smell from what's-his-name: aromatic pipe tobacco mixed with new wood.

And we did talk scripts. He was a screenwriter too (and at a certain point I suddenly recognized his name), a musician (shades of Danny!), and an accountant, and all sorts of other things. He was also quite wealthy from investments, having successfully navigated the Crash. I don't know why I didn't think he was lying through his teeth.

"I don't know if I trust musicians." I was feeling a little less intimidated after several glasses of good wine and was beginning to gently flirt.

"Had any bad experiences with them?"

"Have I! One of them went to jail for embezzlement."

"Not Danny Hoolihan."

My eyes flew open.

"Where on earth did you get my number?"

"Oh, an old boss of yours — "

"*Don Bishop* gave you my number?"

"For strictly professional reasons."

"So you know about all that mess with Danny? Whatever happened to him?"

"He's doing five to ten for bigamy. Yes, you heard me right! Has a wife on either coast, and they didn't know about each other. What a catfight in court."

"How do you know about all this?"

"Told you, I'm a drummer. You don't believe me, do you?"

"I want to believe you, Michael, but this town is an awful place for confidence men and crooks. As witness Danny."

"I assure you I'm harmless."

"Completely?"

"That depends. Hey, this sounds like a very bad script!" We both laughed.

Gently, we came together, mostly because I loved talking to him: when I was with him, I felt like my best self. I was completely comfortable, and confident I wasn't making a total fool of myself. I kept telling myself it was just a good friendship; he hadn't pressed anything physical, but as I was getting ready for a date with him, looking in the mirror at a dress that had definite pizzazz (if not razz-ma-tazz), I suddenly wanted to stamp my foot.

Why *didn't* he kiss me at the end of these dates? Was I so repulsive to him? Had he been married before? He was at least eight years older than me. What did I really know about him?

And was it possible that he was entirely too good for me?

It's sad but true that no one can do a background check on a boyfriend (unless one wants to hire a private detective). One evening he took me to a small but achingly romantic place, with a spectacular lookout that gleamed and twinkled. I had that precarious feeling, that sense that I would not be able to help myself much longer.

"Muriel."

"My real name is Jane."

"Yes, I know."

"Michael! Have you set a detective on me?"

"It doesn't matter. I wanted to know everything I could find out about you before I let myself fall in love with you."

This is the sort of thing men don't say, and it almost knocked me out of my chair.

"Michael, don't — "

"It's too late, Muriel."

My mind spun crazily: too late for what? Too late for falling in love with me?

"How do you feel about me? Tell me honestly. How do you feel when you're with me?" His directness shocked me.

"I feel . . . oh, Michael." Tears flooded my eyes. I felt like an idiot. "I just feel completely accepted. I feel like I can be who I really am. I feel . . . (I had to spit it out before it was too late) beautiful."

"So I'm just reflecting back the real Muriel. The real *Jane*."

"I don't know. I've had lousy judgement in men up to now. I suppose you know everything about the fiasco with Harold Lloyd."

"Harold Lloyd. You know *Harold Lloyd?*" His incredulous expression tipped me into slightly hysterical laughter.

"I was another person then. Starstruck."

"You were just a kid."

"Then you must know everything about the scandal, the murder — "

"None of that matters, Muriel." His warm eyes wore a new expression that I recognized. I was seized with a feeling so powerful, I didn't even try to analyze it. Terrified at my lack of sophistication, I let him lead me, and when I opened the door of my apartment and led him across the threshold, I knew there was no going back.

∽∽∽

The term "late bloomer" seems to have been made for me: both happiness and success very slowly began to accelerate after Michael and I were married. When I sold my first novel I was ecstatic, and when Sterling Prescott (of all people!) offered to adapt it into a movie, I wondered if I had beaten the curse on my life at last. And when he asked Michael and I to adapt it, I thought: my cup runneth over. I prayed Harold Lloyd wouldn't be cast in it — and he wasn't — which was a good thing, because I was afraid my Lloydsickness would return after all these years.

I was thirty-nine when I became pregnant again, and everyone I knew held their breath. It wasn't a good time: we had given up on that particular dream a long time ago. At that time people spoke of "mongoloid" babies who were retarded and had to be institutionalized (for a retarded baby was a judgement on the mother and simply couldn't be seen in public).

When Anna Louise Anderson was born, she was perfect, and my heart was ready to burst with gratitude. All the riches and treasures that had been held back from me were spilling into my lap, and though I still felt bewilderment, Michael had taught me to open my heart and receive.

But lest you think my irrational love for Harold had completely dissipated with the years, be aware that I still felt a little start every time I saw his picture in a magazine. Even after his supposed retirement, he seemed to be as driven as ever, charging through life as if he were on a perpetual fox hunt.

One of the most frustrating aspects of this situation was that I never got to see the movies from his glory days. He kept a tight hold on them, no doubt fearing they would be adulterated like too many of the best classic comedies, with the result that no one got to see them at all.

But Lloydsickness is a malady that has no cure. One day Michael was rummaging around the apartment looking for something, probably a script, while Anna (known to her friends as Anniekins) toddled all over the living room. He strode into my office and began to rifle through dog-eared scripts.

"Hey! Get your hands off that stuff, it's private property."

"Wait a minute. What's this?"

"Give that back!"

He had unearthed my most humiliating secret. It was an old, yellowed scrapbook full of pictures of Harold that I had cut from magazines, some from the days before I first went to seek my fortune.

"Oh Michael. You creep. You found me out."

He looked at the most recent entry.

"Well, what do you know. This is from last week."

"No it's not! Give me that." I was flushed and ashamed.

"Hey, Janie, don't be upset. Do you know how much those pictures are worth?"

"Yes. They're irreplaceable. To me."

The magazine photos were all I had. I knew I would never see him again, not even on that new magic box which threatened to overwhelm the entertainment industry: television. His memory began to recede even as my life moved forward. But I never threw the scrapbook away.

In the interim, a modest Harold Lloyd revival had begun. A new wave of film buffs emerged, eager to pry open the vault and see those remarkable films for the first time in several decades. Harold was invited as a special guest to silent film festivals and presented with lifetime achievement awards, receiving them with self-deprecating speeches that belied his fierce pride. When asked to comment on the resurgence of his masterpieces, he shrugged. "My pictures are so old, they're new."

So it delighted me to read in *Photoplay* that he was preparing a compilation of his best screen moments for his fans (who after forty years of waiting must have either become very impatient, or died). After all the years apart, after the frustrated passion, the anguish, the moments of exhilaration, the decades of living and experiencing and rising and falling, what would it be like to see him on-screen again?

I had kept track of his post-picture life in my usual obsessive manner, observing with some amusement his myriad hobbies and interests, the thousands of three-dimensional photos he had taken of beautiful nude women, the abstract painting which kept him up all night, the fantastically-expensive antique cars, the dogs (over eighty Great Danes at one point), the movie marathons in which he raced from one theatre to another, the massive room-filling Christmas tree (left standing all year) which was said to have 20,000 ornaments. Not hundreds for Harold, but thousands. His motto seemed to be: more, more, *more!*

I had read severe criticisms of his larger-than-life way of living in the massive and somewhat run-down estate that reminded some journalists of the echoing mansion in *Citizen Kane*. The movie articles were reports of a self-absorbed eccentric who rode his hobbies to death, dropped them, then went on to something else, much like a bright but easily distracted little boy. And he *was* a boy: a boy genius, much like Orson Welles, who was quoted in an article in *Photoplay* as saying, "Someday he'll get his proper place — which is very high. I got to know Lloyd through magic — we were both members of the same magical fraternity. What a lovely man!"

The theatre was packed, to my satisfaction, not just with older people but college students, adolescents and children. I was profoundly grateful to find that Harold's compilation was far superior to anything I had seen before: no cow-bells or whistles, appropriate music, no narration whatsoever, and decent-length, coherent excerpts rather than clips of only a few seconds. The laughter rose and fell, but when people weren't laughing, I could feel them enjoying and appreciating, as I did.

Forty years later, it was delightful to see the mad race to the church from *Girl Shy*, the crazy tooth-pulling scene with the giant in *Why Worry*, and the manic final football game from *The Freshman*, in which Harold the underdog miraculously saves the day. Interestingly, though it was referred to at the beginning, the clockface scene was not particularly emphasized. In this, Harold was communicating with his audience, as if to say, "Listen, we know *Safety Last!* is the picture everyone remembers me for. But what about these? They're every bit as memorable."

I wanted to see *Harold Lloyd's World of Comedy* again, and vowed to get in one more viewing before it left town, but as it ended (provoking a small groan from the audience, who obviously wanted more), an officious-looking man appeared on the stage at the front of the theatre (for this was one of those old picture palaces which had once doubled as a vaudeville house).

"Ladies and gentleman. We hope you have enjoyed this presentation of excerpts from Harold Lloyd's classic comedies. I'd like to announce that we have a special treat for you tonight." Great, I thought, a cheesy photo of Harold holding a football or hanging off a clock.

"As you leave the theatre, you will be presented with a complementary photograph from one of Mr. Lloyd's classic films. But that's not all. Tonight you will experience a rare opportunity: Harold Lloyd has honoured us with his presence tonight, and will be signing autographs in the lobby." This inspired an audible gasp, and a burst of applause. And a crazy leap in my heart that made me shake my head.

The scene was surreal, but somehow congruent with all that had come before. The cheesy photos weren't cheesy at all — in fact, they were beautiful — and we had a choice: a matinee-idol closeup from the peak of his magnificence in 1923, a frantically funny pose from *The Freshman*, the inevitable clockface from *Safety Last!*, and — surprisingly — the "clinch" from *Why Worry?*, the only really passionate kiss in his whole career, in which he practically lifted Jobyna Ralston off her feet.

I didn't need to decide which one to take (and I noticed several people taking more than one). The lineup was a dense smother of people — I knew this would make him happy — but since he spoke individually to each person, the wait was interminable. I wasn't going to say anything to him, to test whether he remembered me. But how could he recognize the slip of a girl I had once been in a woman of over fifty, her waist thickening, her hair greying, and crinkles around her eyes?

I could see from a distance how splendid he was at nearly seventy. There was something about him that defied normal ageing, the line of his jaw, the fine eyes, the smile like a sudden illuminating flashbulb. He was not "still" good-looking or "still" charismatic or "still" anything. That was for museum pieces. This man would be splendid until he died. The most complicated man I had ever known, the most difficult, the most enthralling, heart-tugging, paradoxical . . . but here it was nearly my turn.

In spite of what most people seem to think (and what I used to think, when I was younger), being in your fifties does not exclude you from longing and desire. As I stood waiting in that interminable line, I was somewhat taken aback to realize I was not just excited, but aroused. Obviously part of me had never grown up. Perhaps I would always be a Wendy to his Peter Pan.

And there he was. Looking up. Looking up at *me*.

He looked.

And something clicked.

"Muriel."

He held out his hand. His right hand, the deeply damaged one that had miraculously served him for so long. I knew he did not do this for everyone, that it was a sign of closeness, of trust. I held it gently in both my hands. I had promised myself not to cry, but tears rushed into my eyes as I smiled at him.

"Remember what Hal Roach used to call you?"

"The little girl who smiled while she was crying."

"You haven't changed."

He was still the master of the gracious lie.

"Oh, Harold, you haven't either. You're the same old charmer."

"Well, I guess the 'old' part is accurate. Oh Muriel, have dinner with me tonight, there's so much to talk about."

"I don't think . . . look, I'm holding up the line."

But time had stopped. I still felt the same familiar yearning, and wanted to say yes so badly. I wondered what Michael would think. It was absurd, really — this wasn't an affair, just a couple of old friends reminiscing. But there seemed to be something illicit about it. Maybe it was that slightly bedroomy look in his eyes, still in evidence after all these years.

"The line can wait a little longer. Muriel, I'm so proud of you! Everybody knows about you now. Four novels, and one of them made into a movie. You should've got that screenwriting Oscar you were up for, but I know you'll get it next time. Oh, how I wish I were fifty years younger!"

"I thought you were." As usual, I couldn't say what I really felt.

"I'll be at the Waldorf at nine o'clock tonight. I'd love it if you'd join me. Do whatever you decide, but I'll be there."

I wasn't going to do it. Absurdly, I hadn't told Michael about the whole thing, as if I needed to keep it a romantic secret.

But I couldn't eat dinner that night. I told Michael I had a migraine. I only got them in the morning, so he looked a little skeptical.

It occurred to me that he might have seen the notice about the movie in the paper and put the pieces together. But in any case, his lack of questioning was the grace I needed to move past the barricade in my heart.

"I'm going to the library," I told Michael. He didn't ask where my migraine had gone.

There is nothing quite like the sensation of being on the outside of a fancy restaurant looking in, especially when it's winter. It's a kind of paradise denied. I looked through the window and saw that the restaurant was quite full, with thick smoke hanging in the air. I looked and looked, didn't see him, and felt foolish and humiliated. I wondered if he'd toy with me like that after all these years.

Then I saw someone wave. He didn't look his age: not any age, or perhaps he was every age. Decades fell away. A silly smile insisted on having its way with my face.

I pulled the door open, and a rush of warm air enveloped me.

I walked to his table, sat down, and we looked at each other face-to-face.

Author's Note

The Glass Character is a fictional account of a woman's experiences in Hollywood from approximately 1921 to 1962, in which she pursues an obsessive relationship with silent film comedian Harold Lloyd. In his day, Lloyd was at least as popular as Chaplin and Keaton, celebrated for his bespectacled "everyman" screen persona. Though the specs had no glass in them, Lloyd always referred to his alter ego as the Glass Character.

Even after nearly a century, the iconic image of a meek, ordinary man desperately clinging to the hands of a huge clock twenty storeys off the ground has never quite faded from public consciousness. But Lloyd's own personality, fiery, brilliant and seductive, was infinitely more complex. My purpose in writing *The Glass Character* was to explore the hopeless romantic longing such a great star can inspire, an obsession that can seize the soul and consume a lifetime. At the same time, I wanted to communicate atmosphere: the excitement, exuberance and joy of those "high and dizzy" times.

Because this is a work of fiction, I sometimes found it necessary to improvise on history. Though I did extensive research in exploring the era in general and Lloyd's life in particular, this story is not intended to be biographical. In some cases, dates have been gently moved, details tweaked, the players rearranged and certain things invented in the service of story. Even with these changes, my hope is that the spirit of this unique and remarkable screen artist comes through — the Harold Lloyd I fell in love with.

Margaret Gunning's experience in print journalism includes hundreds of columns and book reviews in such publications as the *Globe & Mail, Vancouver Sun, Victoria Times-Colonist* and *Montreal Gazette.* Her poems have appeared in *Prism International, Room of One's Own, Capilano Review* and many others. Gunning's first novel (*Better than Life*), described by the *Edmonton Journal* as "fiction at its finest", celebrates the joy and anguish of family in small-town Ontario. Her second novel (*Mallory*) explores issues of bullying and social ostracism. Gunning currently lives in Coquitlam, BC.